PONGA BOY

Also by Philip Reed

The Marquis de Fraud

Bird Dog

Low Rider

In Search of the Greatest Golf Swing

Free Throw

Ponga Boy

By Phil Lebherz & Philip Reed

Epic Press
San Mateo, CA

For information about this book address Epic Press LLC, 1600 West Hillsdale Blvd, San Mateo, CA 94402.

ISBN: 978-0-615-20184-9

Library of Congress Control Number: 2008927650

For the people of Los Barriles,
whose beautiful village
and love of life
was the inspiration for this book.

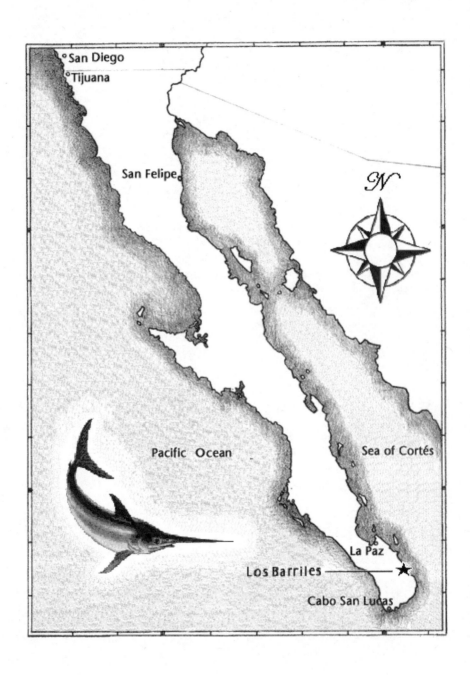

San Diego

Tijuana

San Felipe

N

Pacific Ocean

Sea of Cortés

La Paz

Los Barriles

Cabo San Lucas

Chapter 1

On the tip of the Baja Peninsula, on the Sea of Cortez, there is a small village called Los Barriles. Most of the local people don't have a lot of money, and yet they consider themselves very lucky to live here. Every day they watch the news on television and see a world in turmoil. But here it is peaceful. The rocky, dry mountains are dotted with yucca and palo blanco plants. And there is the beautiful green-blue sea, teeming with dolphin, marlin, tuna and dorado. And then there is a steady stream of hot, sunny days, one much like the next, but each wonderfully different, too.

It is the fishing that attracts people to this place. The fish caught in these waters feed families across Mexico and people all over the world. Americans on vacation also like to come here for the sport fishing. Every morning at dawn, charter boats come to the pier that stretches out from the Hotel Palmas de Cortez, their diesel engines growling as they maneuver up to the dock. The shouts and whistles of the captains and deck hands are like a cheerful song greeting the rising sun. As the fishermen climb aboard, lugging coolers, rods and reels, smaller boats dart among the larger charter boats. These are the ponga boats. And the men who work the ponga boats sell live bait to the sport fishermen who hope to hook a wahoo or a marlin.

Only a short distance from the dock, in the middle of the village, is a small soccer stadium. The field is made of concrete and the small goals are steel bars solidly planted in the ground. The bleachers were once a light blue, but most of the paint has been blistered by the hot sun and has chipped off. Floodlights are mounted on poles that rise above this little stadium and the lights blaze all night long.

It was on this field that a group of boys played soccer one hot summer night. Most of the boys were about 16 years old and they were tall, with long, muscular legs. But one of them was much younger and smaller than the others. Despite his size, he was the best player on the field, dribbling between the larger boys, displaying amazing speed and balance. His name was Pichu. He had been playing here for hours and now it was time for him to go home. But whenever he started to leave a chorus of protests would rise from the other players.

"Pichu! Pichu! Come back!" The older boys called to him as he tried to leave the soccer field to go home.

"It's late! I have to go home," he answered.

"Pichu! We can't win without you!"

Tico, a tall boy with black, curly hair, passed the ball to him just inside the line. Pichu knew he had to leave. But here was the ball right at his feet, tempting him to stay. His feet responded. He caught the ball on his instep and cradled it for an instant. Then he dodged an onrushing defender and sprinted down the open wing. His bare feet slapped the cement as he ran.

"Pichu!" he heard someone yell. He looked across and saw Tico open in front of the small goal. Pichu knew he had to loft the ball over the heads of the other players so Tico could head it into the opposite corner of the small goal that was filled by Rudolfo, the chubby son of the grocer. Actually, Pichu didn't think any of these things. Instead he sensed them and his feet reacted.

"Pichu! Mira!"

"Si! Ahi!" Pichu shouted back.

Pichu turned sharply, set the ball, kicked it and knew it was good. He didn't have to see what happened. Instead, he kept running and ran right out of the little soccer field and onto the dark streets of Los Barriles as the cheers of his friends erupted behind him.

Pichu ran and ran. He ran past the Hotel Palmas de Cortez, where he would arrive with his father the next morning at the first light. He ran past the storage yard where the old boats lay on their sides on the beach, tilted crazily, sad and forgotten. He ran past Tio Pablo's, where three gringos were leaving the bar, walking unsteadily and talking loudly in English. Finally, he arrived at the wall that was a shortcut to his house on top of the hill.

The wall was taller than Pichu and was made of adobe bricks. It ran up the side of the mountain, enclosing the hacienda where the rich man from the North came to vacation. The men on the docks said this man was the mayor of Tijuana. As the men spoke, their voices were low with respect and no jokes followed their words. Pichu sensed the power that this man, this mayor of the great city, must have. After all, Tijuana, to the north, was almost to the United States. And the United States must be —

Well, Pichu didn't really know what the United States was like. But he knew it was supposed to be wonderful and filled with riches. He had seen many pictures of it in the magazines his mother brought home that were left by the tourists at the hotel where she worked as a maid. Looking at the pictures, Pichu knew that in the United States all the women were blonde and all the men were tall. Everyone was rich and they all drove big new cars that cost a lot of money.

Pichu took two quick steps, sprang off a rock, and landed on top of the wall. His bare feet, tough with calluses, gripped the rough surface as he scampered up the wall, up the side of the mountain, taking the shortcut to his house. At the top of the rise he paused and looked back. He could see the water under the moonlight. This was the Sea of Cortez. If he looked carefully, he could see his father's ponga, the Maria (named after Pichu's mother) bobbing on the waves near the dock.

The Maria was a white and blue wooden boat, 22 feet long and graceful, with an outboard motor mounted on the back. His father had saved for months to get the money for a down payment on the boat. Each month, he carefully set aside enough cash to make the loan payment. It was so important to Pichu's father to know that the payment was made that he made it in person, in cash, at the small bank on the main street of Los Barriles. After all, the boat was the pride of his life and all the money he earned to feed and clothe Pichu and his seven brothers and sisters came from the fish he caught from his ponga.

"Pichu! Is that you?" a voice whispered.

"Yes, Angelina. I'm home."

He looked down from his perch on the wall and saw her standing in her yard in her long white nightgown. Angelina lived just on the other side of the wall, in the house next to his. She was a year younger than Pichu, and she had been there ever since he could remember. And she was always waiting when he came home from the soccer games in the village. When he looked at her face, a pale oval in the darkness, something moved inside him. It made him think of the way a fish would jump from the sea, visible for a moment, then disappear below the waves.

"You are home early, Pichu," she said.

"Yes. I have to get to bed early tonight. Tomorrow I get up before dawn. It is my first day."

She nodded seriously. "The first day. You must sleep well and be rested."

Angelina was leaving when he called to her: "Angie! Mira!"

As she turned he did a cartwheel on top of the wall.

"Pichu! Careful!" But she said it with laughter in her voice, her hands clapping lightly. "Now please, Pichu, you better sleep. Sleep, so you will be ready for your first day."

He jumped lightly to the ground inside his yard. His house was already dark. His father and mother were asleep in their bed.

Once more, Angelina's voice came to Pichu from over the wall. "I am glad you are home. Sleep well."

Chapter 2

A crack of light appeared under the doorway of Pichu's room early the next morning. Moments later the door opened and his father was bending over him saying, "It is time, Delfincito." His father began calling him this name when he first began swimming. He said Pichu moved with the waves like the dolphins that swam alongside the fishing boats in the clear water.

In the kitchen, his mother kissed him and said, "Be a help to your father." Her voice was heavy, and Pichu saw the pride in her eyes as she enjoyed this special moment. She pressed a rolled up tortilla into his hand and told him breakfast would be on the table when the sun was up and his work was done.

Pichu's father pulled on his dark blue baseball cap, the one with Mexicana written across the front. His father's face was deeply tanned and weathered and he had a bushy black mustache that twitched as he talked. But he didn't talk very often. When he was on the sea, in his boat, he was silent, his eyes alert, watching the surface of the water.

"Vamonos," his father said, and they walked out into the darkness. Although the sky was black, Pichu could feel the day coming. It was just over the horizon, over mainland Mexico to the east. Soon the sun would be shining on the sea and then it would warm the water, the fish, and their boat here in Baja Sur.

The door of his father's truck complained like an old man as it swung open and then closed. The engine roared to life, and they set off down the bumpy dirt road. No cars were on the road this early, but they had to avoid dogs lying in the dirt. The dogs woke up and sleepily moved aside to let them pass. His father was silent beside him, only humming a melody now and then. Pichu could smell his father's special smell, a mixture of sweat and soap and coffee, and he could see his strong forearms corded with muscle like steel cables as he worked the big wheel of the truck.

When they reached the Hotel Palmas de Cortez, his father drove the truck out onto the flat, hard sand of the beach. The headlights shone on the docks where the other fishermen were loading their boats and checking their lines. They needed to have everything in place and ready. At dawn, the clients would wake up and come down from their rooms in the hotel, moving slowly and carrying mugs of coffee. Then the boats would take them far out into the sea where they would try to catch the marlin. Pichu had seen the marlin on the wall above the bar in the hotel. He went there in the afternoon to watch soccer matches on TV, and he looked at the stuffed marlin and the dorado and the rooster-fish on the wall. They were posed like they had been hooked and were fighting. He also saw real marlin hanging from the scales on the dock where excited Americans posed beside the dead fish, telling the story of how they caught it.

Pichu followed his father onto the wooden dock that stretched out into the bay. This dock held many happy memories for him. It was where all the boys gathered to listen to the men from America speaking English. Sometimes the men would hire the boys for small jobs. The boys who knew the most English phrases were chosen, so Pichu learned all he could. His mind picked at the words and remembered them, and he could put them together in sentences that grew longer as time passed. Sometimes, when the boats came back, the fishermen from the United States would give Pichu their coolers to carry back to their rooms. And when he got to the room, they would hand him a dollar. He would take the dollar and go to the Super Mercado (where they accepted American money too) and buy a Coca-Cola. He would sit in the shade and drink it down as slowly as he could, and then go back to the docks hoping to carry another cooler for another fisherman.

But this morning he was not here for errands. He was here with his father to do a man's work. The air around them was heavy with diesel exhaust. The men whistled and called to each other as the boats turned and backed and the heavy engines growled. The men joked and laughed. Watching all this, Pichu's chest filled with pride and happiness as he realized he was now a part of this world.

"Hey, Chuy!" one of the men called to Pichu's father. "Chuy" was his father's nickname on the dock, although his formal name was Lorenzo.

"Hey, Chuy. What is that following you? Is that a little dog or something?"

"This is my son, Pichu," his father said. "He turns 10 years old today. So now he will work with me in the mornings."

Another man laughed. This was Herman. He often told people his name was "Herman the German," even though he certainly wasn't from Germany. In fact, he had never gone farther north than La Paz, which was only 130 kilometers away. And when he got there he became nervous for being so far north and he quickly returned home.

"But what can he do?" Herman said. "He's only a boy."

"A boy who can work is no longer a boy," his father said. "He is a man. Pichu, show them. Bring in the boat."

Pichu knew it was a test and he had to prove himself. He wanted to succeed and make his father proud in front of the other men. He looked for his father's boat, the Maria, and saw it was moored off the dock, the last in a string of pongas. He jumped down into the first boat, then ran quickly across the seats. When the waves tossed the bow, he used the motion to spring across to the next boat. In this way he moved easily from ponga to ponga, his feet moving lightly, never landing for more than an instant. The men watching from the dock were amazed. The boy seemed to be dancing across the boats, floating in the air above the bobbing pongas as easily as a hummingbird moves between flowers in the sunlight. They weren't really sure they had seen what their eyes told them they were seeing.

"Ayi!" Herman whistled. "The boy is a cat."

"No," his father said. "He is smarter than a cat."

"But nothing is smarter than a cat."

"A dolphin is smarter than a cat. A dolphin knows everything that is around him at all times. That's why I call him Delfincito."

When Pichu brought the boat to where his father stood on the dock, he saw his father staring at him with a look he didn't understand. But years later, recalling this moment, Pichu would realize it was the going away look. His father knew his son had a special gift. He was proud of the gift, since it had come through his blood. But he also knew that the gift would take his son away from him to places that were not as simple and good as this life in Los Barriles. And in those places, his son would be hurt and changed and things would never be like this wonderful moment ever again. This was the expression he saw in his father's eyes as he looked up at him standing on the dock.

Soon, they were both in the ponga and moving across the surface of the sea, which was glassy in the early morning. There was a bank of clouds on the horizon and the light came from around the clouds in golden rays, making the water glitter. A spray of salt water cooled Pichu's arms as the boat cut through the waves. His father's eyes caught sight of something moving below the surface and he circled around and brought the boat to a stop. His father grasped a steel lever, turned it, and saltwater began to gurgle into the boat, filling the center section between the two seats. When a foot of water was inside the boat, he told Pichu to shut off the valve. Then, they stood on the bow and looked down at the tiny fish that swarmed like grass in the wind. They scooped the sardines and the mullets and mackerel with long-handled nets and dumped them into the water inside the boat. In this way the sardines would stay alive and they would sell this bait to the fishermen trying to catch the great marlin.

Pichu and his father continued working as the sun rose, netting the bait fish and dumping them into the water inside the ponga. Pichu struggled to work the net since he weighed little and the long pole was heavy. But he did not want his father to think he was not able to help with the catch. He swung the long handle back and forth in the water until the muscles in his back ached and the palms of his hands were red. When his father said, "That's enough," Pichu was relieved.

As his father struggled to start the engine, Pichu sat in the bow and watched the fish in the boat swirling like seaweed in the current. They tickled his feet and darted mysteriously, all turning in one direction, then another. His father wound the cord around the starter and pulled hard. The engine coughed and sputtered, but didn't start. The spring mechanism had snapped and it took time to wind the rope by hand. Muttering, his father wound the rope again and pulled once more, cursing softly when it wouldn't catch. Pichu was afraid of his father's anger even though he knew it was not directed at him. Finally, the engine started and the boat nosed forward.

Pichu turned to let the breeze cool the sweat on his forehead and the water slid under the bow. As they approached the dock, the men in the large fishing boats yelled, "Ponga! Hey, Ponga! Aqui! Aqui!" Pichu's father maneuvered the ponga alongside the larger boats. He told Pichu to use the long-handled net to scoop up the wriggling sardines and hand them to the fishermen who dumped them in their live bait tanks. Money changed hands as Pichu and his father went from boat to boat. Pichu found that he was counting the money his father collected, adding it in his head. He didn't try to do this — he did it without thinking. And he realized that his father was making what seemed to him like a lot of money. After the fishermen got their bait, the engines of the big boats roared and the bows climbed out of the water. They headed off toward the sun and soon were only white dots on the horizon.

When Pichu and his father returned home several hours later, the kitchen was filled with the smells of breakfast: chilaquiles, huevos rancheros and homemade tortillas. His little brothers and sisters were awake now, and they were running around in the kitchen. His mother moved easily, avoiding the little children as she carried hot pans and sharp knives. When the food was ready, they all sat down. They all made the Sign of the Cross, said a quiet prayer and began eating. Pichu hadn't realized how hungry he was until his mother put a plate of food in front of him. The food had never tasted this good in his entire life.

"Did Pichu work hard?" his mother asked.

"He worked like a man," his father said. "With his help, I got more fish and sold them more quickly. And all of the men on the docks were amazed when Pichu ran across the pongas so quickly. They said it was impossible."

His mother smiled and looked Pichu. "You run across walls, you climb trees, you jump on boats moving in the sea. How do you do it?"

"I don't know," Pichu said between mouthfuls.

"How do you know where to put your feet?" she persisted.

"I just think where I want to go. My feet know where to step. And soon I am there."

His mother and father exchanged a look he didn't understand. But he sensed it was a look of love and approval.

"After breakfast, we have to go into Cabo San Lucas," his father said. "I need the starter recoil system for the boat. And I can pick up the food for the party tonight."

"Can I come, too?" Pichu asked.

His father chewed in silence for a moment, then said, "Yes. You can help me with the numbers. I always wonder if the merchants in Cabo are cheating me when I buy from them. They talk so fast and use so many numbers. Yes, you can come along."

Pichu had only been to Cabo one other time in his life. So this was a big event. Although he was tired from waking up so early and the excitement of working for the first time, he didn't want to sleep as they drove to the city. Instead, he watched the trees and cactus roll past the truck. The golden trunks of the elephant trees were beautiful in the desert light. And the yucca and palo blanco with their bright blossoms dotted the arid landscape with color. In the background, Mount San Lazarus seemed to watch over the landscape like a soldier, rising higher than the other mountains that shimmered in the heat.

Soon, they passed the airport and the traffic increased. Hotels and restaurants sprang up along the wide avenue jammed with trucks and buses. Many people rushed around on the sidewalks and streets. In one block, there were more people than in all of Los Barriles. Pichu found it strange and a little frightening that he didn't know the names of any of the people. The expressions on their faces seemed impatient and unfriendly, as if something bad had just happened or was just about to happen.

"Why is everyone in a hurry?" Pichu asked.

"They are not in a hurry," his father said. "This is just the city. When you live away from the sea, you lose the heartbeat of the world."

"If there is no heartbeat, how can they even live?"

His father looked at him and smiled. "The sea is not the only thing that keeps people alive. But for our family it is everything."

In Cabo, they drove along the waterfront and stopped in a used-parts boatyard. A man in dirty overalls helped Pichu's father find the parts he needed for his motor. Pichu stood beside them, listening to their talk about mechanical things: springs and ratchets and a new roll pin for the prop shaft. The man began to try to sell his father a new motor for the boat. When the price was mentioned, his father laughed scornfully and Pichu was afraid the man would think that disrespectful. But the man accepted his father's reaction without irritation. Finally, his father set the parts on the greasy counter and waved his hand over them.

"I want this, this and this," he said. "How much for each?"

The man's eyes narrowed and he licked his lips. He began rapidly listing prices. When the man was done, his father looked down at Pichu.

"Nine hundred and seventy pesos," Pichu said. He hadn't meant to add the numbers, but the answer was there when he was asked for it. His father smiled and touched his shoulder. The man whistled, impressed.

"He is very smart for such a young boy," the man said.

"He is my son," Pichu's father said. "But already he can do many things I can't."

When they were finished with their errands, it was late afternoon. They got in the truck and began winding through the tight streets. They passed the same place twice and Pichu felt a moment of panic, realizing that, even though his father hadn't said anything, they were lost. The streets became narrow. Women stood in the doorways calling to men as they passed in the streets. The voices of the women were hard and flat, with a strange note of hunger Pichu didn't understand. Most of the men turned their eyes away and hurried off. But a few of them stopped to talk to the women and then disappeared into the doorways.

"What do the women want?" he asked his father.

"Don't look at them," his father said sharply. Pichu realized he shouldn't ask any more questions. Soon they were back on the familiar road to Los Barriles.

Later that evening, Pichu celebrated his tenth birthday at his home with many friends. Angelina, from the house next door, came with her family. The small yard inside their adobe wall was filled with people and music came from the house. They ate and talked and danced. His uncle, Tio Jorge, who owned the ice factory outside the village, told a joke and laughed until his face shone with sweat. When it came time for the piñata, Pichu hit it with the stick on the first swing even though he had a blindfold on and he really didn't peek. With two more blows, the candy and prizes poured out on the ground and all the children dove for them.

Going to bed, Pichu had many images from the day in his head. But the one that came to the surface was how the women in Cabo had stood in the doorways calling to the men. He described what he had seen to his mother as she sat on the side of his bed smoothing his hair back from his forehead.

"What were those women doing?" he asked his mother.

She looked at him sadly, thinking many different things. Finally, she said, "They are women who have lost their way. And they are looking for men who have also lost their way."

Pichu knew that was all the explanation he would get at this time. But the sadness on the faces of the women and men stayed in his memory for many years.

Chapter 3

ichu was watching a soccer match on the TV over the bar in the Hotel Palmas de Cortez when Rudolfo came running in the door. Mexico City was leading Guadalajara 2–1 in the final minutes. But Guadalajara had the ball in Mexico's penalty area and was threatening to even the score. A shot from the great striker Sanchez had just hit the goal post.

"We need you, Pichu!" Rudolfo said, panting. His face was red and shiny and he was pointing out the door. When Pichu looked outside he saw his brother Neto with the boy named Luis who played on the soccer team with him. And Angelina was with them too. Pichu smiled and waved to Angelina. She was pulling a wagon that had something in it.

"What's wrong?" Pichu said, turning back to the TV screen. He was 12 years old now and he knew that young boys like Rudolfo (who was only 10) would often get excited by small things that didn't really matter.

"I bet Luis that you could climb in the blowhole and when the waves come up they will shoot you 20 feet in the air!"

"Thank you for making me part of your bet," Pichu said.

"You can do anything, Pichu. You turn flips off boats, swing from trees and balance on top of the school house roof. This blowhole trick will be easy for you."

Pichu turned back to the TV as Mexico City cleared the ball down field. Their defenders were too strong for Guadalajara. Time was running out and Guadalajara would probably lose. Pichu slid off the stool and went to the door. Angelina was standing there with Neto and Luis. It was very hot that day. The boys had their shirts off and their skin was shiny with sweat. Angelina wore a pretty T-shirt with brightly colored pictures of fish from the Sea of Cortez. At first Pichu wondered why she didn't take her shirt off too since the sun was strong and the humidity pressed in on them. Then he looked at her again, more closely, and he understood.

"Hola, Pichu," Angelina said, smiling.

"Hola," Pichu said. He turned to Luis. "Qué pasa?"

"Rudolfo is crazy. He says you can get shot out of the blowhole like a cannon ball. I bet him two Cokes and a Corny Bar that you wouldn't do it." Luis waited for Pichu's answer as he added, "You won't, will you?"

All the children waited for Pichu to speak. He thought of the blowhole and the waves that surged into it and then shot skyward. He imagined himself on the wave, riding the forces of nature. He looked at the faces of his friends and said, "Let's go."

They all cheered, because now they had something to do.

The collection of children started walking along the beach toward the rocks at the far end of the bay. Rudolfo was pulling a wagon that carried two watermelons.

"What are the melons for?" Pichu asked.

Rudolfo seemed very proud. "I got them from my father's super mercado. We will throw the melons in the water at the blowhole and see how high they go. Then, you will be the one to be fired into the air!"

Angelina smacked Rudolfo on the back of the head with her open hand. She frequently hit the boys and her sharp blows earned her a lot of respect. "Pichu didn't say he was going to do it." She turned to Pichu and she looked at him with the concern he had seen in his mother's eyes. It was the same but it was also very different. "Please be careful, Pichu."

"You don't learn anything by being careful, Angie," he told her.

Before they even got to the rocks they could hear the booming of the blowhole and see the spray shot high into the air. No wonder they called it "La Bufadora."

"Ayi!" Neto said. "The surf is strong. Pichu will go a mile high!"

"He didn't say he was going to do it," Angelina repeated.

The kids climbed the rocks, lugging the watermelons with them. Soon, they were standing on the rocks looking down at the trough of water that rose and fell with the waves. They watched as a wall of water came rushing up the narrow space and thundered into the rocky cave. A moment later with a great roar, water sprayed into the air and soaked them all. It felt refreshing in the heat of the afternoon.

Rudolfo's red, chubby face was shining with excitement. "Pichu will dive under the waves and swim right into the blowhole. Then the surf will come in and — BOOM! — he will be blown way up into the air!"

"Yay!" Neto said, clapping his hands.

"And then Luis will have to pay me two Coca-Colas and one Corny Bar," said Rudolfo.

"As if you need them," Luis said, patting Rudolfo's round stomach.

"Pichu hasn't said he's going to do it," Angelina said once more.

They all turned to Pichu, who was watching the water move up the trough.

"Get the watermelon," Pichu said. "We have to test it first."

Rudolfo rolled the melon to the edge of the trough and was about to push it in. Pichu stopped him.

"Wait!" Pichu called. "You have to wait for the right wave." They all watched the waves, looking for a big one that would carry the melon into the blowhole.

"Now!" Pichu yelled.

Rudolfo rolled the melon over the edge and it splashed into the sea. The crest of the wave caught it and it disappeared under the rocks. Moments later there was a rush of air and spray of water and the melon shot skyward forty feet. It fell on the rocks with a wet 'splat!' and broke into a reddish pulp.

"Ayi!" Neto screamed. "That was so high!"

"But look what would have happened to Pichu," Angelina said, pointing to the pulpy mess.

"Yes, but Pichu would have aimed better," Rudolfo said. "He could aim over there and — and maybe dive into the ocean. And then I would get two Coca-Colas and a Corny Bar. Right, Pichu?"

All the children turned to Pichu. He said, "Get the other melon."

They waited for another big wave and rolled the second melon into the water. The wave caught it and it disappeared under the rocks. There was a huge spray of water but no melon appeared in the air. A few seconds later pieces of the crushed melon floated back into sight. The reddish pulp glistened in the sunlight. The children were very quiet watching the mess float past them and out to sea.

"I still think you can do it, Pichu," Rudolfo said quietly. "You can do anything."

The children looked at Pichu.

"I can do it," Pichu said.

"No," said Angelina firmly. "This is stupid. You won't do it."

Pichu looked at Angelina and saw something in her face he had never noticed before. And looking at her strong, dark eyes, he knew that what he saw connected him to her in a way he couldn't explain.

"I can do it," Pichu said again. "But I won't do it."

"I knew it!" Luis said. "Pichu is chicken."

"I'm chicken, am I?" Pichu said, calmly turning on Luis.

The boy took a step back. He set his jaw and said, "Yes, you are a chicken."

"Would a chicken dive into the waves from that cliff up there?" Pichu pointed at a rock outcropping above them.

"No one can reach that cliff," Luis said, looking relieved.

"I can reach it," Pichu said. "And I will dive into the waves."

"But it's not deep enough," Angelina said.

"It's deep enough when the waves come in."

He started toward the cliff. Angelina put her hand on his arm. "Please," she said.

"Trust me," he told her. "I know I can do this."

"And then Pichu will get stuck halfway up the cliff and we will have to run home and get our parents," Luis said. Pichu turned on him and Luis added, "It might happen. But then again you might do it just as you say."

The children watched as Pichu picked his way across the rocks. Soon it was steep enough that he was moving on all fours, like the mountain goats that lived on Mount San Lazarus nearby. Then he was pulling himself up the rock wall, picking handholds and footholds in the sheer cliff.

"Ohhhhh," Angelina moaned and turned away. She punched Rudolfo in the shoulder.

"Ouch! What did you do that for?"

"For starting this whole stupid bet."

Pichu was moving upward steadily. He seemed to glide over the rock face with ease, never slowing. The children blinked rapidly, waiting for their eyes to explain what they saw. But they couldn't. Pichu had magic powers and that was all there was to it.

"Aye!" Neto said. "He is so high."

"How will he ever get down?" Rudolfo said.

"He says he will dive," Luis said. But then he added softly, "I would give him three Coca-Colas and two Corny Bars just to be back here safely again."

"Ohhhh," Angelina moaned again clutching her stomach and rocking back and forth. "Pichu, please be careful." She closed her eyes and her lips moved silently.

Pichu pulled himself up on the ledge that was way above the water. Opening her eyes, Angelina felt her stomach drop. But Pichu stood there fearlessly, hands on his hips, catching his breath and looking at the rocks below.

When the waves fell back, the rocks were exposed below Pichu. But when the swells came in, the water was high and smooth. Pichu stood there a long time, watching the water below and then staring far out to the sea, looking for what he needed.

"If he comes back now, I won't even call him a chicken," Luis said.

"Come back, Pichu," Angelina said softly.

Several times Pichu looked ready to dive, but then he backed off again and his eyes returned to the waves in the distance. The kids were silent, watching him. Angelina kept her eyes closed and her lips moved silently. Occasionally, she murmured, "Has he done it yet?"

High on the cliff, Pichu's body became alert. He saw what he was looking for. The children looked out to the sea and saw a massive swell rolling forward. It was much higher than the other waves. When it was still quite a distance from shore, Pichu dove. The wave rolled forward slowly — much too slowly! — and Pichu was falling so rapidly. He was heading straight for the exposed rocks. It looked like he would plunge to his death on the jagged rocks. But then the great wave covered the rocks just as the boy plummeted head first, arms outstretched, in the water. He knifed into the crest of the wave without a splash and disappeared from sight. Had he struck his head on the bottom and been killed? Would his friends ever see Pichu again? They waited for agonized seconds that seemed like hours.

Then, a head bobbed up above the surface. Pichu! He waved to them. The kids ran forward, whistling and laughing, stumbling over each other, running down the rocks and onto the sandy beach nearby. They swam out to meet him laughing excitedly. Even Luis was happy to see the feat had been accomplished.

Later, they sat in the shade drinking Coca-Colas. Angelina slapped Pichu's shoulder, saying, "I was so afraid. Why did you do such a dangerous thing?"

"I've been at that point many times with my father while fishing. The waves funnel in through the opening and grow very big. I knew how to do it so it wasn't dangerous."

"Why didn't you tell me that before you left? I was so worried."

"I told you to trust me and I thought that was enough."

She quietly considered what he said.

"Okay," she said at last. "But you have to remember, there are still things you don't understand. And being smart means knowing you don't know everything."

He saw that look again and knew that her feelings weren't something he should joke about. Instead, he smiled and said, "I'll remember that."

They touched Coke bottles, tipped them up and drank.

Chapter 4

Four years later, Pichu arrived at the dock one Saturday morning and saw that his father's ponga was the last in the string of boats. It had drifted in the night and now floated more than twenty feet away from the nearest boat. He couldn't easily run there across the boats.

"Don't worry," said Herman the German. "If you wait, one of the boats will take you there."

"I don't have time," Pichu said impatiently, pulling off his shirt. Since it was Saturday morning, the dock was already crowded with fishermen eagerly waiting to get out on the water. To wait would mean losing valuable business. And some of the other pongas were already on their way to catch bait.

"What is your hurry?" Herman asked.

"I have many things to do before the game."

"The game, of course, the game. When is the kickoff?"

"Noon," Pichu's father answered. "It will be his first time playing with the upper division. Will you come to the game?"

"Of course," Herman said. "Everyone in Los Barriles will be there. But Pichu, soccer is a different game after you turn 16. It is much faster. And the ball is played in the air more often. You might not have such an easy time of it."

"Everyone tells me that," Pichu said.

"And the boys from Cabo are very strong," Herman continued. "Their team has beaten everyone. What chance do we have?"

"Why is everyone so eager to give me bad news?" Pichu said, eying Herman evenly. He had grown up on these docks and he spoke with confidence even to men who were much older than he. "The game will answer all of these questions. Come and watch and find out. Now let me get my work done."

Pichu jumped down into the first boat. Looking back toward the dock, he saw that Herman was catching the attention of two Americans. One wore a shirt with big letters on it: USF. Herman pointed at Pichu, telling the Americans, "Watch this!"

The waves were lively this morning, so the boats were dancing in the water. Pichu noticed this and let his bare feet adjust to the moving surfaces of the seats, making sure his weight was balanced and not pressing down long enough to tilt the pongas. His feet moved quickly while he watched the approaching waves out of the corner of his eye. He knew that his vision told him many things, not just what he was directly looking at. And if he opened his mind, his senses let him feel everything around him. For example, he knew a big wave was rolling in. It was far out now, but when he got to the last boat it would be here.

Pichu had run across all the boats now and was standing balanced on the bow of the last one, looking across the water to his father's boat, still twenty feet away. He flexed his knees, waited a moment, and then the big wave was under the boat, throwing him upwards. It was like getting a boost from a big friend. Up he went into the air. When he reached the top of his flight he tucked himself into a ball, turned a double flip, then flattened out and dove into the water. He came up beside his father's boat and pulled himself over the rails and into the ponga. He heard cheering and turned to see Herman waving to him and the men on the docks clapping and whistling and looking at each other in amazement.

When Pichu steered his boat back to the dock to pick up his father, one of the Americans was saying to Herman, "Ask him how he does it."

Pichu looked at the man, the one wearing the USF shirt, and said, "It's okay, I speak English."

"Who taught you that?" he asked, indicating the way Pichu had moved across the boats.

"Taught me?" He shrugged. "I guess the waves taught me."

"But how can you balance? How do you think fast enough to know where to step?"

"I let my feet do the thinking."

The man laughed and said, "Yes, of course. But that's totally amazing. I've never seen anyone move like that."

"Excuse me," Pichu said. "I have to help my father now."

"Show them the other trick," Herman urged.

"I don't have time now," Pichu said.

"What? You don't have 30 seconds for some fun?" Herman said with his big smile. He reached into a crate and pulled out two old soccer balls, their leather covers cracked. "Go on, show them."

Herman rolled the ball to Pichu's feet. Pichu couldn't resist. He flicked the ball into the air and started juggling it with his feet.

"Not bad," one of the Americans said.

"You ain't seen nothin' yet, boss," Herman said, rolling the other ball to Pichu's foot. Pichu flicked the second ball into the air and began juggling both balls, his feet moving with astonishing speed.

"Unbelievable!" the American said, awed.

"But that's not the trick," Herman said. "Pichu, do the trick."

Pichu kicked one ball out over the water so it fell in a lazy arch. When the first ball was almost in the water he kicked the second ball in a rocket line drive. It struck the first ball and sent it flying.

Herman turned to the Americans. "Well?"

The two Americans stared at the soccer balls now bobbing on the water. Their mouths moved but no words were heard.

Pichu and his father climbed into their boat and pulled away from the dock. Looking back, Pichu saw Herman talking excitedly with the Americans who had now recovered from their shock.

Later that day, Pichu went to the soccer stadium in the center of town. The team from Cabo, the Scorpions, was already arriving. They pulled up in a special bus with their team name across the side and a picture of a scorpion swatting a soccer ball with its tail. The ball in the picture was streaking into the goal so fast it tore through the nets. The boys from Cabo were all big and their uniforms were bright blue with gold trim. As they climbed from the bus, they looked around and then some of them spat in the dust. They nudged each other and pointed at the team from Los Barriles, the Dolphins. Their uniforms were T-shirts with a smiling dolphin on the back. They had been made by one of the ladies who sold jewelry and Chiclets to the tourists at the hotel. When Pichu had first seen the T-shirt he thought they looked good. But now, as he looked at the boys from Cabo, his uniform suddenly seemed cheap and silly.

The bleachers were packed with people from the village. All around the concrete playing field, with steel goal posts at either end, were faces that Pichu recognized. He looked to the upper row, near the entrance, and saw Angelina. She smiled and waved to him. It was where she always sat and watched the games he played in. His father was also there. And so were Herman the German and some of the skippers from the docks. This was a big game since it was the first time the team from Cabo had come to their village to play.

"Ayi! They are so big!" Luis said to Pichu, nudging him and pointing at the Cabo players forming a circle around their captain. They were stretching in sync and counting in unison as if they were soldiers.

"Okay, so they are big," Pichu said. "That doesn't mean they are good."

"But it does mean it will be a rough game."

"Maybe. But these Scorpions have never played on a field like this before," he said tapping the concrete surface with his foot.

Luis laughed. "We have the advantage there. The first time they try a slide tackle they will regret it."

The whistle blew, and the two teams prepared to take their positions. But first, Pichu's team gathered around its coach, Señor Gallegos. Pichu noticed that even Señor Gallegos seemed impressed by the players from Cabo, how big they were and how expensive their uniforms looked. But then the coach directed his eyes first at Pichu and then at the other players from Los Barriles.

"The whole town is here to watch you play this game," the coach said. "Play the very best you can and that alone will make us proud of you."

The referee blew the whistle, and the two teams lined up. The coach had arranged the team with four players on the line and Pichu, at center forward, trailing behind. In this way, he could help the midfielders with defense but still attack the goal. The Scorpions were kicking off and they quickly pushed the ball out to the edge of the field where it was trapped by the wing. The wing easily threaded his way through the defense, worked his way free in the corner and crossed the ball. A striker flew in and headed the ball into the net. The players high-fived each other as they ran back to the center of the field. Except for the celebrating Cabo players, it was very quiet in the little stadium.

"Not even a minute has gone by and they have already scored," Luis said to Pichu as they prepared for the kickoff.

"Yes, but now we have the ball," Pichu answered.

The referee blew the whistle, and Luis rolled the ball forward to José. The Cabo players were converging on him from all sides. He heeled the ball back to Pichu, who was standing in the middle of the field.

"Go, Pichu! Go!" the crowd yelled.

But Pichu did nothing. He stood there watching the Scorpions closing in on him. One Scorpion came in hard with his feet, trying to sweep the ball and Pichu's legs. Pichu tapped the ball up over the attacker's legs and jumped free. The Scorpion screamed in pain as he fell on the concrete surface. Then, furious, he jumped up and charged again. This time Pichu leaned as if he were going to the right, then dodged left. Once again the Scorpion flew past him without getting the ball. Another player sprinted forward and Pichu dodged him too. Still, he hadn't advanced the ball down field at all. He stood there in the middle of the stadium looking around him. All motion suddenly stopped. The Scorpions were winded and confused. They didn't know how to get the ball from Pichu.

And that's when the fans began to react. They weren't cheering. Instead, they were laughing. But it wasn't mocking laughter, it was amazed laughter. They enjoyed seeing Pichu take control of the ball and evade all the attackers so effortlessly.

"Okay, let's go," Pichu called to Luis. He tapped the ball to him and ran behind the Scorpions' line in a give-and-go play. Luis saw the opportunity and fed the ball back to Pichu once more. He trapped it, then guided it with the outside of his foot, spinning it to the wing, José, who took it deep into the Scorpions' territory. The other team had come alive again and was rushing him. A Scorpion defender tried a slide tackle, but José was too fast. He touched the ball once more and then lofted it in a perfect cross, the ball hovering in front of the goal. But no one was there to head it home. Still, the game seemed more even now, and the Los Barriles Dolphins were playing with heart.

At the end of the first half the score was 3–0. But each goal the Scorpions scored was hard-earned. Also, the Dolphins had taken some good shots and had unlucky breaks. Once, José's shot hit the post and came straight down. It bounced in front of the goal for several tantalizing moments but no one was there to send it home.

During the halftime break, the Los Barriles players gathered in the shade at one end of the broiling hot stadium. They drank water and poured what was left in their bottles over their heads, letting it drip down their necks and dribble onto their T-shirts. Rudolfo's father came running down the hill from the super mercado carrying a plastic bag of oranges cut into sections.

"I hear you are giving the Cabo boys a real contest!" he said, his round face red and sweating.

"But the score is three to nothing," someone said, dejectedly.

"Yes, but if you score even one goal it will be a great victory for our town. I have to go back to the store but I'll listen for the cheering from there." He ruffled Rudolfo's hair and went running off again. Pichu watched him go. And as he looked toward the entrance, he saw the two Americans who had been on the dock that morning, the one in the brightly colored shirt and the other one with the letters USF on his shirt. They threaded their way into the top row of the bleachers and took a seat.

At the beginning of the second half, it was the Dolphins' turn to kick off. As soon as Luis touched the ball, a Scorpion tried to tackle him. Luis slipped past and was breaking free when the boy grabbed his T-shirt and pulled him back. He lost his balance and fell backwards, landing on his butt.

"Hey!" Luis cried, looking at the referee. But the referee's view was blocked and he didn't blow the whistle.

"Baby," the Scorpion sneered at Luis as play continued. "Cry little baby!" he mocked again, leaning close to his ear. Luis threw an elbow at the player and connected on the side of his head. The Scorpion punched Luis and knocked him to the concrete, where he lay dazed and barely moving. José came running from the wing and jumped on the bigger boy's back, riding him to the ground. Players came running from all over the field. The referee and the two linesmen waded into the group, pulling the boys apart.

Off to the side, a Scorpion had singled out Pichu and was taunting him. Pichu didn't respond but stood there watching the fighting players. The player pushed him again, taunting him, his fists balled. Alfonso, the Dolphin team captain, saw what was happening and said, "Come on, Pichu! Get him!"

Pichu turned away. Alfonso's voice grew louder. "Pichu, they hurt your teammate! You have to fight."

Pichu said nothing.

Soon the game resumed, and the Scorpions scored again almost immediately. As they were running back to center field they mocked the players from Los Barriles. Seeing this, Alfonso ran over to Pichu and said, "If you don't learn to fight like a man, Pichu, you can't be part of this team."

"Really?" Pichu said. "I thought this was a soccer team. I'll show you the way I fight."

The game continued with no more goals until there were only a few minutes left. The crowd was quiet, and the Scorpions were threatening continually. The Dolphins' goalie, Rudolfo, who wore heavy pads to protect him when he fell on the concrete, was playing the best game of his life. Although he wasn't as quick as many other goalies, he seemed to sense where to be even before he had to be there. Many times he broke up plays before the Scorpions had a chance to shoot.

One Scorpion took a pass and broke through the defense. He was one on one with Rudolfo, but he took one too many dribbles and the goalie slid in, breaking up the play. The ball rebounded to Luis who passed it to José on the wing. José crossed the ball to Pichu who was in front of the net. However, there was a much taller boy guarding him. Instead of trying for a header, which would have been blocked, Pichu trapped the ball on his chest and lightly dropped it to his feet. The defender waited for Pichu to make his move. Pichu remained motion-less. The crowd saw the other Scorpions rushing back to break up the play. Without looking, Pichu sensed them closing in on him and dodged to one side and circled back. He pushed the ball out to José on the wing again. José didn't trap the ball. Instead he one-touched it, sending the ball lofting back to Pichu again who was still guarded by the taller play-er.

People in the crowd weren't quite sure what happened next. The people knew what their eyes told them, but their brains said it was impossible. It looked like Pichu ran in a circle around the taller defend-er and then, turning sharply, he jumped high, did a flip, and while he was upside down, connected with the ball. His actions were so unex-pected that the other players stood there dumbfounded while the ball rocketed through the corner of the goal post into the back of the net.

Everyone from Los Barriles jumped to their feet, clutching their heads in amazement, screaming with all the air in their lungs. Moments later, the whistle blew, signaling the end of the game. But the cheering didn't stop. People jumped up and down on the steel benches, making a huge racket. Rudolfo's father came running down the hill into the sta-dium with his apron still around his big belly.

"What happened? Did we win?" he exclaimed, searching the faces around him for an answer.

"No. We scored a goal!" Herman cried. "Pichu scored a goal against the team from Cabo!"

"And what a goal it was!" said Señor Gallegos. "Pichu jumped and, well, he — I don't know. But he scored a goal against the team from Cabo."

That night, before Pichu went to sleep, his mother sat on a chair beside his bed. She noticed that he seemed subdued.

"What are you thinking about?" she said, stroking his forehead. Most of the time he felt he was too old for this. But Pichu allowed his mother to do this just before bed.

"Today, in the game, they said I should 'fight like a man.' But why does fighting make you a man?"

"It doesn't. Sometimes, it's the worst thing a man can do."

"Why?"

"You might get in trouble. You might hurt someone badly and be sent to prison. Then you would not be there to help your family. Instead, you should learn to love like a man. That means you will always be there to feed your family, to help them and protect them. That's what a real man does."

His mother's words were comforting. As he drifted off to sleep, the words, "Love like a man," echoed in his ears and settled deep into his memory.

Chapter **5**

The next day, when Pichu came back home from the docks, he saw a car parked in front of his house. Pichu had stayed to tether their ponga boat and rinse the salt water from their nets while his father went to his second job as a fix-it man at the hotel. The fishing had been poor lately and he needed the extra money to cover the payments on his boat, the Maria. Now, walking up the dusty road to his house, Pichu wondered whose car was parked there.

"Americanos," Angelina said as she watched Pichu walking up. She said the word in a sad way, as if there was a meaning to it he didn't yet understand.

"Why would Americanos visit my father?" he asked. As he talked to her, he noticed that she was taller now and dressed like a woman. He saw her every day, but this was the first time he had noticed this. She didn't run around in bare feet wearing shorts and a T-shirt anymore. She was neatly dressed and her hair was longer, held back with a silver barrette, and she was very pretty.

"The Americanos are not here for your father. They are here for you."

"Me?"

"Yes, I heard them talking over the wall."

He smiled at her. "You were spying on us?"

She pretended to be mad, balling her fist as if she would punch him. "I wasn't spying! You know how Americans are — they talk so loud."

Pichu's younger brother Joaquin came flying out the front door and across the yard, creating a small cloud of dust as he ran. "Pichu! Come quick!" He grabbed his big brother's hand and began tugging him into the house. "Americanos! For you!"

Pichu looked back at Angelina. She was watching him go. And for some reason, there was sadness on her face.

Inside, Pichu heard strange voices in the living room. His father was using his limited English to try to talk to the two men seated on the couch. His mother stood by, looking worried and not understanding anything being said. When Pichu walked into the room, the two men stood up. He recognized one as the man wearing the USF shirt on the dock the day before. He was tall with gray hair and small silver glasses. Pichu felt this man's sharp eyes could see right through him.

"Hello, Pichu," said the man with gray hair. "My name is Ben Jordan. I'm the head soccer coach at The University of San Francisco." He said this as if it would be very meaningful to Pichu.

"It's nice to meet you, sir," Pichu said shaking his hand.

"And this is my friend, Steve Connors," he said indicating the other man, who was bald and round with a loose-fitting, colorful shirt. The man nodded and smiled pleasantly.

Pichu stood beside his father. In Spanish, his father said, "They saw you play yesterday. They saw you score that goal."

Pichu nodded and turned back to the Americans.

"Pichu, do you know where San Francisco is?" the coach asked.

"In California?"

"Right," he said. "Three years ago, we had the best team in the NCAA."

"Yes." Pichu felt like that might seem impolite so he added, "I'm very glad."

The coach smiled. "Thank you. We want to be the best again. So I'm always looking for talented young players. I was telling your parents here that I'd like you to try out for our team. Maybe we can give you a scholarship to come and play at USF. It's a good Catholic school and you'd get a real education."

"But I went to high school here in Los Barriles. I finished last year."

Coach Jordan squinted a little and gave Pichu one of those looks that seemed to go right through him. "What I'm saying is that I can give you the chance to get a real education — a college degree."

"Thank you."

"Would you like that?" Coach Jordan asked, searching Pichu's face.

"I don't know."

"You don't know?"

"I don't think I need a degree to work the ponga boats."

The two Americanos looked at each other and laughed a little. Then Coach Jordan turned back to Pichu. "What I'm saying is that this would be a chance to improve yourself. Do you understand?"

"Yes."

"The university would pay for you to come and play on our team in the fall. You could practice your English and get a college degree. From there you can do anything you want. What do you think you want to do with your life, Pichu?"

"I want to be a fisherman, like my father."

"Well, we offer classes in marine biology. Would that interest you?"

"I don't know."

"I think it would. I think it would be fascinating for you to learn about things you've seen all your life."

Pichu said nothing.

"What we want is for you to fly to San Francisco and try out for our team," Coach Jordan said. "Of course, we would pay for your trip and you can stay for free in the dormitory. If you play as well as you played in that game yesterday, I know there would be a place for you on our team. You could stay on and practice with the team. And then you could start school in the fall."

"I'm sorry, but my family doesn't have money to pay for such a university."

"Everything would be paid for. And they would give you some money to live on, too."

"That's very nice. But why would they do that for a boy from Los Barriles?"

"Because of your talent. Because you are a good soccer player. Would you like to do that?"

Pichu's head was suddenly filled with all the pictures he had seen in the magazines his mother brought back from the hotel. Blond women and tall men. Expensive new cars and green lawns. He felt a strange feeling he'd never experienced before, as if a door were opening to a new world that was inviting but dangerous. He was curious and afraid at the same time. Then he thought of something.

"I'm sorry, I can't come," Pichu said, "I have to stay here to help my father."

His father smiled at him and said, "Pichu, I have to talk to you." He stood up and motioned for Pichu to leave the room with him. When he joined his father in the kitchen, the older man put his hand on his son's shoulder. The hand was warm and firm and made Pichu remember how it was to be a boy when his father's hand both punished and protected him. Standing here in the kitchen, eye to eye with his father, he realized for the first time that he was the taller one. But the weight of his father's hand was still heavy on his shoulder.

His father spoke in a serious voice he didn't often hear.

"Pichu, you have a special ability that God has given you and the ocean has perfected. You are very good at many things. All of these things make you the best soccer player I've even seen. You love the game. You love to play. And I know you want to be the best. But you cannot ever find out how good you are until you play against the strongest opponents. Only then will you find out what is in the deepest place inside you."

"But Papa," Pichu said. "Señor Gallegos says we will play against the team from La Paz. They are the best in all of Baja Sur. They have some guys over there you wouldn't believe."

His father shook his head. "This man from San Francisco is offering you something your mother and I could never give you."

"But who will help you work the ponga boat?"

"Your brother Ernesto turns ten next month."

Pichu laughed. "Neto? He's too small."

"He is as big as you were at that age. And he needs to learn."

His father's big hand touched Pichu's cheek. The hand was rough from pulling in the fishing nets and working the ponga boat. But the touch comforted Pichu and somehow made him feel both connected and free to go.

"You owe it to yourself to go," his father said. "Go and find out what is inside you. And when you come back, Los Barriles will still be here, just as you left it."

Pichu hesitated. "Are you sure, Papa?"

"You can never be completely sure about anything in life. But, yes, I believe that this is the right thing to do."

"Okay," Pichu said, feeling jumpy and excited and almost dizzy as he realized his life was going to change so quickly. "I will tell them I will try out for their team." He turned and walked back into the living room where the men from America were waiting for his answer. He told them he would accept their offer and they all shook hands.

That night Pichu had trouble sleeping. It seemed so hot in his small room. His brothers, sleeping around him, groaned and whimpered as they dreamed and tossed in their beds. It seemed like the air above Pichu's bed was filled with visions of America. When he closed his eyes, he saw a country that was alive with color and music and expensive things. And he saw himself wandering lost and confused across a strange landscape.

In just two weeks, he would be landing at San Francisco Airport. What would it be like to fly in a jet? How would he know where to go when he got there? Would they speak English in a way that made it hard for him to understand? And if he didn't know what they were saying, would the blond women and the tall men laugh at him?

Pichu climbed out of bed and padded through the quiet house. The moon was shining through their open front doorway and Pancho, their dog, was sleeping across the threshold. When Pichu stepped over the dog, Pancho raised his sleepy head and watched him walk out into the yard. Pichu found a handhold on the rough adobe surface and placed his right foot on the edge of a heavy earthen flowerpot. He swung up and landed on top of the wall. The adobe was cool on his back and he could lie balanced on the wall and look up at the moon and stars. He closed his eyes and dozed off.

"Pichu!" came a whisper sometime later.

He opened his eyes and saw Angelina standing below him.

"Hola, Angie."

"I knew I would find you here."

"How did you know?"

"When your mind is crowded, it's hard for you to sleep."

Pichu swung his legs around so he could face her. He saw that she wore a long T-shirt and a pair of shorts.

"Where are you going?" he asked, his voice playful.

"Oh, I don't know…"

After a moment he said, "I will meet you on the road out front."

Pichu jumped down inside his yard. Pancho, the dog, watched him go with a look on his face that said, "I'd like to go with you, but I'm just too sleepy."

Angelina was waiting for him when he reached the dirt road that ran between the houses and led down the hill to the beach. They walked slowly along together toward the water. Somewhere along the way, Pichu took her hand and held it, feeling a very special thrill that came from touching her. He squeezed her hand and she squeezed back in a way that made his heart pound. They continued walking, holding hands, and soon the course sand was rough under their feet. The water was glassy with only a few small waves lapping at their toes as they sat in the sand.

After some time, Angelina said, "American women are beautiful."

"Very beautiful," Pichu said. "And very sexy, too."

She punched his shoulder. He pretended that it hurt a lot. Then he put his arm around her shoulders and she leaned against him so he felt the warmth of her cheek against his neck. This was the first time she was so close to him.

"So you will probably like America so much you will never come home again," she said.

"Is that what you think?"

"Well, it is obvious. Why would you want to come back here when you can live in a big house with doors and windows that close and lock and make you feel very safe?"

"Our doors here don't close. And we are safe."

"That's because there is no one here to hurt us. But in America, there are a lot of crazy people over there. So you need to lock the doors." She turned her face up to him and said, "Pichu, promise me you will always remember to lock the doors."

"No crazy people are going to get me."

"Just promise me you will remember to lock the doors when you are in America."

He looked at her in the moonlight. Her face was truly worried so he realized this was not a time for joking. "I will remember."

"Remember what?"

"To lock the doors."

"Good."

She relaxed a little but continued looking at him. And looking at her face made him think how, soon, they would be separated. He realized then how, all these years, they had been connected. It was in the same way he was connected to the water. The water was always there, and it would always be there. Angelina had been there since his memory began. And, although he was going away, she would always be here for him. At least, he hoped she would, he suddenly thought, feeling a pang of insecurity. Thinking these thoughts, and feeling the separation even before they were apart, he took her face in his hands and kissed her. He didn't plan all this out, but it felt right so he did it. It was the first time he had kissed her and it was like diving off the cliff, hoping a big wave would be there to catch him. They were awkward for a moment, their lips touching but motionless. But then he moved and she moved with him and they fit just right together and he knew this was how it should be. And he desperately hoped it would always be this way.

Pichu's doubts and his determination made Angelina's kisses so much sweeter. He was so close he could hear her breathing and smell the honest scent of soap on her skin. She was right there, looking at him, just the two of them alone by the sea in the middle of the night with the moon watching over them, holding off the terrible darkness of separation that lay ahead.

Chapter 6

The day soon arrived when Pichu was to leave for San Francisco. His mother wanted him to stay home from fishing and pack his clothes. But he insisted on getting up before dawn and working with his father as he always did. The men on the docks joked with Pichu about all the things that would happen to him in America. And Herman the German did an imitation of an American woman trying to flirt with Pichu. He used a high voice and made his body sway like a woman's. All the men laughed until Pichu thought they would fall into the water.

Pichu's father didn't join in the laughing. And when they were alone in the boat, as they had been every morning for the past years, his father was strangely quiet. Usually he hummed a little melody as he worked. It was a song that came naturally from the happiness inside him because he was doing what he loved most. But today there was no humming. No song. And Pichu knew his father was thinking deeply about what his future held.

Some time later, his father turned off the motor and sat in the back of the ponga boat looking at the horizon. He turned to Pichu and said, "Before you go, there are several things I must tell you."

"But we are losing time. We have to get the bait to the fishermen."

"The other pongas can sell their bait," his father said. "It's more important that we talk now. And here in our ponga is the best place for talking."

Pichu put down the long pole with the net on the end. He sat down and waited for his father to speak. He became aware of the waves picking the boat up and gently setting it down again. The sun was just coming up over the surface of the water to the east. It was orange but when it reflected off the water it was a reddish gold. The sun was warm on the side of his face. He felt a pang of sadness that he soon would be separated from his family and all this.

"Soon you will be going away to the United States," his father said, pushing his hat back on his head. "You are very talented. And your talent will be rewarded in many ways. But you must not give in to the temptations of the world. You will learn about life but you must not compromise who you are. What your mother and I have taught you is now in your soul. It will be your foundation and it will become the roadmap of your life."

Pichu watched his father's face as he spoke. He saw that speaking this way was very difficult for him. But he also knew it was necessary because a good father will always do everything he can to prepare his son for the future.

"You will learn about other people and women and most importantly about yourself," his father continued. "There will be girls, too. Lots of girls. Not girls like Angelina who come from strong families and understand our way. But girls who want something from you that you can't give. Don't fall in lust and mistake it for true love. Love is sacrifice and self-discipline. When you lose your self-control, you lose your self-respect. And when you lose your self-respect, you have lost yourself."

His father was silent, but Pichu knew he wasn't done. He waited patiently for his father's words as he felt the motion of the boat and heard the lapping of the waves on the side of the ponga.

"How you act when you are alone is who you really are," his father continued. "You cannot hide from yourself. Self-discipline is what makes things work. It is harder to be self-disciplined in life than it is to be undisciplined. The man who cheats on his wife while acting macho in front of his friends is actually the weakest man in the group. The man who laughs at the stories and asks for more is the next weakest. Love does not tolerate or promote this type of behavior. Trust yourself and everything will work itself out. I love you, son. I love you, but I need to let you go. I am proud of you. I will miss you."

His father pulled his hat brim low over his eyes and blinked rapidly several times. He turned to the sun, and the warm light was kind to his weathered face. For several minutes, he stared toward the rising sun and together they felt the sea rocking the ponga boat.

"Let's finish our work," his father said, and stood up again.

Some time later, Pichu said, "Papa?"

"Yes, Delfincito?" It was the first time he had called Pichu that in years.

"I will always remember what you told me just now."

"I know you will remember it. But I also hope you will use it."

They sold their bait to the last remaining fishermen who paid them in U.S. dollars. Pichu's father pressed the cash into his hand saying, "You will need this in America."

After they tied up the ponga boat and washed and put away the nets, Pichu stood on the dock and looked around. It would be the last time he saw it for a long time. Herman the German saw Pichu's expression and seemed to understand it. He came over and said, "Pichu, did I ever tell you the story of the dog from Tijuana?"

"Yes. Many times."

"Okay. But let me tell it to you again. Because it is important for you to understand it. And maybe it will take that serious look off your face."

Herman cleared his throat and began.

"This is a story about a dog named Pépé who lived in Tijuana. Pépé lived a very happy life. He ate wherever there was a taco stand. And he hung around with the other dogs. And he had a very happy temper." While he was telling the story, Herman acted like a dog, panting and sticking his tongue out. It made Pichu smile, even though he had heard this story many times before.

"One day, this dog came up to Pépé and said, 'Hey, man, we can smuggle you into the United States.' So they took him over the border. And he found a home where his owners bathed him and gave him bones and fed him breakfast, lunch and dinner. And Pépé was very happy. But every night he went out into the yard and he stood there. And he looked across the border at the lights of Tijuana." Herman made a sad dog face that made Pichu laugh.

"After about a year went by, he decided to go back to visit his dog friends in Tijuana. He found the same dogs he used to hang out with. But they didn't recognize him because he looked really nice and he didn't have any skin problems anymore. He said, 'Hey guys! Don't you remember me?' The other dogs looked at him and said, 'Who are you?' He said, 'Don't you know me? I'm Pépé!' So all the dogs gathered around and asked him, 'What was it like in the United States?' So he said, 'Over there I have people who love me. My owners pet me all the time. They take care of my nails and brush my teeth. And I have lots of sexy girlfriends.' And the other dogs were drooling, listening to the stories. But finally one of the dogs said, 'Hey, if it is so great in America, why did you come back to Mexico?' And Pépé looked at him and said, 'I came back to bark.'"

Herman waited for Pichu to react. But he just stared at him.

"To bark," Herman repeated. "Don't you get it? You see over there he couldn't bark after 10 p.m. or they would shoot him. He couldn't poop in someone else's yard or he would be fined. He couldn't get tacos from the garbage can at the taco stand. So the moral of the story is that in Mexico we may not have all the stuff they have in America but at least we are free."

"Free?" Pichu asked. "Free to do what — bark?"

"Exactly! What does a dog want to do more than anything else? Bark!"

Pichu heard laughter and he turned to find his father leaning on a post, shaking his head and chuckling.

"Herman, have you been to America?" Pichu asked.

"Ayi! No," he said, turning away for a moment. "Those guys are crazy over there!"

"Then how do you know that we are free and they are not?"

"My uncle was up there one time. He said they are all crazy over there. So, Pichu, watch out."

"Pichu can take care of himself," his father said proudly.

"Fine, maybe. But remember, when you need to bark, come back to Los Barriles."

"Owwww!" Pichu howled like a dog.

"You will see," said Herman the German.

When they got back home, the smell of his mother's tortillas filled the air. Pichu felt that he was experiencing everything more vividly than ever before. As he stepped inside, his brother Neto tried to punch him in the stomach. He caught the smaller boy's fist.

"What's that for?" he said, holding him.

Neto struggled free and ran away. Pichu turned to his mother for an explanation.

"He's sad that you are going away," she said, drying her hands.

"So he tries to punch me?"

"Neto doesn't know how to put things into words. He's confused right now. So Pichu, you need to be kind to him."

They all sat down at the table for lunch and bowed their heads. His mother said a prayer and Pichu noticed that candles were burning beside the statue of The Virgin Mary on the shelf above the TV set. They ate in silence, glancing at the clock on the wall. The food tasted better than ever before, but Pichu's stomach was tight.

After lunch, they all climbed into the truck for the long drive to the airport in Cabo San Lucas. He sat between his father and his mother in the cab while his brothers and sister rode in the truck bed. Neto sat next to Pichu's suitcase and protectively guarded the bag of food his mother packed for him. When Gustavo, the littlest, tried to steal a tortilla, Neto made him cry.

At the airport, they marched into a big room with many people waiting for their flights. The room was filled with American tourists coming back from Cabo San Lucas. The men and women were sunburned and wore T-shirts and carried tubes with fishing rods in them. They bought bottles of tequila and silver jewelry from the stores that lined the big room.

Pichu felt all the American tourists were looking at him and his family and thinking they had no right to be there. Soon, a voice on the loudspeaker announced the flight to San Francisco. It was time for Pichu to say goodbye. He hugged his mother, whose face trembled and a tear ran down her cheek. She wiped it away, sniffed and said, "I didn't want to do this. And now look — " She turned away quickly. His father hugged him, too, his mustache brushing Pichu's face and his strong arms holding him tightly for a moment, as he sternly said, "Remember the things I told you." His brothers and sisters hugged Pichu's legs until he thought he would topple over.

Only Neto remained to one side, his arms folded across his chest, pouting. Pichu held his arms open but Neto turned away. Pichu waited for a moment, then slowly turned and headed down the tunnel that led to the plane. Suddenly, he felt arms hugging him from behind. It was Neto. He awkwardly reached back and patted his brother's head. They faced each other for a moment longer and Pichu said, "It's up to you now to help Papa in the ponga boat." Neto straightened up, met Pichu's gaze and nodded. They shook hands and Neto rejoined his family. They stood at the entrance to the jet ramp and watched as Pichu disappeared down the long tunnel that led to the airplane — and to America.

Chapter 7

The engines roared and the big jet lumbered down the runway until it reached an unbearable speed. Then, suddenly, it lifted into the air and Pichu was pressed back into his seat. He sat there, rubbing his hands together and feeling the sweat on his palms. He was afraid to look out the window because he knew they would be higher than he had ever been before. But when he did risk a glance, it wasn't scary at all. They were soaring over Mount San Lazaro, and he could see the whole coast and the water in the distance at a point he thought was Los Barriles.

The jet moved and bumped beneath him. It reminded him of being on a ponga boat in the ocean. But the waves they hit were invisible and the jet lurched without warning, giving him quick flashes of panic. When he looked around at the other passengers, none of them seemed to notice the irregular motion of the flight. They yawned or slept or read magazines while sipping drinks from plastic cups.

After an hour, Pichu heard someone behind him say, "There's San Diego." He looked out the window and saw an amazing city spread out below him. It lay on the ocean with bridges soaring over inlets and sailboats gliding along cutting white wakes in the water. There were wide roads everywhere, jammed with cars that sparkled in the sunlight.

"So this is America!" he thought. "It looks as beautiful as they said."

A few moments later, they were flying above another city. This one was even bigger than San Diego, so big he couldn't see the end of it. Pichu knew that it must be Los Angeles. Somehow, it lacked the green purity and the sparkling excitement of San Diego. Instead, he saw warehouses and parking lots and small bungalows with dusty yards. And even more roads with more cars — so many cars that they were barely moving. He couldn't help thinking of what the people back home had told him about America: "The people over there are crazy."

Slowly, the great city gave way to mountains and desert and Pichu felt a connection to the familiar landscape. Small towns dotted the landscape and he could see roads running as straight as a stretched fishing line all the way to the horizon. As they droned on, Pichu could see the hills below had dark shapes on them. The shapes were rambling trees with branches reaching out in all directions. The grassy slopes were tan and the trees were brown and it was very pretty.

"We will be landing in San Francisco in approximately 15 minutes," a woman's voice on the loudspeaker announced. "Please fill in the appropriate forms so you can get through customs quickly."

There was a loud bump from under the plane that made Pichu jump. The man beside him saw his reaction and said, "Don't worry, that was just the landing gear."

The great motors grew quiet, and the jet seemed to hang in the air. Then, as they descended, the houses below seemed to come up quickly. The jet rocked and swayed then hit the ground with a bump. The engines roared louder than ever as the huge weight of the jet tried to hurtle forward. With a groan that shook the plane, it came to a complete stop. In the silence, the calm voice of the woman came over the loud speaker: "Ladies and gentlemen, welcome to San Francisco."

"I'm in America now!" Pichu thought, straining to look out the window to see what it was like. "I'm really in America."

In the airport, Pichu watched the suitcases going around and around for a long time. He was beginning to panic, thinking that his suitcase would never arrive. But then he saw the brown bag with the duct tape holding it together all by itself in another baggage area. He had been waiting in the wrong place. He had to stand in several long lines. Finally, he waited in another line that led to a customs agent. Pichu held his passport ready. He had driven to La Paz with his father to obtain it. They had waited all day and filled out many forms. When he returned to his house with it, all his brothers and sisters had wanted to touch it and pretend it was theirs.

When he reached the tall desk the man looked at him and said, "Passport." The man wore an official uniform and a disapproving look on his face. Pichu was pretty sure he was Mexican and he spoke with a slight accent.

"Come to work?" the agent demanded in English.

Pichu didn't understand him. "I'm sorry…"

"Did you come here to work?" the man demanded impatiently, speaking this time in Spanish.

"I'm — I'm just visiting," Pichu said. Then for some reason he added, "I might go to college at USF."

The man slowly looked up at Pichu. His expression seemed to say he didn't believe a word that Pichu said. He stamped the passport and shoved it back at Pichu saying, "Have a nice visit."

A stream of people carried Pichu down a long corridor. When he turned the corner, he was surprised to see he was in a large room jammed with waiting people. Some were Mexican but many were other nationalities that he had never seen before. Some wore long white robes and had cloth wrapped around their heads. But everywhere he looked, there were signs with people's names on them. Some were simple little cardboard signs and others said, "Welcome home!" with balloons and flags attached. As people emerged from the customs areas, there would be shouts and running and then families hugged wildly. It was such a scene that Pichu stopped walking and stood still, taking it all in.

"Pichu!" a voice called.

He looked around and a waving hand caught his attention. He saw Coach Jordan with his gray hair and his silver glasses and the sharp look in his eyes. He waved back and carried his suitcase toward him. They shook hands and Pichu saw a woman standing beside the coach, smiling at him.

"Welcome to America, Pichu."

"Thank you."

"This is my wife, Irene."

Pichu shook the woman's hand. It was a very strong handshake. She was tall and unnaturally thin with brown hair cut short. She was wearing a dark blue Adidas running suit.

"Pea-shoe?" She asked. "Am I saying it right?"

"Pichu. Yes."

Coach Jordan put his arm around his wife and said, "Irene coaches the girl's lacrosse team."

"Yes."

They looked at him oddly. "Do you know what lacrosse is?"

"No."

Irene said, "It's a game with goals, like soccer, but you use sticks and a small rubber ball."

"Okay," Pichu said, but he couldn't visualize it at all.

"You'll have to come and watch one of our games sometime. We have some very pretty girls on our team."

He smiled but said nothing.

"Do you know what 'pretty' means?"

"Yes. I can speak English very well. But sometimes I don't know what to say."

They laughed kindly. Coach Jordan pointed at Pichu's suitcase. "Is that all you brought?"

"Yes. Except for this." He held up the bag of food his mother had packed. He had been so excited on the plane he forgot to eat it.

"Okay. Let's go to the car." As they walked, Coach Jordan said, "Here's what I had in mind. Tell me if it's okay with you…" He continued talking as they walked outside. It was cool with a nice wind blowing. It was almost too cold, Pichu thought. Still, the sky was bright blue and the buildings around him were very clean and colorful. All the cars passing in the road were new and many were tall trucks or four-wheel-drive style. There was no dust on the cars and their windshields were not cracked.

"…and after we hook up with the admissions department, we'll swing by and show you the field," Coach Jordan was saying. "There's no practice today, but I thought you'd get a kick out of seeing where you'll be playing."

"Who was your coach in Mexico?" Irene asked.

"Señor Gallegos," Pichu said.

"What kind of drills did he have you doing?"

"Drills?"

"You know, for shooting and dribbling and passing. One-on-one."

Pichu thought about it for a long time. Then he said, "We just played."

"Oh," she said, disappointed.

"But we played a lot," Pichu added. "Sometimes, after I was done with my work, I played until midnight."

They arrived at a big silver car that said Lexus on the back and was high off the ground. It didn't have any dust on it, either. Ben swung open the back door and put Pichu's suitcase in the back. He reached for the bag of food but Pichu shook his head and continued to hold it.

As they drove on the busy roads, Pichu was amazed at how many houses there were. He could look from one horizon to the other and see nothing but houses, roads and cars.

At one point, when the road ran along by the water, he asked, "Is this the ocean?"

Irene laughed. "No, this is just the bay."

"But where is the sea?"

"We're on a peninsula here, Pichu," Coach Jordan said. "The ocean is way over those mountains."

Pichu looked in the direction he was pointing and saw that eventually the houses ended and a forest began. But it wasn't like the elephant trees and yucca and the palo blanco at home. There were pine trees that were thick and green. And above the trees cold gray clouds appeared, moving rapidly. He felt the chill the clouds would bring.

That afternoon, Coach Jordan and Irene took Pichu to a big office building where he was introduced to the admissions officer, George. He was a black man with a large stomach, a very deep voice and friendly eyes.

"It must be very different here for you," George said, studying Pichu's expression.

"A little bit," Pichu said, in such a way that made them all laugh.

"Well, we're going to try to make you feel very much at home," George said. "Coach Jordan has told me that you'll be working out with the team. In the meantime, we'll be getting your transcripts together. You will probably have to take some tests before we can formally admit you. You have to do your best, but don't worry too much about them. They are just a formality. The main thing for you to do is to follow Coach Jordan's instructions. He'll guide you through this process. Okay?"

Pichu sensed there was hidden meaning in George's words. There were many things that he didn't understand. But he nodded and said, "Okay. Thank you."

The next stop on the tour was the soccer field. They parked the big Lexus and walked through a tunnel and out into a huge stadium. Rows of bleachers surrounded a bright green field with white goal posts and nets. An odd little man with a crooked walk was walking behind a machine that put a white line at the edge of the field. He looked up at Pichu and smiled, then returned to his work. Pichu couldn't help noticing that the field was carefully lined with chalk to show the boundaries and flags were at the edges where the corner kicks were taken.

"A little different from your field in Los Barriles," Coach Jordan said. "We play on grass here, not cement."

"It's so big," Pichu said.

"And wait until it's filled with screaming fans. Soccer is a big sport on campus. Our players are real celebrities."

Coach Jordan let him gaze out over the vast area for a few more minutes. Then he put his hand on Pichu's shoulder and said, "Let's go. I bet you're hungry."

They drove through a busy shopping area and then turned onto side streets that ran through large houses that all looked the same. Finally, Coach Jordan guided the big car up a driveway and stopped.

"You'll stay with us tonight," Coach Jordan said. "Then tomorrow I'll get you settled in one of the dorm rooms. I think you'll be very comfortable here."

When they opened the front door, a dog with reddish hair jumped up on Pichu and tried to lick his face.

"Skipper! Down, Skip!" Irene said, disapproval making her face suddenly look much older.

Pichu petted the dog and was amazed at how smooth its coat was. There were no skin problems with the dog at all. And it smelled like a woman, not a dog.

Irene gave Pichu a tour of the house. All the floors were covered with thick carpet and the house was very, very quiet. She pushed open a door to a room and said, "You'll be staying here with our son, Tod." A boy slightly younger than Pichu was playing a video game, pressing the buttons and saying, "Die! Die!"

"Tod, this is Pichu," Irene said. "He's going to be staying here with us tonight."

"Hey," Tod said, without looking away from the screen. He began furiously pressing buttons on the controller and saying, "I'm going to kill you all!"

Irene laughed nervously and smiled at Pichu. "Here is your bed," she said to Pichu. It was a single bed next to a sliding glass door and a patio outside. There was a thick blanket on the edge of the bed, and the covers were so smooth there were no wrinkles. Pichu was afraid to sit on it. Off to one side was a small bathroom.

"And these towels and this washcloth are yours," she said, laying them on the edge of his bed.

The evening passed very slowly for Pichu. First they ate a dinner of steak, baked potato and salad. The steak was very easy to chew and there was no fat on it at all. For dessert, they had something with a strange name that looked like flan but tasted more like ice cream. Tod immediately disappeared, leaving his plate on the table. After dinner they watched highlights of World Cup matches while Coach Jordan often jumped from his chair to point out things on the screen, telling Pichu where the players should have been.

Finally, they asked Pichu if he was tired. He said yes, even though he wasn't. As he was leaving, Irene said, "Oh, Pichu, before you go to sleep, remember to lock the sliding glass door in your room."

"Yes," he said. Then he added, "You have been kind to me today. Thank you."

"We're happy to have you here," Irene said.

"Yes, we are," Coach Jordan added. "And tomorrow's a big day, so get a lot of sleep."

Pichu went into his room and closed the door. Tod had fallen asleep with the game controller next to him and the TV on. Figures from the video game were still on the screen running back and forth and shooting at each other. A cool breeze was coming from the open sliding door. He would have liked to lie in bed and feel the air on his face as he slept. But then he remembered what Irene had said about locking the door. That reminded him of the night he sat on the beach with Angelina and how she worried about crime in America. If he left the door open, a crazy person would come in while he was sleeping and try to hurt him. He slid the door closed and carefully locked it.

Chapter 8

A whistle blew and a rough voice yelled, "Okay, listen up!" Pichu looked around to see who was yelling. It was a short, stocky man wearing shorts, a USF T-shirt and soccer cleats. He was clapping his hands and impatiently motioning the players to gather around him. Standing beside the short man was Coach Jordan, who carried a clipboard and wore tan-colored pants and soccer cleats.

As the players jogged over, some of them looked at Pichu with cold expressions, sizing him up. They had mostly ignored him when he arrived for practice. Coach Jordan had told him to "loosen up" but hadn't introduced him to any of the other players yet. Pichu found a ball and began juggling it by working the ball up his body — first his foot, then his knee, then his chest, then his head. He also played a game where he kicked it over his head, then struck it with the heel of his foot in such a way that it came back over his head and onto his foot where he caught it on his instep. While he was doing this, he noticed that some of the other players were nudging each other and pointing at him.

"All right, listen up," the stocky man was saying. "Coach wants to say a few words before we break into squads and run some drills. Coach?"

"Thank you, Coach Connors. I want to welcome you all to the first practice of the season. And I know it's going to be a great year. We've got a lot of players returning this year. And we have some new recruits, so we're going to have a great season. Before we get started, though, I wanted to let you know that we have a young player who will be working out with us today and maybe joining the team permanently. His name is Pichu and he comes from the Baja Peninsula of Mexico."

Pichu felt the eyes of the other players on him. Some of them smiled and nodded. Others curled their lips and looked him up and down noticing his old shorts, faded T-shirt and the worn soccer shoes he had brought from home. The coach had said he would get Pichu new equipment and he had waited eagerly for the new uniform. But nothing had been given to him yet. And now that the eyes of the team were on him he felt ashamed.

Coach Jordan continued: "I saw him play in a game in his hometown and I was so impressed, I invited him to come and work with us today. I expect you all to make him feel welcome."

A stocky player with straight black hair reached over and shook Pichu's hand, saying, "Hey, Pichu. I'm Bart. Fullback."

A tall, thin player with curly red hair held his fist out to Pichu waiting for him to do something. Pichu made a fist and touched his. It seemed to be the right thing to do because the player smiled and said, "All right, bro. I'm Kevin, the goalie. Welcome to Los Estados Unidos."

"Thanks, Kevin."

"All right now, guys," Coach Connors said, standing with his feet planted wide apart and picking up a clipboard. "We're going to run some drills and then do some light scrimmaging. Here's how we're gonna break it down." As he read off a list of names, the players jogged away to join groups at the midfield or near the far goal. When he had read all the names, Pichu was left standing there alone. The two coaches talked rapidly together and Coach Connors said, "Pichu, join the strikers over there." He pointed toward a group of players at the opposite goal. As Pichu jogged toward them, he was disappointed to see that Bart and Kevin were not among them.

"So we get stuck with the new hot shot," one of the players was saying as Pichu arrived. He was tall and powerfully built with thick brown hair and small patch of whiskers in the center of his chin.

"Yeah," said another player with red blotches on his skin, "Another one of Jordan's brainstorms. When is this place going to get a real scouting team? We keep winding up with these bozos that can't even speak English."

"I speak English," Pichu said.

"Oh, that'll help," he said sarcastically. "But do you know how to pass? Or are you one of those hot-dog juggling acts?"

Pichu said nothing since he knew that his words kept getting turned around.

A lanky player with curly hair and an easy smile came up to Pichu with his hand out. Pichu shook hands with him. "Don't worry about Moore," he said, pointing to the player with the strange strip of whiskers on his chin. "He's in a slump now, so he's taking it out on everyone around him. I'm Peter Devins but the guys call me Pete. I'm the winger — well the third string winger anyway." Pichu shook his hand.

"What's a brainstorm?" he asked Pete.

"A what? Oh. See, Coach has had a lot of different players try out. He's trying anything to get us out of the basement. Three years ago we were NCAA champs. Now — " He made a thumbs down gesture and dropped his voice. "Word is this'll be Coach Jordan's last season unless we start winning. Every time someone tries out, Moore and Shields think they're going to get cut. So they give the new guy a hard time."

"So if I don't do well, they will be happy?"

Pete looked at Pichu for a moment, then smiled. He turned his head, thinking about what he had said. "Well, yes. But that's their problem. If I were you, I'd play my best and try to get a spot on the team."

"Why?"

"Girls, man. Girls," he said. "The starters on this team can get any girl they want. See?" Pete pointed to the stands. Three girls were leaning on the railing watching practice.

"The blonde in the white top — that's Moore's girlfriend." He shook his head. "She is so hot. One next to her, short black hair, that's Shields' girlfriend." He pretended to pull a knife out and drive it into his heart. "To die for, man. To die for."

A ball hit Pichu in the side of the head. A wave of pain blurred his vision. He heard laughter and looked around to see it came from Shields and Moore. Moore shrugged and said, "Sorry, man. I tried to warn you."

The pain made Pichu's head seem to swell, and he felt anger rising in his chest. He jogged over and retrieved the ball.

"Here you go," he said and fired the ball at Moore. It was a rocket and would have taken his head off, but Moore ducked, turned, saw the ball fly high into the stands. His face darkened. He charged Pichu.

"Hey, junior. No one pulls that on me and gets away with it."

He shoved Pichu in the middle of the chest, and he went down on his butt. He started to scramble to his feet, but Moore hooked his ankle and dumped him again. Shields and Moore stood above him laughing. Suddenly, their expressions grew serious. Pichu saw why — Coach Jordan was coming.

Moore extended his hand to help Pichu up. "No hard feelings, huh? We don't have anything against you. We just don't want you here."

Pichu took Moore's hand and felt himself being lifted onto his feet. But before he was fully on his feet Moore released his hand. Pichu fell backwards and had to scramble to recover his balance. He brushed the grass off his shorts.

Coach Jordan looked sharply at Moore. "We're not going to have trouble again, are we?"

Moore rolled his eyes. "Coach, come on. You know me — I'm a mellow guy."

Coach Jordan turned to Pichu. "Are you okay?"

"Fine," Pichu said. "Your team is just welcoming me."

Pete laughed.

"Okay. We're going to start with a few shooting drills. Pete, I want you to cross the ball either on the ground or to the head. The rest of you, I want you to trap the ball and shoot."

Pete jogged over to the corner and Coach Connors, the assistant coach, rounded up balls and rolled them over to him. Pichu was eager to show what he could do, but Moore and Shields elbowed him aside so they could be first in line. Pete sent a high cross floating across the goal. Moore chest-trapped the ball, let it drop to his feet and pounded it into the goal. The next ball came on the ground to Shields. He touched it once, evading an imaginary defender, then kicked it high and into the corner with his left foot. When he circled back to the group, he got into Pichu's face and said, "There's juggling and there's scoring, little bro. That was scoring."

It was Pichu's turn now. He ran at an angle to the goal while Pete kicked the ball. It floated over his head, too high to make a play. He started to turn back to rejoin the others.

"Take another," Coach Jordan said.

This time the ball came at waist level and hard. Pichu trapped it with the inside of his foot and hit the ball solid before it touched the ground. The shot exploded off his foot with no spin. The black and white patches were clear as the ball sailed wide of the goal. He turned back to the group hoping for a response but he saw that Shields and Moore were looking away, waving to the girls in the stands.

"Nice shot!" Pichu looked around and saw Coach Connors giving him a thumbs up.

They ran a series of shooting drills for an hour. But it seemed every time the ball came to Pichu it was too hard to handle. Besides, he felt the grass was slowing everything down and throwing off his timing. He felt frustrated and confused, as if he wasn't really himself.

"Okay guys," Coach Connors said. "Water break! Then we're gonna scrimmage a little. But don't kill each other. This is just so Coach can get a look at you. He might be moving some of you around a little, shake things up a bit, see if we can't get better results this year."

The players grumbled and looked at each other, understanding the remark even though Pichu didn't.

"All right. Here's what Coach wants." He began reading off names.

As each person was called, he clapped his hands and ran out onto the field, relieved to be included in the starting lineup. Then Coach Connors began reading off what he called "The B Team." These players didn't clap or run onto the field. They took their positions on the other end of the field.

"The rest of you, take a seat," Coach Connors announced.

The players shuffled toward a line of benches, grumbling. Pichu saw that Pete was one of the players that wasn't on the starting team or the "B" team. Pete saw Pichu looked at him and shrugged.

"Same position as last year, " Pete said, "ridin' the bench."

Another of the benched players said, "Yeah, I guess you got that position covered."

"Yeah, just watch me cover it," Pete said. He slowly took a seat on the bench.

"You're all over it," the other player said and laughed.

Coach Jordan saw Pichu standing alone and put his hand on his shoulder. "I'm going to sub you in here in a few minutes — see what you can do. Just sit tight for now and get a feel for how we play." Then he gave Pichu one of his sharp looks, his eyes crinkling behind the glasses.

"You doing all right?"

Pichu thought about Moore and how he had pushed him down. For a second he wondered how he had gotten here and what he was doing. But he couldn't put any of this into words so he nodded and said, "I'm good, Coach."

"Good." Coach Jordan looked back out at the field and said, "There are some big egos on this team."

"I'm sorry?"

"Egos. Some of the players might resent you being here. They feel you will take their position. Just play your game. Don't let their attitude throw you."

"But if they don't want me here, then why am I here?"

The coach looked at him, forming an answer that he decided not to give. Instead he just said, "You'll see. It will all work out."

A whistle blew and the B team kicked off. Pichu watched as the ball went back to the midfielders then out to the wing. A short, muscular player sprinted up the wing. Pichu was amazed at how fast he was. But then, without much effort at all, a defender stripped the ball, controlled it and jogged back up field with it. He looked around, saw an open player on the opposite side of the field, and launched a long pass that landed softly at Shields' foot. The lanky player steered the ball around a charging halfback and took off at about half speed.

Man, these guys are great, Pichu thought. They are big, they are very strong, and their control is impressive. And it even seemed like they weren't really trying. Pichu felt small and insignificant in this vast field with the thick grass and the goals that were so much bigger than the goals on his own little concrete playing area back in Los Barriles. He watched the players moving effortlessly, gliding above the grass like gods. How could he ever hope to compete against them?

But the more he watched, the more he realized that something was different about the way they moved here. And when he realized what it was, he knew that he could definitely play against these players even though they seemed so superior. A small feeling of hope rose inside him like an air bubble from an oyster at the bottom of the sea. The hope rose until it finally reached his face and curled his lips up slightly. The smile was still there when Coach Connors turned to him and said, "Okay, Pichu, I want you to go in for Frasier. I want to see how you and Shields and Moore work together. Let's see what you can do."

Chapter 9

Pichu jogged out onto the field, feeling the thick grass beneath his cleats. The other players watched him, their chests heaving as they caught their breath. Some players leaned forward with their hands on their knees, drops of sweat falling from their noses and their chins. It looked like they needed to get in better shape before the season began, Pichu thought.

"Frasier?" Pichu said to the center forward. "Coach wants me to take your place."

Frasier was tall and thin, but his features were pinched tightly together in the middle of his face as if he'd just sucked on a lime. He glared at Pichu and said, "Sure, take my place in practice. Do it in a game and I'll kick your ass."

Pichu looked around at his teammates — Moore on one side and Shields on the other. He nodded to them and said, "My name is Pichu."

The two insides ignored him but a winger, a short guy with bulging thighs said, "I'm Tommy Revinski. They call me Rev."

The ball was in the penalty box ready for a goal kick.

"Okay guys, let's go," Coach Connor said. He blew the whistle.

The fullback ran up and kicked the ball. He miskicked it slightly and the ball sailed low across the field at about head level. Pichu didn't think he could reach it but he ran and jumped anyway, reaching for it with his outstretched foot. The ball struck the toe of his soccer shoe and fell straight down. Pichu fell to the ground beside the ball. He scrambled to his feet and saw a clear path to the goal. He took the shot. The ball hugged the ground, the black spots clearly visible showing that there was no spin on the ball. The goalie dove and knocked it down, then dove and pounced on it before Shields could follow up with another attempt on goal.

Pichu felt good about what he had done, hoping that Coach Jordan was pleased with a quick show of his talent. But when he looked over the coach was bent over his clipboard as if he hadn't seen what happened. A second later, Moore ran past him and said, "Didn't you hear me calling for it?"

"No."

"Open your ears. You're on a team now, you know. There's no chance of scoring from way out there."

Pichu wanted to tell him he'd scored from there many times. But his words burned inside him, unspoken. He put his head down and ran back to midfield. The halfback was bringing the ball up so Pichu called for it. But he forgot where he was and yelled, "Mira! Mira!"

Across the field he heard Moore laugh and say, "Oh yeah, he speaks real good English."

The ball was passed off to Rev on the wing. He moved down the field gracefully, his powerful legs moving easily. The defender challenged him but Rev threw a fake, touched the ball between his legs and broke free. Pichu followed the play, lagging behind Shields on his right and Moore behind him. He knew the ball would be coming across the top of the penalty box and he wanted to have room to move in for the head ball or to take a shot.

Rev drew in another defender and cut the ball back across the field. Shields reached for it but missed and suddenly the ball was on Pichu's foot. He trapped it, sensing that a fullback was coming in from his left. He cut sharply and let the defender shoot past. He was open with the goal in front of him. Yes, he had been right about playing on this grass. It was incredibly slow. The ball didn't bounce high and the players moved slowly. It was nothing like the field in Los Barriles, where the ball skipped and slid. There, even the slightest touch made the ball dart off unpredictably.

Another fullback moved in, guarding him, refusing to commit. "Over here!" Moore screamed. But when Pichu glanced left he saw Moore was covered by a fullback. Shields was shouting for the ball too, but he was blocked. All Pichu had to do was draw in the fullback, beat him and take the shot. He drew the ball back, started to his right, then cut sharply so his back was almost facing the goal. He planted his right foot, pivoted and fired the ball. It curled and hit the top of the cross bar.

Pichu was running in to take another shot when something unexpected happened. He was hit hard from the side. Everything broke into pieces for a few seconds and his eyes were blurry. When he focused again he was looking up from the ground into Moore's red face. He was shouting down at Pichu.

"I was wide open, you little ball hog! When I call for the ball you give it to me! Understand?"

Rev stepped in front of Moore and offered his hand to help Pichu up. He pulled Pichu to his feet and said, "Don't mind Moore. He was top scorer last year. He doesn't want anyone taking that away from him."

Pichu looked over and saw Coach Jordan had taken Moore aside and was talking to him. He had his head down, nodding and kicking the ground, but didn't seem to be very sorry about what he had done. He nodded once more and jogged back onto the field and past Pichu.

As Moore passed, he softly said, "Don't forget what I told you, hot dog."

The rest of the scrimmage Pichu was careful not to intercept any passes. He did very little dribbling. Instead, he moved the ball out to Shields or Moore as soon as he had the chance. At one point, he was wide open at the top of the penalty box with no one guarding him. He glanced up and saw the goal and knew exactly where he could have put it. In his mind he could feel the ball solid on his foot and see the nets flying. But instead he held the ball until a fullback rushed in, then passed it to Shields who mis-kicked the ball, sending it spinning wide.

When the scrimmage was over he stayed on the field with Coach Jordan as the other players jogged past him in groups, talking and laughing. When the field was empty the Coach put one foot up on the bench and leaned forward on his knee.

"So what do you think?" he asked.

"I think you have a very good team," Pichu said. "But they don't want me here."

Coach looked at him, his sharp eyes stinging him. Pichu was afraid to look straight at the Coach.

"Pichu, I didn't see the same..." he paused, thinking, "...the same spark I saw when you played in Los Barriles."

"Yes, Coach. I played poorly."

"I didn't say that. It's obvious you have amazing ball control. And your passing was solid. But something was missing. I had expected you to be more of a playmaker. Is there anything bothering you?"

Pichu had many things he could say. But he knew it would be wrong to say any of them. He had to do this on his own, or not at all.

"Thank you for this chance to play with your team, Coach," he said, hoping that would end the conversation.

Coach Jordan laughed in an understanding tone of voice. "You'll have other chances, Pichu. In fact, we're playing a preseason game against Santa Clara on Saturday. I'm hoping you'll be up for that. Maybe the competition will draw out your A game."

He glanced at his watch and seemed surprised. "Shoot. I'm running late. I'm going to have Coach Connors take you to your room. I'll see you tomorrow at practice." He started to turn away. Then paused and added, "You've taken a big step today. You can't expect it to happen all at once. Be patient."

"Yes, Coach."

Pichu stayed in the shower until most of the players were gone. Then, when he was dressed, Coach Connor came out of his office and said, "I'm supposed to show you to your new digs."

"My what?"

"Your room. You're going to camp out in the dorm for the rest of the week. Get your things and follow me."

Pichu picked up his suitcase and the bag of food that his mother had packed. When he was almost out the door someone called his name. He turned and saw Rev smiling at him.

"Dude, you like to party?"

"I don't know."

"There's gonna be a party tonight. Lotta the guys from the team will be there. Wanna go?"

Coach Connors nudged Pichu and said, "You should go. Get to know the guys."

"Okay."

"Sweet," Rev said. "I'll come by your room and get you. We can walk there."

Suddenly, Coach Connors' voice changed. "Revinski."

"Yeah, Coach?"

"No funny business."

"What are you talking about?" he asked in a tone of mock innocence.

"I think you know. I'm holding you responsible. Coach Jordan'll bounce you off the team if anything happens to this kid."

"Don't worry, Coach. It'll all be good clean fun."

"Okay." The coach pulled a key out of his pocket and looked at it. "He'll be in room 207 over at Jock Hall."

"Sounds good. I'll take real good care of him. Later, Pichu."

Rev smiled. Pichu suddenly noticed that Rev's teeth were perfect and very white.

Pichu followed Coach Connors out of the locker room and they walked together across the campus. It was quiet with people occasionally passing by on bicycles. The trees around them were very tall. There were many large brick buildings with red tile roofs.

"A week from now, this place'll be packed," Coach Connor said as they walked. "Right now, the only ones here are athletes like you. You'll be in a dorm with the football players. They get pretty rowdy sometimes. So watch out."

They kept walking and Pichu saw that gray clouds were blowing in over the tops of the buildings. He felt cold and the empty brick buildings made him feel lonely. It was almost dinner time and he couldn't help thinking of how everyone was sitting down at the table at home. Angelina and her family would be eating dinner next door. Pichu's mother would be putting the tortillas on the table and setting out pots filled with refried beans and rice and fried fish. After dinner he would call to Angelina and they would meet out front and go for a walk on the beach. On special nights, Pichu's father would let him borrow the truck and he and Angelina would drive up the coast.

"I saw that first shot you took today," Coach Connor said. "It was a bullet."

"Thanks, Coach."

"You got game. No question about it."

Pichu didn't understand, so he didn't answer.

"But soccer's a team sport. I hope you can fit in with the other guys. Lord knows we need something to give us a kick in the butt. Well, here you are: Jock Hall."

They had stopped in front of another tall brick building. The pulsing beat of music was coming from several different places inside. Coach Connors held the door for Pichu and they walked up to the second floor. In the hallways were three huge men with their shirts off. Their chests and shoulders were lumpy with muscles and Pichu felt they were looking down at him as if he were a child. The coach unlocked a wooden door to room 207 and held it open as Pichu walked in. The floor was linoleum and a small metal frame bed was along one wall. Sheets, a pillow and blankets were all at the foot of the bed. The one window looked out on a parking lot and a tall building. Beyond that Pichu could just see the edge of the soccer stadium with the mountains in the distance and the gray clouds above the mountains.

"You can use this meal pass downstairs in the cafeteria," Coach Connors said, handing him a plastic card. "They're probably serving dinner in a few minutes."

Pichu set his suitcase down. He saw there was a small refrigerator so he put in the bag of food his mother had given him. He sat down on the bed.

"Here's the key," Coach Connor said, placing the key on the desk. "All set then?"

"All set, Coach."

"See you at practice." He paused at the door. "Have fun at the party. The guys are okay once you get to know them."

"Yeah, they seem like nice guys," Pichu said. He hoped it sounded like he was telling the truth.

Coach Connors closed the door after him. Pichu stood in the middle of the room for a few minutes, trying to decide what to do next. Finally, he lay down on the bed and closed his eyes, thinking that he might be able to fall asleep. The sound of the pounding bass was coming through the walls. He heard the men laughing outside. A door slammed somewhere. The music was turned off and the room became very quiet. The silence intensified and Pichu opened his eyes and looked at the cinder block walls all around him. His chest heaved once, as if he was struggling to get rid of the loneliness inside him. His stomach turned and he found himself wondering what his mother was serving for dinner back home in Los Barriles.

Suddenly, it occurred to him that he could telephone his house. He took the room key and made sure he had his wallet with the money his father had given him. Much of it was in pesos but he knew he also had some American money that tourists had given him. He walked out of Jock Hall and along the street until he was off the campus. The houses were made of wood with porches and yards with thick grass, like in the soccer stadium. No dogs were walking on the streets. There was no dust or garbage and everything was clean and very beautiful. He wondered why it didn't make him happy. He came to a small store that looked a little like the Super Mercado in Los Barriles. Some of the signs in the window were in Spanish.

Inside, behind the counter, a tall man with dark skin wore a piece of cloth wrapped around his head. He watched Pichu suspiciously as he entered.

"I need a phone card," Pichu said. Herman the German had told him about phone cards. He had never been to America. But he said his cousin had worked in San Diego. All the Mexicans bought phone cards so they could call home.

"How much?"

"I need a phone card. To call Mexico."

"I know what they're for," the clerk said impatiently. "But for how much? Ten dollars, twenty dollars, fifty dollars?"

Pichu was confused. He pulled out some money and held it out. The clerk said, "Okay, just twenty dollars then."

He took Pichu's money and handed him the card. Pichu stood there uncertainly.

"Phone's out front," the man said. Then, in a softer tone he added, "Follow the directions on the back of the card. It'll tell you what to do."

Pichu had to dial several times. He kept getting strange noises over the telephone receiver. But then suddenly it was ringing!

"Hola!" It was Neto.

"Neto! Hola! Soy Pichu!"

"Pichu!" Neto said. Then Pichu could hear him yelling to the rest of the house, "Pichu is calling from the United States!" There was a lot of shouting and bumping, and everyone was fighting to talk into the phone. Pichu laughed, imagining everyone running for the phone. His brothers and sisters shouted many questions into the phone. Then there was the sound of his father's voice, angry, telling them all to go back to the table and eat their dinner.

"So how is America?" his father asked.

Many different feelings flooded through Pichu. He knew he should be grateful for this chance with the hopes of his family on his shoulders.

"Papa, you can't imagine what it is like. The cars are all new and the windshields aren't even broken. And they don't have dogs on the street."

"No dogs on the street? Where are the dogs then?" his father asked.

"They are kept in the houses. And they are given baths and they even smell nice with no skin problems."

"And how is the soccer? Have you played? Have you scored? Did they see how good you are?"

"The soccer is not good."

"Why not?"

"They don't want me here. They won't pass the ball to me. And if I shoot, they knock me down."

His father thought this over. Pichu imagined him rubbing his bushy mustache with his rough fingers and frowning as he thought.

"Papa, I want to quit. I want to come home."

"Yes, you can quit, Pichu. But it's important for you to quit at your time. Not at their time."

"When will that be?"

"I don't know. But it isn't now. You have to wait."

"But Papa — "

"Wait. Be patient. And then you can come home when it is the right time. Besides, if I — "

Pichu heard his mother's voice in the background.

"Your mother will speak to you now. Goodbye, Delfincito."

His mother's voice came on the line. It made Pichu realize how far away he was. And how he had always taken things for granted.

"Something has happened," his mother said in a tone of voice that frightened him.

"What is it?"

"Everyone is talking about it."

"What are they talking about?"

"Even the maids and bus boys in the restaurants talk of it. For days, all the boats have come back empty. They did not catch any fish."

"But there have been many days where they didn't catch a marlin."

"Not just marlin, Pichu. They didn't catch any fish at all."

"Not even dorado?"

"Not dorado. Not rooster fish." She paused, and said in a voice that brought up a fear that had been with him for some time. "The fish are gone, Pichu."

Pichu heard the words but they didn't fully sink in. There had always been fish in the sea, so many fish you could run across their backs all the way to the shore. True, there had been some bad days recently, but then the next day of fishing was fine. Now, his mother's words frightened him. A horrible image flashed into his mind of a still, lifeless sea, an empty sea. And it made him panicky and hot.

"How can this be?" he asked.

"People are saying it's the long-liners — the fisherman that string a line three miles long with thousands of hooks. It's the long-liners who have ruined it with their greed. Your father is very worried. He is trying to find work but he doesn't want to work in a factory."

"My father is a fisherman," Pichu said angrily.

"Your father will always find a way to feed his family."

"Please, Mamá. Don't let him do that. I will help with the money. And you will see. The fish will return."

There was a long silence as his mother seemed to be considering his words. In the background, he heard the chatter of his family around the dinner table. Finally, his mother simply said, "Thank you, Pichu." They said goodbye and he hung up. Standing there at the pay phone outside the store, the isolation closed in on him again and he found himself cut off from his family in a strange country that he didn't understand.

Chapter **10**

When Pichu walked into the dining hall he saw that it had a very high ceiling with big chandeliers hanging down. On the walls were paintings of athletic events that had been held at the university over the years. Some of the paintings showed football players dressed in old-fashioned helmets or muscular baseball players swinging at pitches. There were no paintings of soccer players. The late afternoon sun streamed through the tall windows that looked out on the soccer stadium and the green grass practice fields. The smell of food was in the air and the clatter of plates and silverware came from the kitchen.

Pichu took a tray and slid it along a gleaming metal counter as he picked out his dinner. He was happy when he saw they were serving enchiladas and rice. He was also amazed to see that he could take as much Coke as he wanted without paying. He carried his tray back out into the dining room, looking for a place to sit. There weren't many open seats. At one long table a group of large men sat hunched over plates heaped with food. He moved to the end of the table as far away from them as he could. But as soon as he set his tray down one of the men turned and glared at him. He had a shaved head and sunglasses hooked into the neck of his tee shirt.

"Hey!" the man said, his face twisted in anger. "Football players only! No soccer wimps! Shove off!"

As Pichu picked up his tray to leave, all the men broke into laughter. Their laughter followed him across the hall until he found an empty table in the corner near the kitchen. He took a bite of enchiladas. It was mushy and tasteless. The rice was a little better, but it was overcooked. He had taken several flour tortillas so he rolled one up and bit into it. It had the right texture and it tasted okay. But it didn't taste at all like the ones his mother cooked. He continued eating, head down, hoping no one else would see him.

From where Pichu sat he could look into the kitchen and watch the workers doing their jobs. The students brought their trays up to a window and left them on a stainless steel counter. A worker would spray water onto the dirty plates and then place them in a rack. In the background, other workers scrubbed pots and pans. The kitchen staff wore white pants and T-shirts with nets covering their heads. They joked with each other and laughed as they worked, talking in Spanish.

When Pichu was done eating, he took his tray to the window and handed it to a worker, a young guy who looked as if he was about his age. The worker had black hair and Pichu assumed he was Mexican. As he took the tray, he smiled briefly at Pichu and nodded.

Pichu stood there watching the worker take his tray and rinse off his plate. When the guy turned back to the window he was surprised to see Pichu still standing there.

"Can I help you?" the worker asked, speaking with a slight accent.

"Yes," Pichu said. "Can I ask you a question?"

"Sure."

Pichu hesitated. "Can I come into the kitchen?"

"Okay."

Pichu found the entrance to the kitchen and walked in. The worker was waiting for him.

"Do you speak Spanish?" Pichu asked.

The worker nodded.

"I need your help," Pichu said in Spanish. "Can you tell me how I can get a job here?"

"You have to talk to Señor Vargas."

"Can you introduce me?"

"Sure. Follow me." The worker called to one of the others and said, "Cover the window for a second!" He led Pichu past large tin cans of beans, peaches and other food. He saw large machines for mixing dough and baking bread. They reached an office door. Inside the small, hot office a fat man with thinning greasy hair was writing on papers held on a clipboard.

"Señor Vargas? I have a student here who wants a job."

"A job?" Señor Vargas said, looking up impatiently. "What kind of a job?"

"Anything to make some money," Pichu said. "I'm a good worker."

"You done kitchen work before?"

Pichu's heart sank. He felt that he would be turned down. Then he realized that, in a way, he might still have a chance. "In my hometown in Mexico, I worked at a hotel." Pichu felt this was truthful because the dock where the boats left from was at the hotel. Occasionally, he had helped out in the kitchen as a bus boy.

Señor Vargas's eyes seemed to soften and lose their impatience. "What town are you from?" he asked in Spanish.

"Los Barriles."

"The fishing there is the best in the world. I'm from Cabo. I used to go to Los Barriles to catch the rooter fish. The rooster fish is the best fighter in the ocean." Señor Vargas's thick fingers played with the pen he had been writing with. "We can always use an extra worker at breakfast. But you have to be here at 5 a.m. to help set up. Can you do that?"

"I promise I will be here at 5 a.m.— much earlier if you need me."

Señor Vargas laughed. It was a deep, warm laugh.

"We only pay six dollars an hour. But you are paid every week. Let me see your green card."

Pichu's heart sank again.

"I don't have a green card. I'm just visiting to try out for the soccer team."

"You're going to be a student here?" Señor Vargas asked. He seemed surprised and he looked at Pichu more closely.

"Yes."

"And play on the soccer team?"

"Yes."

"I go to all the soccer games here," Señor Vargas said. "If you're on the team you must be a great player. Okay. If you're a student you can work without a green card. Be here at 5 a.m. And wear a white T-shirt and rubber-soled shoes. The floor gets slippery."

"Thank you, Señor Vargas," Pichu said, shaking his hand enthusiastically.

Señor Vargas laughed, amazed at his enthusiasm for the job. Then, as Pichu walked away, he added, "I'll come to the games and watch you play. I'm a huge soccer fan. Soccer is the greatest sport in the world!"

Chapter **11**

When Pichu climbed the stairs back to his room on the second floor, he saw Tommy Revinski waiting in front of his door. Pichu suddenly remembered he was supposed to go to a party with him.

"Dude, I thought you flaked on me," Rev said.

"I was eating dinner," Pichu answered.

"The food sucks, huh?"

"Maybe. But there is a lot of it," Pichu answered, not wanting to be disrespectful.

Rev laughed. "You got that right." He looked at Pichu and said, "So, ready to party?"

Pichu saw that Rev was wearing an expensive looking blue shirt and shorts that showed off his tanned, muscular legs. Pichu suddenly felt that his own clothes were ugly and looked cheap. He felt everyone at the party would think he looked different. They would know that he was from Mexico and that his family didn't have money. But when he tried to think of what to wear he realized he didn't have anything that would make him look like Rev or any of the other players. In fact, he really didn't want to go to the party at all. But then he thought of Coach Connors saying, "You should go. Get to know the guys."

"I'm ready to party," Pichu said.

"Right on," Rev said and smiled. When he smiled his lips pulled back and showed his teeth, which were straight and unnaturally white. His smile made Pichu think of the pictures he had seen in the magazines his mother brought home from the hotel.

As they walked out of the dormitory and across the campus, Rev said, "So you're from Mexico?"

"Yes."

"What do you do there?"

"I work with my father. I'm a fisherman." But as he said this he thought of what his mother had said: The fish are gone. He felt the same hot, panicky feeling again.

"I went fishing down in Cabo on Spring break last year. Got a marlin. Is that what you catch?" Rev asked.

"Oh, no. We catch the bait for the fishermen. I'm a ponga boy."

Rev laughed. "A what?"

"Ponga boy," Pichu said, feeling sorry that he brought it up. "We work in a ponga boat. Catch live bait."

"A ponga boy," Rev said again, thinking it over and smiling. "I remember that from when I was down there. The little boats came around to the fishing boats and sell bait for 10 bucks. That's what you do?"

"Yes," he said uncertainly. But then, hoping to impress his new friend he added, "My father has his own boat."

"His own boat, huh?" Rev answered. "Wow."

They walked until they reached a row of large brick houses.

"Here we are," Rev said. "Party palace. Gonna be lots of ladies here tonight. You might get lucky." He nudged Pichu. "Lucky. Comprendo?"

"Lucky is good," Pichu said, and smiled. But he didn't know what Rev was hinting at.

They walked in the front door and Pichu heard the thumping bass of a loud stereo. As they climbed the stairs, he could hear voices and people shouting. He smelled spilled beer. It was the same sour smell at the hotel in Los Barriles when he passed the bar and the sun was coming up and heating the tile around the bar stools where the Americans sat drinking late into the night.

Rev opened another door and suddenly all the sounds were much louder. People were everywhere — in the hallway, going in and out of rooms and in the stairway. Most of them held plastic cups and they all yelled so they could be heard above the music. He saw Moore and Shields with two girls. They were the same girls who had been watching practice from the grand stands that afternoon. As Moore spotted Pichu, he pointed at him and said something to the girls. The four of them laughed.

"Hey, Pichu!" a voice said. He felt a hand on his shoulder. He turned and saw Pete, the third string winger, with his long curly hair.

"Hey, Pete."

"Did you meet the guys?"

"Many of them," Pichu said, wondering if he could slip away from this party without being noticed.

"You've got an awesome shot, man," Pete said. "Pow! That low knuckler — drives goalkeepers crazy."

"You have a good shot, too," Pichu said, even though he actually felt that Pete moved awkwardly.

"Yeah, right. Thanks anyway. I try hard — that's my thing. I try hard and maybe someday, I'll get off the bench. You know what they say, 'The sun shines on every dog's ass once in his life.'"

Pichu laughed. For a moment he thought about telling Pete the story of the dog from Tijuana. But then he decided against it.

"Look, I wanted to ask you something," Pete said, looking serious. He lowered his voice. "Can I practice my Spanish with you?"

Pichu was surprised by the question; why would anyone in the U.S. want to learn to speak Spanish?

"See, here's the thing," Pete continued. "I tutor these kids, low income, Hispanic. If I could speak with them in their own language, maybe they'd listen to me. 'Cause they need help. They really, really need help. So, habla en Espanol?"

"Claro," Pichu said.

Pete smiled excitedly and shook Pichu's hand. "Gracias. Gracias. Por favor, quieres una cervesa?

"No gracias."

"Coca Cola?"

"Si, gracias."

"Una Coca Cola por el jefe," Pete said. He pushed his way through the crowd and disappeared. Pichu suddenly felt uncomfortable standing there alone, as if everyone was looking at him. He took out a pack of Chiclets from his pocket, popped one into his mouth and nervously began chewing. Looking around he noticed that everyone here was dressed in clothes that looked casual but were actually expensive. The T-shirt and shorts Pichu was wearing felt out of place, as if he was a little boy. He wished that Pete would return. He would drink his Coke and then leave. He needed to get to bed early so that he could wake up in time for his new job.

"Ponga boy!" a voice called. He looked around and saw the tall thin striker called Frasier coming toward him. Out of the corner of his eye, Pichu caught a glimpse of Rev smiling and watching him.

"That's what you are," Frasier said, standing close to Pichu. "You're a bait boy. Right?"

"I'm a fisherman," Pichu said.

"No, you aren't. You're a bait boy," Frasier said, his small features pinched together angrily in the center of his red face. He held a plastic cup in his hand and beer sloshed over the side. Moore and Shields saw what was happening and gathered around along with their girlfriends.

"I catch live bait. I sell it to the fishermen," Pichu said.

"I told you!" Frasier shouted to the others. "He's just a ponga boy."

"But my father owns his own ponga boat," Pichu blurted out.

"His own ponga boat?" Frasier mocked. "He must be a very important man!" Then he jabbed Pichu in the chest and said, "You know who my father is? Huh? My father's the CEO of American Electronics. And he owns a yacht. He could buy your father and his ponga boat and everything you own with one week's salary. What do you think of that, ponga boy?"

"I think you should keep your hands to yourself when you talk," Pichu said, feeling his anger rising.

"What are you going to do if I don't?"

"I'm going to make you sorry."

Frasier pretended to cry. "Oh please, Ponga Boy. Please don't make me sorry." Moore and Shields laughed and the girls giggled and clapped their hands. But another girl nearby with short black hair said, "Leave him alone, Frasier. God, you're such an idiot."

"Shut up, Christy. Ponga boy comes up here, thinks he can take my spot on the line, thinks he can tell me what to do."

He pushed Pichu in the chest again.

"I told you to stop that," Pichu said.

"And I said I'd do anything I want to you." Frasier pushed Pichu in the chest again. "There. What're you going to do?" Then he started singing, "Ponga, ponga. Ponga boy." He turned around as if dancing and shoved Pichu in his chest, knocking him backwards. He continued singing, "Ponga, ponga. Ponga boy." Everyone was laughing. "Okay, Ponga boy. Bring it on." He shoved him again. "Come on. Take a shot."

Pichu's face felt like it was exploding with anger. The laughter was ringing in his ears. It made him feel like the walls were caving in on him. The circle of faces leaned in, mocking him. He wanted to ram his fist right into Frasier's sour face. And he knew he could do it, too. Frasier was bent over him, wide open. And it would be so easy. Just — bam! — and Frasier would be on the floor. He felt his fingers curling into fists. The muscles in his shoulders tightened.

"Come on, ponga boy. Fight like a man."

The words suddenly cut through Pichu's anger, dissolving it. He thought of what his mother told him long ago. Instead of learning to fight like a man, you should learn to love like a man. Then you would always be there to help your family. It was very important for him to help his family now. If he punched Frasier now, he would be sent home. And if he was sent home, he couldn't help his father and his family when they really needed him.

"What's the matter, ponga boy? Can't you fight like a man?" Frasier spilled beer on Pichu. "Now what are you going to do?"

"I'm going to teach you a lesson," Pichu said.

"How are you going to do that?" Frasier said, leaning into his face.

Pichu moved so quickly no one knew what was happening. It looked like Pichu had punched Frasier in the nose. But what he had really done was take the gum from his mouth and stick it on the end of Frasier's nose.

"Why do you put your gum on your nose?" Pichu said, laughing. He plucked it off and stuck it on Frasier's jaw. "Do you like it there better?"

"Hey!" Frasier tried to catch Pichu's hands. But Pichu was too quick.

Pichu was dancing like a boxer now. Picking the gum off Frasier's jaw and putting it under his eye. Then on his nose again. The people around Frasier were laughing, pointing at Frasier as he tried to stop him.

"Cut it out!" Frasier shouted, and took a swing at Pichu. But Pichu ducked to the side and moved the gum back to just in front of his ear, then stretched some out and looped it to his other ear forming a big gooey grin.

"Look. A big smile!" Pichu said.

Frasier threw a flurry of punches but Pichu was never there. Moore put his arm around Frasier and steered him away.

"What's going on?" It was Pete, holding a can of Coke for Pichu.

"Don't worry," someone said. "It's over now. Ponga Boy took the fight out of Frasier."

Pete handed the can of Coke to Pichu. He said, "Frasier's got some real issues. You have to ignore him."

"No problem," Pichu said, feeling very relieved and oddly happy, as if he had narrowly escaped catastrophe. He felt a hand on his arm. He turned and saw Rev smiling at him.

"Dude. That was very cool."

"But it wasn't cool you told everyone I am a ponga boy," Pichu said, his anger flaring.

Rev shrugged. "Hey, no hard feelings. Okay?"

Pichu took a sip of the Coca Cola. It had never tasted so good. He calmed himself down, smiled at Rev and said, "No problem, dude."

Chapter **12**

Pichu was waiting by the door to the kitchen when Señor Vargas arrived for work the next morning at 5 a.m. It was dark and cold waiting here, but Pichu wanted to show his gratitude to Señor Vargas for giving him this job.

"You're early," Señor Vargas said, smiling approvingly. "Good. Follow me." They walked through the kitchen, turning on lights as they went. They arrived at a small office door behind all the stacked boxes of food. Señor Vargas took out a big ring of keys and opened his office door. He pulled out a clipboard with several forms on it. He handed it to Pichu along with a hairnet.

"You'll have to wear this whenever you're serving food. But today you'll probably be at the window. New workers always start at the cleanup window. Fernando will be here in a few minutes, and he'll show you what to do."

When Pichu was done filling out the forms, he looked up and saw Fernando walking in, yawning and rubbing his eyes, which were puffy with sleep. They went to the cleanup window and Fernando showed him how to take the trays from students and scrape the plates into the garbage disposal. Then he had to spray off the plate and stack it in a rack that went into a dishwasher.

"Just wait until the girls come to the window," Fernando said excitedly. "They wear these loose shirts. And when they bend over to put their trays down — I'm telling you, it's all right there!"

Fernando stuck his tongue out and acted dizzy. Pichu laughed.

"But they hate us," Fernando said abruptly.

"Hate us? Why?"

"They hate Mexicans. They think we're dirty. So sometimes we play tricks on them. When they bring the tray up, we get a hand full of garbage. When we take the tray, we put our hands on their hands and smear all that crap onto them." He imitated the girl's revulsion. "They scream — iiieee! It's so funny. Uh oh. Time to eat now. I'll show you where we go."

Pichu took a tray and followed Fernando through the cafeteria line. They loaded their plates with scrambled eggs, bacon and hash browns. He followed Fernando to a table in the back where other kitchen workers were eating. They were all Mexicans and were speaking in Spanish. Pichu recognized accents from all over Mexico. But most of the men were from Mexico City and the mainland.

Señor Vargas appeared carrying a plate so loaded with food that pieces of eggs and hash browns fell on the floor. He said, "Amigos, this is Pichu. He's going to be playing on the soccer team."

One of the workers looked up and spoke with his mouth full. "If you're good enough to play on the team, why are you stuck working here with us?"

"To get extra money to send to my family," Pichu said.

All the men nodded and accepted this without further questions. They asked Pichu where he was from. Then they talked about where they were from in Mexico and how their families needed the money they earned here in the United States. Then the subject turned back to soccer. The men were eager to tell Pichu what soccer teams they liked best. This led to a loud argument about which Mexican team could beat other Mexican teams. Then there was another argument about who was the best player in the Mexican league. Most of the players who were favored were the top scorers. But some of the others said it would be foolish to forget the goalies and great defensive players who dominated the center of the field. Finally, Señor Vargas stood up, burped and looked at his watch. "Aye!" he said. "We better get to work."

Pichu took his place at the window, where he could look into the dining hall. Students were coming in and picking up trays. They reappeared moments later with steaming plates of food. They took their seats and began eating. Soon, trays stacked with dirty dishes were being handed to him through the window. He became very busy trying to keep up, scraping the garbage and stacking the plates in racks for the washer.

"Check it out, man!" Fernando said. He pointed through the window. Pichu looked and saw a table of girls eating breakfast.

"They are so hot!" Fernando said. "Keep a sharp eye on them and you'll see something you can think about tonight while you lie in bed." He made a rude gesture and laughed hysterically.

"Hey, I'll do you a favor," Fernando said. "Go out and get the cart over there in the corner." He pointed at a stainless steel cart with dirty dishes in it near the girls' table. "Go on. Get the cart. And while you're there, check out the ladies, man. They're so hot!"

Pichu left the kitchen and walked out into the dining hall. He felt uncomfortable in his white T-shirt that was now blotched with food. His rubber-soled shoes, which were wet, made squeaking noises as he walked. The girls at the table saw him coming and one of them looked around. When she turned back to her friends he heard her say, "That's the Ponga Boy," and they all laughed.

Suddenly, Pichu wished he wasn't out here. He wanted to be back in the kitchen where he was invisible, where he could work hard and speak Spanish. He noticed that the girls were talking to some of the football players who had just come in. They were the ones who called him a "soccer wimp" yesterday. He looked around for the quickest way to get back to the kitchen. But when he looked through the window he saw Fernando motioning him to bring the cart back.

Dirty plates were stacked everywhere around the cart. One plate of food was heaped with scrambled eggs and hash browns and was almost untouched. What a waste, Pichu thought. He picked it up and was holding it front of him. He was about to put it into the plastic tub when there was a loud smack and suddenly he couldn't see. Cold scrambled eggs were everywhere — in his eyes, on his face, dripping from his chin. As he was wiping it all off, he heard laughter. He looked across the hall and saw the football players laughing. They had thrown a canned peach at him that hit the plate of food and sent it flying all over him.

The laughter was growing and growing, spreading from table to table. Soon, everyone in the hall was laughing at him. Everywhere he turned, he saw laughing faces. The football players were pounding the table and gasping for air. At the door to the dining hall, Moore and Frasier were just walking in and they looked around to see what was happening. They saw Pichu covered with food and they pointed at him and began laughing too, yelling, "Pon-ga boy! Pon-ga boy!"

Pichu walked back into the kitchen pushing the cart with dirty dishes. He shoved it at Fernando who said, "Hey man, it wasn't my fault." Pichu kept walking until he reached the back of the kitchen. He opened the large freezer door and stepped inside. The heavy door closed after him. It was quiet here in the freezer but somehow he could still hear the laughter. He stood in the freezer thinking how, within a few days, his world had completely changed. Nothing like this had ever happened to him in Los Barriles before. Life was easy and he understood the people. Now, everywhere he turned there was trouble. He wanted to walk out and just go home. But he thought of his father's advice, how he couldn't quit on their terms — he had to do it on his. His family was counting on him to succeed. He was trapped.

Pichu stayed in the freezer, letting the cold dissolve his anger. Finally, he couldn't stand it anymore and he returned to the cleanup window. The dining hall had returned to normal. The girls at the table were getting up and bringing their trays to him.

"Here come those girls that laughed at you," Fernando said. "Do the thing I was telling you about."

"What thing?"

"Smear garbage on them."

"Why?"

"Man, they laughed at you," Fernando said. "You should mess them up."

Pichu saw the girls coming, and he remembered their laughter. The anger began to rise inside him. He wanted to get back at the girls even if it was only in a small way. He looked at the bucket of garbage beside him. It was filled with hash browns and coffee grounds and eggs all swimming in greasy water. He looked back at the girls with their blond hair and their perfect white skin and red fingernails. He pictured the garbage dripping from them and making them ugly. He imagined that Rudolfo and Herman the German were here with him and they were all laughing at these girls. Thinking these thoughts, he felt something he had never felt before. It was an ugly, dark feeling that seemed to rise up from a place inside him he had never known was there.

Pichu scooped up a handful of garbage and waited.

The first one to the window was the dark-haired girl from the party last night. She was the one they called Christy, who'd said Frasier was an idiot.

Christy reached out and handed the tray to Pichu. He was about to smear her hand with garbage when she looked him in the eye and said, "Are you okay?"

Pichu stared back at her, waiting.

She said, "I'm sorry about what they did to you. It wasn't right."

It was so surprising that Pichu didn't know what to say.

"Are you okay?" she asked again.

Pichu nodded. He took her plate and turned away. He felt ashamed.

Fernando had been watching this and said, "Man, you missed your chance! You could have messed her up, big time."

"You said they hate us because they think Mexicans are dirty," Pichu said. "So you want me to do something dirty to them? That doesn't make sense."

"But they laughed at you, man," Fernando said. "You've got to get even."

"I'll get even," he said, stepping toward Fernando. "But I'll do it my own way. Okay?"

"Okay. Jeez. Chill out, man."

Pichu turned back to the window and looked across the dining hall. Christy was standing there looking back at him.

After the dining hall closed, Señor Vargas asked Pichu to mop the floor. He put the chairs on the tables and began to work. Working the mop made him think of scooping the mackerel and mullet from the sea and putting them in his father's ponga boat. He was looking down at the tile floor, but he was seeing the sparkling water of the Sea of Cortez. He was hearing the whooshing of the dishwasher in the kitchen. But in his imagination, it was the waves breaking on the rocks near the blowhole. He thought back to the afternoon when he went there with Rudolfo, Neto and Luis. And Angelina was there, too, telling him to be careful. She seemed to hang in front of his eyes and speak to him in Spanish in her soft voice. She seemed to be here in front of him and yet was not here at all. Why did he have to come here? he wondered. He could be home with his family and Angelina. He could be with people he understood and people who loved him.

"Pichu?" a voice asked.

He turned and saw a tall, thin man with glasses and a kind face. "Are you Pichu?" the man asked in Spanish.

"I am Pichu," he answered in Spanish.

"Coach Jordan said I would find you here. But I didn't expect you to be working. Didn't they give you a stipend?"

"I don't know stipend."

"Didn't they give you extra money?"

"I have enough money," Pichu said defensively.

"Then why are you working?"

"To get some more money for my family," Pichu said, feeling that he had been trapped. But this man smiled understandingly. Besides, he spoke Spanish with an accent that sounded familiar to Pichu. So maybe he was here to help him.

"I am Professor Baca. Coach Jordan asked me to help you with the admissions process. I have your transcripts here." He waved the folder of papers. "Pichu, you are a very good student."

"Thank you."

"When I heard about you, I thought you would be another dumb jock," he said, using the English phrase. "But your test scores are very high."

"What is a dumb jock?" Pichu asked.

Professor Baca laughed. "It's hard to explain." Then, the tall thin man was quiet, looking at Pichu standing here in his dirty T-shirt holding the mop. And he seemed to understand what Pichu was feeling.

"Is this your first time in America?"

"Yes."

"Have you ever been away from your family before?"

"No."

"You must be homesick."

"Yes. Very much."

Professor Baca was quiet for a moment, thinking. He took off his glasses and rubbed them with his thumb. His black hair was long and uncombed and it fell in his face.

"Pichu, why don't you get changed and meet me in a few minutes at the student union? We'll go over your records and talk about the tests you have to take."

A few minutes later, Pichu found Professor Baca seated at a table in a shady area outside the student union. He looked up at Pichu, smiled, and told him to sit down at the table. They talked for a long time while they drank Coca-Cola. It turned out that Professor Baca was a visiting professor from the University of La Paz. He had grown up in San Felipe, where his father was a doctor. As they talked, Pichu forgot about his loneliness and all the trouble he had gone through since he arrived. He relaxed, knowing that his words wouldn't be twisted into something to be used against him. And he knew that this man was not looking at his clothes and thinking how he must come from a poor family.

Finally, Professor Baca leaned forward and said, "Pichu, why are you here?"

"To get a real education."

Professor Baca nodded as if he expected that answer. But then he said, "Is that why you're really here? You said you already know what you need to know to be a fisherman."

Pichu felt a moment of panic. Was this a test? He didn't want to lose the trust of his new friend.

"I'm here to play soccer."

"But you can play soccer in Mexico."

"Here, I can play against the best. I can find out how good I am."

Professor Baca nodded. "That's important. But I want to give you some advice. I understand you are very talented. But you always have to remember, your talent is not who you are. Who you are is what you become. Do you understand?"

The words seemed to hold great wisdom, yet Pichu couldn't really grasp the meaning of what he said.

"No..." Pichu said at last.

"Who you are is what you become through hard work and studying. Looking at your tests and your grades, I see that you have a fine mind. Your mind needs to be developed just like your soccer skills. So please don't settle for just being a dumb jock. The world doesn't need another dumb jock. The world needs someone who can think and solve problems and set a good example for other people. Will you remember what I said?"

"Yes."

"Good. Now, let's get down to these tests," he opened the envelope and laid the pages in front of Pichu along with a yellow pencil. "If you do as well as I think you will, the next step will be to choose classes for you."

Pichu picked up the paper and looked at the first question. He was lost in thought when he heard Professor Baca speak as if from a great distance. He said, "You can start the test now, Pichu. Good luck."

Chapter **13**

Pichu was in the locker room putting on his uniform for the pre-season game against Santa Clara. He laced up his cleats just the way he liked them and tucked in his new shirt which was a little too big. He crossed himself, said a short prayer and started walking toward the door to go outside. As he passed Coach Jordan's office, he heard a voice call his name. He turned and saw Coach Jordan motioning him to step into his office.

"I need to speak with you," the coach said, pushing his glasses up on his nose. Pichu stepped into the office

"Close the door, please."

Pichu closed the door on the noisy banging of lockers and the players yelling back and forth. He stood in front of the coach's big wooden desk. The bright light from a window behind the desk made it hard for Pichu to see Coach Jordan's expression. Pichu's cleats clicked on the tile floor as he nervously shifted his weight.

"Are you comfortable in your dorm room?" Coach Jordan asked.

"Yes, sir."

"I understand you're working in the kitchen now. If you needed more money, you should have told me."

Pichu sensed his disapproval. "You've done so much for me already."

"But you're here to play soccer. And to study," he quickly added. "Besides, what will happen if you have to travel to play a game? You'll have to miss work."

"Señor Vargas is a huge soccer fan," Pichu said. "I know he will understand."

Coach Jordan held Pichu's eyes with his sharp gaze. After a long pause he said, "I'm not starting you today."

Pichu understood that this meant the coach was disappointed in him. He shifted his weight again, hearing his cleats on the tile floor and feeling the tight muscles in his legs.

"I've, well... I've been a little confused about what I've seen from you in practice," Coach Jordan said, squinting as if in pain. "I see the talent but there are no sparks." He paused, as if waiting for an answer.

Pichu thought how, at the last few practices, they never gave him the ball. He thought of how he avoided shooting because of Frasier's threats. And so he found himself doing little more than taking those balls that came to him by chance and then passing off as quickly as he could. Still, he knew he had to make the team. He had to succeed here — not just for himself, but for his father and his whole family. Even for Angelina, too.

"You know, Pichu, I took a big chance bringing you up here. I really stuck my neck out. And I'm still willing to give you the chance to prove yourself. But I just want to know if there is something going on that I don't understand."

As the silence grew, Pichu realized that the locker room was now quiet. That meant that the team must be on the field now. He wanted to be out there too, on the grass, where things were simple. Either the ball went into the net or it didn't. He couldn't pretend something was really something else. He knew exactly where he stood because it was all there in front of him. But off the field he understood nothing about his life and the new people he had to interact with.

"I can do better, Coach," Pichu said, looking down.

"I know you can, too," Coach Jordan said. "But will you?"

"I'll try."

"This isn't about trying. It's about doing," he said, fixing Pichu in his gaze again. "Okay, we need to get out there." He put his hand on Pichu's shoulder as they walked out into the locker room. Pichu was reminded of how his father's touch felt. It was heavy but it made him feel he was saying, I'm here if you need me. Coach Jordan's hand was only heavy.

They pushed through a door and out into the sunlight. As Pichu was jogging away, Coach Jordan called after him. "Pichu! Professor Baca called me this morning. He said your test scores were very good. He was impressed."

Pichu smiled and nodded. He ran between the bleachers and out onto the field. As he emerged into the vast open space, he realized the stands were filled with people. He slowed down, turning and taking in the crowd. When he got to the goal, he found Pete enjoying his amazement. "Pretty cool, huh? The crowd gets you pumped."

"Pumped?"

"Pumped up. Psyched, you know? Whatever. Okay, better warm up — kickoff is in five minutes."

Pichu jogged around the goal, feeling the muscles in his legs coming alive and the blood beginning to flow. The grass felt thick under his cleats and dragged on his feet, slowing him. He looked down to the other team from Santa Clara. The players wore white and gold uniforms and were running precise drills. Their two goalies were putting on their thick gloves and walking into the nets.

"Tough break, Ponga Boy," a voiced shouted. Pichu turned and saw Frasier pointing at him. His face was pinched in anger and he seemed to be spitting the words at him. "You're riding the bench with the other losers."

As Pichu kept running, the angry words settled in his stomach as if he had swallowed something bitter. He shuffled from side to side and then ran backwards, feeling his body growing warm and the familiar pounding of his heart. He joined the other strikers and took a few shots on the goalie. The ball came toward him slowly and it felt soggy as it came off his foot. He wished they were playing on the slick pavement of his field at Los Barriles. There the ball was alive, dancing happily with the lightest touch and exploding off your foot when you took a shot. He watched as Frasier took a pass, trapped it and shot. The ball stayed low and found the corner of the net. As he ran back to the line he pointed at Pichu and said, "Watch and learn, Ponga Boy."

"How can I learn from that?" Pichu muttered. "You'd never get that much time in a game." Pichu heard laughter from behind him and realized that Pete had overheard him talking to himself.

"His shot's nothing compared to yours," Pete said. "I see you in here at night practicing. You never do that stuff in the scrimmages. Why?"

"Soccer is a team sport," Pichu said. "I focus on passing and setting up my teammates."

"Yeah, okay," Pete said. "But why not take a shot now and then? It's not like they would mind if you scored."

"How about you?" Pichu said. "Why don't you score?"

"I'm not exactly going to score from the bench," Pete said bitterly. But then he cheered up. "I hustle. That's my thing. I try hard."

"Maybe you'd do better if you didn't try so hard," Pichu said.

"What?"

"You put too much strength in your shot and you kick only from the knee down. Use your weight and the muscles of the hips and trunk to whip your leg through with explosive speed. Like this."

Pichu teed off on a ball and it shot forward at waist level, then dipped into the goal. Pete laughed.

"Unreal. But I want to see that goal in a game."

"You will," Pichu said. "But just remember, the secret is that when your power increases, so does your accuracy. If you hold nothing back, your body gives you everything. Come here some night and we'll kick it around together."

"Sure! Okay," Pete said, excitedly. "I'd like that."

The referee blew the whistle, and the players jogged back to the sidelines. They huddled around Coach Jordan.

"Okay guys, it's the start of a new season," Coach Jordan said. "Let's get things off to a great start. Today's game doesn't count on the season record. But I'll be making some decisions based on what I see out there. So let's focus and concentrate. Okay, Coach Connors has the starting lineup."

Players' names were read. The crowd cheered as the USF players began to run out onto the field. The players stood at their starting positions, stretching or swinging their legs in smooth high kicks. It would be Santa Clara's kickoff. The referee placed the ball down on the center mark and backed away. He blew the whistle.

The ball was tapped forward by the center, who then pushed to the halfbacks. A long cross found the wing open and the winger dribbled deep into USF's territory. The wing was very fast and accelerated with unexpected speed. He beat the defender and went all the way to the end line before he crossed it back sharply. A striker slid in, hooked his foot around a fullback and found the ball. It shot toward the goal, but hit Kevin full in the chest and bounced off. Luckily, a fullback was there to clear the ball out of danger. Kevin angrily yelled at the fullback, who yelled something back at him, then walked away with his head down.

Pichu heard the two coaches talking. "This isn't the start I was looking for," Coach Jordan said, folding his arms tightly across his chest and squinting through his glasses.

For the first half, the gold and white Santa Clara players always seemed one step ahead of the USF team. They kept the ball in USF's half of the field and always seemed on the verge of scoring. But it was only Kevin's alert goal-keeping that kept them scoreless. Then, with five minutes to go, Kevin kicked the ball to Moore, who saw Rev open on the other side of the field and sent him a long lead pass. Rev reached it a second ahead of the goalie, who had sprinted out of the net to cut it off. Rev flicked the ball up over the sliding goalie then collided full force with him. The two players writhed in pain as the ball trickled into the net for a goal. The crowd exploded, cheering and waving. Horns blew. It was even louder than a game Pichu had once seen in the great city of La Paz.

The ref called a time out, and the two players slowly got to their feet. The Santa Clara goalie limped back into position. Rev tested his leg, but couldn't put any weight on his foot. Two players helped him back to the bench where the trainer bent over him, probing his ankle. Pete jumped to his feet and went to the coach.

"I'm ready, Coach," Pete said hopefully.

Coach Jordan looked past Pete, still scanning the other players on the bench. "In a second, Pete."

The coach pointed at Pichu. "Go in for Rev. But tell Frasier to move out to the wing. I want you inside. And Pichu — try to get something going."

Pichu saw the disappointment on Pete's face. He met Pete's eye and said, "Lo siento, amigo."

Pete smiled weakly and said, "Esta bien."

Pichu ran out onto the center of the field. Before he could speak, Frasier said, "You better not tell me I'm out."

"Coach wants you on wing," Pichu said.

"Jeez! Why? They need me in the middle," Frasier whined. He kicked the ground as he moved to his new position.

Santa Clara kicked off. They moved the ball up the field with a series of short, accurate passes that USF couldn't intercept. The wing cut the ball back to a waiting striker who was wide open. He pounded it into the upper right corner of the net. It was so fast that Kevin couldn't even dive for it. Kevin ran after the ball and angrily booted it down field as he yelled and gestured at the fullbacks for not covering the open player. They were lining up for the kickoff when the referee blew the whistle, signaling the end of the first half. Pichu hadn't even touched the ball.

Chapter 14

At the start of the second half, Pichu decided he had to do something different to show his teammates he was capable of winning the game for them. The first chance he got, he would dribble through the defense, shoot and score. Then, he thought, his teammates would recognize his talent and they would come to like him.

The referee put the ball down on the center of the field for the kick-off. Moore and Shields came in on either side of him. Moore's blond hair was wild and darkened by sweat. Shields' face was flushed and his acne was so red it looked painful.

"I'm going to pass the ball to you, Ponga," Moore said. "Then I'll run behind their strikers and you hit me. Just a simple give-and-go, okay? Think you can handle that?"

Pichu had never heard the term "give-and-go," but he nodded anyway.

"Well, do you?" Moore demanded impatiently.

"Yes. Okay." Pichu answered.

The referee blew the whistle. Moore tapped the ball forward and took off running down field. Pichu controlled the ball, dodged the first challenge, then looked for Moore. He wasn't open. He avoided another gold and white player and looked for someone to pass to. No one was open! He was bumped off the ball, fought for it, then was brought down by a slide tackle. As he scrambled to his feet, he watched the Santa Clara players moving the ball with their short passing game. They carried it all the way to the top of the penalty area, then passed off to the wing. The USF fullback charged in too aggressively and the wing neatly cut the ball to one side, then lofted a perfect centering pass. A tall striker headed it down and under the diving goalie's arms and into the nets for a goal.

"See that?" Moore screamed at Pichu, his face red and his blond curls flying. "That goal was your fault. Are you happy?"

Pichu's plan to score had backfired on him. For the rest of the game, he tried not to make any more mistakes. He dribbled the ball in the midfield but as soon as he got near the goal he passed it off to whoever was open. A couple of times, as they were running back after a goal kick, one of his teammates yelled, "Nice play," or, "That's more like it." Pichu felt encouraged. Late in the game, Frasier took it deep into the corner. He beat the defender and sent a low pass across the goal mouth. Pichu dove head first and hit it solid. The ball flew past the goalie but hit the post and bounced back. For a second, Pichu was sure there would be a follow up shot. But Moore was standing still, his face exploding with anger.

"That was my ball!" he yelled at Pichu. "Didn't you hear me calling? I was wide open."

"Then why didn't you take the follow up shot?" Pichu answered, struggling to get the words out.

Moore shoved Pichu, knocking him back on his butt. Pichu looked up into Moore's red face as he hissed, "You lost this game for us — Ponga Boy."

A few minutes later, the final whistle blew. The Santa Clara players jumped into the air and began hugging each other, celebrating. Pichu joined his teammates, who were huddled together near the bench.

"What can I say?" Coach Jordan's voice was hollow and sounded tired. He looked at all the players. Pichu felt the coach's eyes on him as he said, "We gave this game away. We're gonna have a lot of work to do on Monday. And you guys better get set because the first game is next Thursday. You play like this, Westford is going to eat us alive. Okay. That's it."

The players headed for the locker room. Coach Connor began putting the equipment into the large net bags that held the balls. Pichu stood there watching as the fans left their seats and quietly melted away. With each person who left, Pichu felt he was losing another chance for success. What was wrong, Pichu wondered. Where did the magic in my feet go? Where is my balance and my speed? The last group of fans was at the exit now. They paused and looked back, then threw an empty cup down among all the other trash and left.

Coach Connor was still gathering up the equipment when Pichu approached him. "Coach Connor," Pichu said. "I want to practice a little more."

"What? Now?"

"Yes. I need to work on something. Can you give me two balls?"

Moore heard what Pichu said and snarled, "Yeah, because he doesn't have two of his own."

Shields caught the joke and laughed. Then he said, "Ponga Boy," and shook his head in disgust.

Pichu waited until he was alone on the field. Then he began juggling the ball. He moved it up his body using his foot, his knee, his chest and his head. Then he took it down using his head, his chest, his knee and his foot. Then he got the other ball and began working that one at the same time. He would kick one ball twice while kicking the second ball higher in the air. It was difficult, and it took all his attention. And somehow it freed his mind from all the trouble he had suffered in the past few days. He lost track of where he was and his mind drifted back home. He imagined Angelina standing in front of him, laughing and enjoying his tricks.

"So what was it like in America?" he heard her ask.

Tap, tap. Kick! Tap, tap. Kick!

"Oh, you wouldn't believe it over there," Pichu heard himself tell her. "The houses are so big. The cars are so new. The stores are all filled with things you can't even imagine. And there are no dogs walking in the streets."

"And what are the girls like in America?"

Tap, tap. Kick! Tap, tap. Kick!

"Aye!" he would tell her. "They are so hot. And they have new clothes and tight jeans. And they think Mexican men are very sexy."

After he teased her in this way, she would always try to punch him. He pictured her chasing him, and it made him laugh. He dropped the ball he was juggling. He bent down to get the ball and suddenly heard Angelina say, "So, if you love America so much I guess you don't want to see me anymore."

"No, Angelina. Please don't go," Pichu said. He felt his throat tighten as the vision of her began to evaporate. "Please stay and watch my tricks a little longer."

But she wasn't there anymore. So he would have to do his best trick to try to bring her back. He got both the balls in motion again, then he kicked one high in the air. As the first one was falling, he set the second ball, drew his foot back and fired it. It hit the first ball, and it ricocheted into the back of the net.

"Did you like my trick, Angelina?" Pichu said to the retreating vision. But she had disappeared. It was very quiet and Pichu felt more alone than ever before. He felt he was falling through space alone and forgotten.

"Did you do that on purpose?"

Pichu turned around and saw a strange figure walking toward him, a small, nearly round man who was barely five feet tall. His shoulders were hunched and he seemed to permanently lean to one side. He reminded Pichu of the pictures he had seen of those bears from Australia, the koala bears, except he was puffing on a cigarette and dragging a plastic bag filled with trash. And when this man spoke, his voice was low and rumbling as if stones were rolling around in an empty oil drum.

"Did you do that on purpose?" the man asked again, peering up in Pichu's face with a look of amazement, a haze of smoke hanging round his face.

"Yes."

"That's unbelievable!" the man said with a huge smile. His face was the color of a potato and his nose was lumpy like a cauliflower. "I've watched soccer my whole life, and I've never seen anyone who can do that." He stuck out a chubby hand. "Humberto. They let me pick up after games and lock the gates. I live in the little house next door with my mother."

"I'm Pichu."

"I was just finishing my last cigarette and I figured I'd watch the show. This is the last cigarette I'll ever smoke, so I wanted to make it a good one. And you made it a truly great one!"

Pichu watched as Humberto took a long pull on the cigarette. He savored the taste and then stubbed it out on the sole of his sandal. He carefully put the butt in the black plastic bag he was carrying.

"There, I'm not a smoker anymore," Humberto said. "Now let me see you do that trick again."

Pichu got the two balls dancing then launched one into the air. He fired the other ball at the falling soccer ball, and it caromed into the net.

Humberto laughed and clapped his hands. He did a little dance of celebration, humming a song that sounded like rump-ta-dump-ta-dee and turning around in a circle. The laugh was friendly, and the dance was so funny, it made Pichu forget how heavy his heart was. He laughed, too.

"You know," Humberto said, cocking his head at an angle and looking up at Pichu, "a player who can do an amazing trick like that, can — can, why he could do anything!"

Pichu was quiet.

"Can you do things as amazing as that in a game?"

"Sometimes."

"When will you do it?" Humberto asked, still standing close to Pichu and looking up into his face. "Because I want to be here when you do it. I'll laugh and do my little dance and get everyone laughing and cheering."

"Nothing is working now," Pichu said.

"Nothing?" He seemed amazed. "I can't believe that."

"No. Nothing. Everything I do is wrong. I can't even score."

Humberto frowned and pulled on his lumpy nose. "Well, if you can't score, why not make your teammates score?"

"What do you mean?"

"What do I mean?" Humberto echoed, surprised. "The one who puts the ball into the net gets all the attention. But the one that passed the ball to the scorer is even more important. Pichu, don't worry about scoring. Don't worry about how you do at all! Soccer is about the team — not about you. Turn your teammates into superstars! Then there will be much scoring. And I will laugh and do my dance and everyone will have the best time."

Humberto began dancing around in a circle again and singing rump-ta-dump-ta-dee. Then he danced away and as he left he said, "I'm locking the field now, Pichu. You have to leave."

The next morning Pichu lay in his bed in his dorm room, thinking about yesterday's game. He didn't feel like getting out of bed at all. He had never felt like this before. It was Sunday morning and there was no practice and he wasn't scheduled to work in the kitchen. There was nothing for him to do. He wanted to call his family, but he knew they would be at Mass. Thinking of this, he realized that he needed to go to Mass, too. Maybe, if he said a special prayer, he could figure out what he was doing wrong and find a way to fit into the team.

Pichu got dressed and went downstairs and out onto the street. He began walking without paying any attention to where he was going. He just hoped that eventually he would find a church. Soon, he found himself in a busy section of the city. It was a major intersection, and Mexicans in work clothes were standing around. Pickups would slow down and look at the men. The men would stand up straight and look back at the men in the trucks. Pichu decided he would ask these men if they knew where a church was.

"You! Hey, you!" a voice from behind called him. Pichu turned around and saw a man leaning out of a pickup truck window.

"Come over here. And you, too!" the man said, pointing at one of the waiting men. The man jogged over to the truck and stood next to Pichu.

"Interior painting. Six bucks an hour. Ever done it before?" The man was looking at Pichu. But Pichu didn't understand what all this was about. He said nothing.

The other man spoke to Pichu in Spanish. "He wants to know if you have ever painted inside houses."

Why would he want to know that? Pichu wondered. He still didn't say anything.

The man seemed impatient with Pichu. "Well? Have you painted before? Habla Ingles? Oh, forget it. You! I'll take you instead." He pointed to another waiting man who quickly jogged over. "Six bucks an hour. Painting. You done it before?"

"I paint anything, boss," the man said, smiling happily.

"Jump in the truck."

The two men jumped in the bed of the pickup and they drove away. Pichu turned to the other men who were still standing on the corner waiting. One of the men was very short and his skin was deeply tanned. He wore a black and silver Raiders baseball cap.

"Painting — that's easy work," the short man said in Spanish, using an accent Pichu didn't recognize. "I like to paint. But all they ever want me for is gardening."

"My last job was breaking up concrete," another man told Pichu. He wore jeans with holes in the knees. "Aye! That will break your back!"

One of the other men looked at Pichu. "Did you just get here?"

Pichu thought it was a strange question since they had all seen him walk up. Still, he didn't want to be impolite. "Yes. I just got here. I want to know where there is a church. I haven't gone to Mass."

"I go to St. Anthony's. But it's a long way from here."

"Where is it?" Pichu asked thinking how he might fill the time by walking.

"It's in that direction." The man pointed. "But watch out — it's a rough area."

The short man looked at the passing traffic and pushed his hat back on his head. "It is slow today. No work. No work. Anyone want to go to the park?"

"I'm going to wait a little longer," the man with torn jeans said. "I really need the money. My mother in Guadalajara is sick. The medicine is very expensive. The only way we can pay for it is with American money."

All the men nodded sadly. Pichu said goodbye and began walking again. He was thinking of how strange this country was. People just walked up to you and gave you a job. And six dollars an hour! That was a whole lot of money.

Pichu began walking in the direction where he was told the church would be. The houses became smaller and he noticed that there were steel bars on their windows and doors. The tiny yards were fenced and short, powerful dogs snarled at him as he walked past. Soon, he found himself in front of a large church where a line of people was forming out front. He joined the line and shuffled inside where he saw that it was truly a large, important church. All the seats were taken and many people stood in the back dressed in jeans with their hats in their hands. The voice of the priest echoed in the vast interior, amplified by a microphone. People were forming a line to take Communion. Pichu found

something familiar about the droning voice of the priest and the service that comforted him. He crossed himself and repeated the prayers.
For a moment the gnawing loneliness subsided.

"Pichu!" a voice whispered to him.

Pichu was startled out of his thoughts. Who could be calling his
name? He turned and saw Pete from his soccer team motioning to him
from a side door. He walked over to Pete and stepped into a long hallway.

"Some of the kids saw you," Pete explained, leading him along the
corridor. "They wanted me to introduce you to them."

"Kids?" Pichu asked.

"The kids I tutor here," Pete answered, opening a door. Inside were
about twenty children of various ages. They were running around the
room, laughing and pushing each other. They saw Pete and stopped.

"Back in your seats!" Pete said. "Everyone sit down or you won't get
to meet our special guest."

This had an immediate effect on the children. They quickly found
seats and folded their hands in front of them. Pichu looked at the expectant faces and realized that they were all either Mexican or from Central
or South America.

"This is Pichu," Pete said. "He plays soccer on the USF team and he
is here from Mexico. Pichu, can you tell them a little about how you got
here?"

It became very quiet in the room as Pichu looked at the children.
He couldn't help thinking how much they looked like his brothers and
sisters back in Mexico. But something was different — the expression
on their faces. How could he describe it? They were angry and defiant,
yet somehow so hungry for his words. The children gazed at him,
unnaturally quiet, waiting for him to speak.

"My name is Pichu and I come from Los Barriles in Baja Sur. My
father is a fisherman and — "

"Pichu," Pete interrupted. "I think they would like it if you
addressed them in Spanish. I can follow along."

Pichu continued in Spanish telling them about how he had gotten a
scholarship and was now attending university — something his family
could never have afforded. The children listened closely and when Pichu
was finished speaking, they all clapped.

In Spanish, Pete said, "Does anyone have any questions for Pichu?"
His accent was flat and the kids giggled at his awkward attempt to speak
their language. Pichu suddenly felt sorry for Pete and he hoped that the
children would not openly mock Pete.

A boy of about twelve raised his hand. Pete said, "Yes, Adrian?"

"What kind of car did they give you?" Adrian asked.

"Car?"

"So you would play for the team," Adrian explained. "They recruit players by giving them cars, yes? I heard that on the news."

"Oh, I see," Pichu said. "What I get for free is my education and my room and meals. That would be very expensive and my family could never pay for it. But I didn't get a car."

"Why don't you forget about college and just turn professional?" a boy asked. "Then you get a car and money and lots of ladies."

A very pretty young girl punched the boy in the arm. "Juan, you are so stupid!"

"Conchita, please," Pete said. "Juan, let's have serious questions."

"No," Pichu said. "I want to answer that." He thought back to what Professor Baca had told him. He smiled at Juan and said, "I believe it is important to develop your mind, just as an athlete develops his body. Learning is very important. So, even if I could be professional now, I would want to finish college first."

"But if you want to be rich you have to be a pro," Adrian said. "I'm going to be a boxer. I have a fight every day and I have never lost."

A loud cry of ridicule greeted this statement. One boy called out, "I could beat your ass any day I want."

Adrian was on his feet in a second. The boy who challenged him jumped up and the two boys were suddenly standing eye to eye, their chests pressed against each other. The kids cheered and whistled urging them on. It was obvious to Pichu that the boys were showing off for him, trying to impress him with how tough they were. Knowing this filled Pichu with conflicting emotions. Why was his opinion valuable to them?

"Juan! Adrian! Stop it!" Pete yelled, pulling them apart. He turned on the boy who had made the challenge. "Juan, go home. Now! I've told you before, we don't use language like that in here. Now go!"

Suddenly, all the machismo vanished from the boy's face. He was like a little child again, a child who might almost start crying. "Please let me stay!" he begged. "Please, Pete, can I stay? I'm sorry. I really want to stay."

"You know the rules. Get out!" Pete pointed to the door.

Juan's shoulders slumped and he headed for the door. He kicked a chair leg on his way out and slammed the door behind him.

"I'm sorry, Pichu," Pete said, looking shaken. "But thank you for stopping by. We're going to get back to our work now. Kids, can you thank Pichu for coming by?"

A chorus of voices thanked Pichu as he walked to the door and back out into the corridor. When Pichu reached the church sanctuary, he saw that the service was over.

Outside, Pichu stood on the front steps and waited for his eyes to adjust to the sunlight. Across the street he noticed a group of teenage boys hanging around by the gates to a housing project. Juan was talking with the teenagers as they leaned against parked cars and looked around, bored. The older boys were dressed in black and silver Raiders jackets and their baggy pants drooped on their hips. Their baseball caps were turned sideways. Pichu caught Juan's eye and waved to him. For a second Juan's face brightened and he seemed about to return the greeting. But then he remembered the company he was with and he turned aside without acknowledging Pichu.

Chapter **16**

After Pichu left the church, he walked aimlessly. He wasn't sure what he was looking for — or even if he was looking for anything at all. When he had walked for another hour or so, he suddenly became very hungry. Either that or something had just reminded him of food. He stood on the sidewalk sniffing the air. Yes, there it was again. A wonderful, familiar smell. It smelled almost like —

Pichu turned down a side street, following his nose. The smell was getting stronger. He turned again and found himself at the edge of a park. There was a wide square of green grass and families were sitting on blankets, eating picnic lunches. While the women served food, the men and boys played soccer in pickup games all around them. Nearby, Pichu saw a plump woman kneeling on a blanket unpacking grocery bags of food. Out of the bags came dishes of rice and beans and jars of salsa. And wrapped in aluminum foil were homemade tortillas. She unwrapped the foil, and a puff of steam rose into the air and floated toward Pichu. When it reached him he felt dizzy with hunger. The smell took him back home. He remembered coming back from the docks after fishing and sinking his teeth into the soft, warm tortillas his mother made. The tortillas he had eaten here didn't taste like that at all. They looked right, but something was missing.

The woman on the blanket seemed to feel Pichu's eyes on her as she served the food to her family. She looked up at Pichu and smiled. He weakly smiled back. He told himself he was being rude and had to leave. He tried to walk away, but wound up circling around the family. She continued serving the food. She spoke to her husband and her husband turned and looked at Pichu. He nodded. Pichu nodded back. His stomach growled so loudly he thought they would hear it. The husband spoke to his wife and she took out an extra plate. She laid out a tortilla and began spooning refried beans and rice onto it. Then she added salsa and an enchilada dripping with sauce and melted cheese. Watching all this, Pichu nearly fell over with hunger. His stomached growled again, and this time it was as loud as a menacing dog. The woman spoke to her son, a boy of only four. The boy jumped to his feet and ran over to Pichu. He caught hold of Pichu's pant leg and began pulling him toward the family. The woman looked up and held out the plate of food.

"Por favor," the man said. "Sit down and eat with us."

Pichu took the plate and sat down. He crossed himself, said a brief prayer, and began eating. With each bite of the delicious, honest food, he felt his strength returning. He absorbed the food and the smell all at once. The woman watched as all the food quickly vanished. She refilled the plate and handed it to Pichu. That plate of food disappeared just as quickly. When Pichu was done eating, the little boy appeared in front of him holding a soccer ball. A game was forming nearby, and they were inviting him to play. On Pichu's team was the four-year-old boy, a fat man of nearly fifty and four boys of about ten years old. The other team was made up of a similar mix of ages. For an hour, they ran and passed and shot and dribbled. The fat man was amazingly fast, and his face became alarmingly red as he played. But whenever he lost the ball, he collapsed on the ground, rolling around and laughing hysterically.

When the game was over, Pichu saw that a group of men had formed on the sidelines and was watching him. Among them was the man who had been on the street corner wearing the Raiders hat. He was holding a soccer ball under his arm.

"I have been watching you," the man said to Pichu. "You are the best player I've ever seen."

"Thank you," Pichu answered.

"Would you please play on our team?" he said, gesturing to the men standing beside him. They all looked at Pichu with great respect. "We are a bunch of guys from Chihuahua. We always play against the other guys from Mexico City. And we always lose. But with you on our team, we could win. Would you play on our team?"

"Of course," Pichu said. "Let's go."

The players from Mexico City were young and fast. They were in great physical condition. But none of them could take the ball away from Pichu. He dominated the middle of the field and easily dribbled through the defenders. All of the Mexico City players rushed Pichu, leaving his teammates open. He waited until the man with the Raiders cap was open and then sent him a beautiful curling pass right on his foot. He trapped the ball, faked a shot to draw the goalie out, then tucked the ball in the opposite corner of the goal. The man fell to his knees briefly, then ran over to Pichu and shook his hand.

"You have given me my first goal I've ever scored against these guys from Mexico City!" he cried. "I never thought I could do it! This is a very special day."

For the next hour Pichu was careful to set up goals for all the players on his team. He sent them head balls, or heeled the ball backwards, or drew the defenders and passed off at the last second. Pichu was deeply moved by his teammates' gratitude after their goals. When the game was over, all the players gathered around him. Even the guys from Mexico City shook his hand and thanked him for playing.

"Are you a pro?" one of the players asked him.

"No. I'm here to play on the USF team," Pichu told them.

"You go to university?" they asked, amazed. "Your father must be very rich."

"Yes," Pichu said. "He is a fisherman, and he owns his own ponga boat."

The men whistled appreciatively. Someone in the back said, "I had an uncle who owned a ponga." But when they all turned to look at him he lost his nerve and added, "With two other guys."

"I'm just starting at the university," Pichu said. "And I'm not sure I can make the team."

"Of course you can make it," said the man with the Raiders cap. "Your skills are amazing. And we will all come and see you play. Right guys?"

All the men cheered.

"And when you make a great play, we will tell everyone around us — we, too, have played with him. We've played with the ponga boy."

Somehow, Pichu found his way back to the university. As he was walking past the soccer field, locked and empty, he noticed a tiny bungalow nearby. It was stucco-colored, with a picket fence, and the front yard was filled with rose bushes. This must be where Humberto lives, he thought. He hoped to see Humberto working among the flowers. But the yard was empty and the front door was closed.

Back in his dormitory, Pichu decided to write a letter to his parents. He started it several times. But everything he wrote sounded like he was complaining and he balled up the pages and threw them away. Finally, he started once more.

"Dear Mama and Papa,

I'm sorry I haven't written sooner. I have been very busy because things are going so well. America is everything I ever hoped it would be! People come up to me on the street and offer me work. And if you are hungry, someone is there with food. My schoolwork is interesting and I've made many friends."

Now came the hard part, Pichu thought. He knew his father would be reading the letter to hear about soccer.

"I haven't scored a goal yet..."

Pichu stopped writing. There was nothing good he could say. He thought back to the game yesterday and the painful memories began to haunt him again. But then he remembered practicing in the empty stadium afterwards. He remembered Humberto, the way he always leaned in one direction and had a rumbling voice. He thought of the little dance Humberto did and how good it felt to laugh after being so sad and disappointed from the game. What was it that Humberto had said about soccer? "Soccer isn't about you. It's about the team. Turn your teammates into superstars." That's what he had done in the park with his friends from Chihuahua — he had given them each a goal.

Pichu watched as his hand began writing again. And he was surprised to see what he wrote:

"... I know what I must do now. I'm going to turn my teammates into superstars. I will get the ball and set up the goals for them. As you know, Papa, soccer isn't about one player — it is about the team."

Pichu pictured his family reading the letter back in Los Barriles. He knew they would all gather around the table and ask his father to read the good parts many times. So he couldn't help adding,

"The stadium we play in is very big and when a goal is scored, the noise is amazing. I would give anything to have you come and see a game! I hope by now the fish have returned and that you are selling much bait. I miss you all very much.

"Love, Pichu."

Chapter

When Pichu arrived for practice and was in the locker room about to get changed, Assistant Coach Connors stopped him. "Better talk to Coach first," he said, looking very serious.

Pichu looked toward the doorway at the end of the long row of lockers. Through the open door he could see Coach Jordan inside reviewing some papers. He looked very stern. Pichu got a heavy feeling in his stomach. He was sure that bad news was coming. Maybe he would be sent back to Mexico. What would he tell his parents and his friends back in Los Barriles?

But, as Pichu watched, an odd figure came in from the outside door and ambled into Coach Jordan's office. It was Humberto, walking in that crooked way that made him sway from side to side. He stepped into the coach's office and began talking, waving his arms excitedly.

"Humberto," Pichu said aloud, surprised.

"So you met him," Coach Connors said. "It's pretty incredible to think of what he did — a little guy like that."

"What do you mean?" Pichu asked.

"No one told you? He was a teacher in a little town in Guatemala. Some guerrillas came in and wiped out just about everyone. But Humberto hid with his family in the jungle. He carried his crippled mother on his back forty miles through the mountains until he crossed the border. That's why his back is messed up like that. Pretty amazing, huh?"

Pichu could see that Humberto was talking excitedly to Coach Jordan. He waved his arms as he explained something. Then he did his celebration dance, turning in a circle. Pichu was surprised to see Coach Jordan smile and laugh. Humberto shook the coach's hand, bowed formally and left the office.

"Okay, better get in there," Coach Connor said with a sigh.

Pichu walked into the coach's office and stood in front of the big desk.

"I was beginning to feel that this just wasn't working out," Coach Jordan said to Pichu. "I was going to tell you that we couldn't fit you into the team. But then I spoke with a friend of mine. He's a little unorthodox but he always gives me a different perspective on things."

Coach Jordan stood and turned his back to Pichu, looking out the window at the soccer field where players were already gathering, kicking balls back and forth or lying on the ground stretching.

"The soccer program is in bad shape," he said with a heavy voice. "The administration is talking about cutting back unless we make a better showing this year. I'm willing to try anything to post more wins. But I'm just about out of ideas."

Coach Jordan turned and faced Pichu. "I know you're talented. And Humberto told me what he saw you can do. That's unbelievable. But how can I use your talent to win games?"

When Pichu had first entered the office, he was sure he would be sent home. But now he saw that there was another chance. And that was all he needed. His mind began whirling, putting together many things. His nervousness and fear evaporated. He took what felt like his first real breath of air since he had arrived in the United States. All the worried voices inside him quieted down, and things became very simple.

"You can relax, Coach," Pichu said. He was surprised to hear his own words. He even thought that he might have shown disrespect.

"Relax? Yes, I'd like to. But why?"

"I know what to do now."

"What?"

"Let me stay at center forward, but I want to play back, almost to midfield. I want to be able to move my position all over the center of the field."

"No one can cover that much of the field."

"I can," Pichu said. "Give me one chance and I'll show you."

"What are you saying?"

"I don't want to say anything. I want to show you."

Coach Jordan looked at Pichu for a long time. His sharp eyes seemed to be trying to cut right through Pichu so he could understand what he meant. Finally, he gave up and said, "I'll give it a try. I don't know why, but I'll try it."

Coming around the desk, Coach Jordan folded his arms. "I arranged a scrimmage against Cal Berkeley. I figured we could use all the game time possible before we go against Westford on Thursday. I'm committed to Frasier in the first half because — well, he has to play. His father is — I don't need to go into all that now. Just be prepared — I'm going to sub you in in the second half. And we'll see what happens."

"Thank you, Coach," Pichu said. "I will make you very glad that you gave me this opportunity."

"Believe me, nothing would make me happier," he said.

The first half was much like Saturday's game against Santa Clara. The strikers couldn't put any plays together, and the defensive players were under constant pressure. Kevin was forced to make many desperate saves. As he cleared the ball, he yelled at the fullbacks, blaming them for not protecting him. The fullbacks yelled back at him, saying it wasn't their fault.

After 18 minutes of play, Cal Berkeley scored on a direct kick that found its way around the wall while the defenders were still setting up. Then, just before half time, Kevin made a diving save and punched the ball wide. The fullback slid in to clear the bouncing ball. But a striker vaulted over his legs and popped the ball into the top of the net. USF was down 2–0 when the referee blew the whistle to end the first half.

Pichu watched the game without surprise. It was much like what he had seen before. But now he understood how he could help. He waited patiently, his stomach jittery. He tried to keep loose by running and stretching on the sidelines. When the ref blew the whistle for the line-up for the second half, he took his place in the center of the field. While he was waiting for the others he juggled the ball and kicked it into the air.

Moore saw what he was doing and said, "As if that crap will help us now."

"You'll see," Pichu said.

"You don't get points for hotdogging," Moore said. "You have to put it in the net."

"Or maybe you have to put it in the net," Pichu said and smiled at him.

The kickoff went to Pichu and he ignored the play that Moore and Shields told him to run. Instead, he controlled the ball in the center of the field, moved slowly up the side and passed off to Rev at the wing. The ball was heeled back to the halfbacks and intercepted by the Cal Berkeley forwards. They began rushing forward, confidently working the ball. The Berkeley striker was looking to make a long pass to the opposite wing. But he hesitated too long, and Pichu came out of nowhere and stripped the ball. He controlled the play, eluding the striker he had stolen the ball from. The pace of play was being slowed by Pichu who, at times, stood motionless as players rushed toward him.

Finally, he sent a long pass to the opposite side of the field. He sprinted down to the top of the penalty box and waited for the cross. He called for the ball and the winger looked up and saw Pichu all alone. But instead, a low pass was fed to Shields, who couldn't reach the ball. The ball rolled across the goal mouth and the goalie easily smothered it.

"Where were you?" Shields screamed at Pichu, trying to cover his mistake.

"Watching you miss it," Pichu said. But then he was sorry he had talked back. So he ran over to Shields and held out his hand for a low-five. "You'll get it next time." Shields looked at Pichu's hand. "Don't leave me hangin', bro," Pichu said, repeating something he had heard Pete once say. Shields rolled his eyes and unenthusiastically slapped his outstretched hand.

The game was being fought in the midfield. Cal Berkeley had several fast breaks but Kevin came far out of the goal and cut them off without any trouble. The USF defenders were starting to come alive, stealing the ball from Cal Berkeley and pushing it up to the strikers. In one case, the ball rebounded to Pichu at the top of the penalty box. Rather than trap it and shoot, as the fullbacks expected him to do, he popped the ball with the side of his foot to Moore, who had threaded his way between the fullbacks and fired the ball point blank. His shot was miraculously blocked by the goalie's legs as he dove wildly.

The goal kick was high and deep into USF's territory. The fullback named Bart lined it up for a header. But at the last second a powerfully built Berkeley player jumped in, crashing into Bart's head. Bart fell to the ground, moaning. Another USF fullback shoved the Berkeley player, who pushed him back. By now, Bart had staggered to his feet and was joining the shoving match. The referee got among the angry players. But now the players were pairing off and pushing each other. One tall, powerful striker from Berkeley cocked his arm and was about to attack Rev, who was dealing with another player. Pichu saw the danger and jumped in, landing on the big player's back and riding him to the ground. The two rolled around until the coaches separated them.

The referee ejected Bart and the Berkeley player who had fouled him. The players returned to their positions and the game resumed. As Rev walked back to his position, Pete shouted from the bench: "Hey Rev, Ponga Boy was watching your back."

Rev seemed surprised. He looked around and found Pichu. He gave him the thumbs-up.

A drop ball was called just outside the USF penalty area. The ball was dropped and a USF fullback gained control and moved it up the wing to Rev. The cross went to Moore, who took a shot. It rebounded off a defender and then bounced again toward the goal. Pichu chased the ball and knew he could reach it first. But he saw he was heading straight into a wall of defenders. There was no way he could get the shot off. Pichu sensed that a fullback was right behind him and closing fast. He put on his brakes as if setting up for the shot. The fullback, coming at full speed, ran right over the top of Pichu, knocking him flat on his face. The referee blew his whistle and motioned for a penalty kick.

"Coach said I take all the penalty kicks!" Moore shouted at Pichu as if expecting an argument.

Pichu got to his feet and said, "Good. Kick it in the back of the net."

"You're damn right I will!" Moore shouted, as if he was still defending his territory.

The players cleared the penalty area and stood with their hands on their hips breathing hard and waiting. The Berkeley goalie took his position on the line, his arms spread wide and his knees flexed. He was watching Moore for a clue about which corner he would choose. Moore stared at the goalie until the ref blew the whistle. He ran toward the ball at an angle and placed it perfectly in the upper right corner of the goal.

Moore ran back to the center line while his teammates high-fived him. Pichu ran over and shook his hand. Moore looked at him, surprised, but didn't say anything.

USF kept the pressure up for most of the second half. But they were still trailing 2–1 and they were quickly running out of time. Pichu guessed the whistle would blow at any second. He knew he had to do something quickly. For a moment, he considered stealing the ball and trying to dribble his way into the penalty box for a close shot. But then he remembered his new strategy and decided to stick to his plan.

The Berkeley players were desperately trying to run the clock out, hoping to hold onto their lead. The goalie rolled the ball out to the fullback. The fullbacks passed back and forth to each other as the USF strikers chased them. Pichu looked for his chance. He saw a slow pass and charged, accelerating with all his speed. The fullback saw him coming and rushed the kick. He mis-hit the ball, and it struck Pichu in the chest and rebounded toward the goal mouth. Pichu chased the bouncing ball as the goalie charged out of the nets. Pichu reached the ball first and saw he had the shot, low and to the left of the goal. But he also sensed that he had Shields to his right. Pichu had one last stride before the goalie was on top of the ball. He dove feet first, hooking his left foot under the ball and popping it over the goalie, who was sliding in sideways. The ball cleared the goalie and bounced lazily toward Shields. Rather than taking a wild shot, Shields saw he was clear and controlled the ball. He kept the shot low and dead center on the empty goal.

"Nice pass, man," Shields said to Pichu.

"Great shot," Pichu answered.

The teams lined up for the kickoff. Cal Berkeley frantically made a last charge and their best striker fired a long shot. The ball missed the goal and sailed harmlessly into the stands. The referee blew the whistle and the game ended in a 2–2 tie.

"Now that's more like it," Coach Jordan said as the team gathered around him afterwards. "You guys are playing like a team for the first time this year. Moore, Shields, great goals. We've still got a long way to go, but at least this is a step in the right direction. See you at practice tomorrow."

The players walked off the field in groups. They were talking and laughing or reviewing key plays. Moore and Shields went over to the stands and talked to their girlfriends, who were with several other girls Pichu had seen around campus. One of them was the girl with dark hair who had spoken to him in the dining hall. She watched Pichu as he walked toward the locker room.

"Nice game, Ponga Boy," she called to him and smiled.

Pichu felt something move inside him. Her dark eyes were exploring him, giving him a secret look that he didn't understand. It was a feeling that had many different colors to it. He nodded to her and was about to turn away, when the girl nudged her friend and said something to her as they looked at Pichu. Both girls laughed and continued staring at him as he walked toward the locker room.

Pichu was getting dressed when Coach Jordan came to his door and yelled, "Pichu! Get in here!" For an instant, Pichu was alarmed. But then he saw a playful smile in the coach's eyes. A few of the players around Pichu laughed and kidded him as he walked toward the coach's office.

When Pichu walked through the doorway, the coach was standing in front of the big wooden desk. Pichu waited for the coach to speak. Slowly, the coach held out his hand.

"Welcome to the team, Pichu," Coach Jordan said and warmly shook his hand.

Chapter 18

"I saw the scrimmage against Cal Berkeley," Professor Baca said. "You played well." Pichu was sitting in the professor's tiny office, choosing his classes for the upcoming semester. The walls were decorated with colorful posters of Spanish and Mexican movies. There were many photographs of the professor's family taken in San Felipe, Mexico. The shelves were lined with books written in Spanish and English and even French. Pichu liked the feeling of this office and he sensed the importance of the knowledge present here. But most of all he liked Professor Baca. He wanted the professor to praise his soccer skills. Perhaps he would describe a specific play that Pichu had made. Or maybe he would express amazement at his speed. But nothing followed his single comment. Instead, the professor turned back to the open college catalog.

"You need to make the most of your time here, Pichu," he said. "This term you will be required to take certain English and science courses. But you will also have elective classes. You can choose from a wide variety of subjects. I recommend you begin to think of what direction you will go in and choose your classes accordingly."

Professor Baca looked up and took off his glasses. "What do you think you want to do with your life?"

"I'm going to be a fisherman," Pichu said proudly.

"A fisherman."

"Yes. That is what I do in Mexico. My father has a ponga boat. We catch bait and sell it to the men who fish for marlin. Or sometimes they catch tuna or dorado or even rooster fish."

"And this is how your father supports you and your family?"

"Yes," Pichu said. "If he needs more money, he goes out in the afternoon and catches trigger fish. He takes them to Oscar, on the beach, who cleans them and sells them to the hotels."

Professor Baca was quiet, studying Pichu's face.

"And my mother works as a maid in the Hotel Palmas de Cortez,"

Pichu added, confused by Professor Baca's silence. "We have a nice house. We have everything we need."

"I'm sure you do." The professor nodded and smiled. Pichu noticed there was a little sadness in his smile.

"Pichu, we live in a changing world. By the time you have a family, the way of life you just described may be gone. Being a fisherman might not be enough."

"What do you mean?" Pichu asked. And then,, suddenly, he remembered what his mother had told him — no one was catching any fish, and the tourists were leaving. But that had to be a temporary situation, caused by a strange ocean current. Or maybe a storm had driven the fish to another area. There were many ways to explain what was happening. But the fish had always been there in the past. And the fish always would be there. He was sure of that.

"Have you heard of the 'long liners'?" the professor asked.

"I have heard that word. I've seen those boats from a distance, working at night."

"When the great American writer John Steinbeck took his trip to the Sea of Cortez, he was so amazed at how many fish were in the waters he called it 'the aquarium of the world.' There is not a place like it on this planet. But now, fishermen from all over the world have discovered this treasure and are destroying it for everyone. I suggest you learn about the long liners and how they are raping your Sea of Cortez."

The professor's choice of words was so shocking that it left Pichu without an answer.

"There are many things that could change the way you live in Los Barriles," the professor continued. "I teach a course called 'Introduction to Oceanography and Environmental Science.' The course has many trips to the field. You will go on boats into the Monterey Bay and off the coast of California. You will study the way American fishermen work. You will study how the U.S. government has enacted fishing restrictions and you can see how they are working. I think you would find it very useful."

"But I already know how to fish. I know how to make my living from the ocean."

"Of course, you can make your living from the ocean," Professor Baca said bluntly. "What I'm suggesting is that you help all people continue to make a living from the ocean for many generations to come. You see, the ocean can be treated like a farm that continually replenishes itself. But some of the things that are being done now will destroy the farm forever. You need to look at the bigger picture, the way all the systems work together, not just your own little world. This is our future — we are becoming a global community."

Pichu was confused. He looked away, letting his eyes travel over the posters and pictures of Mexico on the wall. He found himself staring at the clock and saw that soccer practice would begin soon. It was so much easier to think about soccer than to think about the disappearance of the fish in the Sea of Cortez.

The professor saw Pichu's distraction.

"Do you have someplace you would rather be?" he asked.

"Soccer practice starts soon."

"Yes. I can see that you will have many conflicts this semester between soccer and your classes," Professor Baca said.

"But it is soccer that got me here," Pichu said defensively, as he gathered up his books.

"You have amazing abilities as a soccer player," the professor said. But the way that he said it didn't make it sound like a compliment. "What you don't seem to understand is that you have an amazing mind, too. I rarely see test scores this high. Long after you can no longer kick a ball, your mind will still be active. It will be a long time until your intellect fully matures. It's up to you to choose your elective. But please think deeply about what I said today."

The professor's tone surprised Pichu and hurt his feelings. He had expected support from his friend. These comments felt like criticism. No one had ever talked to him this way before. He took his curriculum sheet, said goodbye and left.

The hallway outside the office was filled with students carrying books. Classes would be starting in another day, and everyone was signing up for courses. Pichu was still thinking about Professor Baca's comments when he felt a warm hand on his bare arm. He turned and looked into the dark eyes of the girl who had waved to him after the game yesterday. "Hi, remember me?" she asked, laughing.

She was smiling at him and acting embarrassed. But the embarrassment made her look very pretty. She was wearing tight jeans and a short white top that showed her navel. There was red in her cheeks and her eyes blinked quickly.

When Pichu didn't answer right away, she said, "No. Why would you remember? I'm Christy. I saw you playing yesterday. It was so exciting. You are an amazing player."

"I remember you," Pichu said. "You've been at many of the games."

"Yes!" she said. "I'm a huge fan. At first, I'm thinking this is going to be such a boring year. But then you started doing those — " she laughed, " — those amazing passes and things. Who taught you that?"

"Taught me?"

"Yes. Didn't you, like, have a coach and go to soccer camp and all that?"

"What is soccer camp?" Pichu asked.

"What's soccer camp?" Christy looked at him in amazement. She began laughing. "You are such a trip."

Pichu glanced up at a clock on the wall. Practice would begin in only ten minutes. She saw him looking away.

"Here I am babbling on and on," Christy said.

"I just need to get to practice," Pichu said.

"I'm walking that way, too." Then she touched his arm again. "If that's okay. I mean, I don't want to be a pest."

"You are not a pest."

She smiled. "Thank you, Pichu. Am I saying your name right? Pichu."

"Yes. Perfectly."

They started walking down the hallway. Coming in the other direction were the girlfriends of Moore and Shields. As they passed, they smiled at Christy in a secret way and said, "Go, girl."

Christy turned and said, "Shut up," and they all laughed as if they shared a secret.

They pushed through a door and stepped outside. It was cool now with wisps of clouds blowing in and hiding the sun. Pichu hadn't gotten used to how much cooler it was here than in Los Barriles. The clouds often gathered, and the nights were cold. The sun seemed weak and provided little warmth.

"After the Westford game, my girlfriends and I are throwing a party for the team," Christy said. "We want to give you guys a boost for the rest of the season."

"Boost?" Pichu had never heard the word before.

"Boost. Yeah, like, you know — " she made a silly motion and then laughed at herself. "How do I explain? We want to help the team. And make you feel good. So, anyway, I was wondering, would you like to come?"

Pichu noticed that Christy had very long, dark eyelashes. It made him think of Angelina, way back in Los Barriles. He felt guilty talking to this girl, since he knew Angelina wouldn't like it at all. She would want to punch Christy. But he needed to be nice to the Americans. Besides, this Christy seemed like a very polite person, and he didn't want to hurt her feelings.

"Yes, I'll come."

"Great! It's at eight o'clock. Our dorm at West Hall."

"Thank you for asking me."

She giggled and said in a formal tone of voice, "The pleasure is all mine, sir."

Pichu knew she was kidding him, but he didn't really understand why. Still, she was very kind, and it was easy to laugh with her. He said goodbye and she walked away, waving to him. He was about to go into the locker room, when he looked back one more time. He saw that Christy was talking to Shields' and Moore's girlfriends. Once again, Pichu had the feeling that they were sharing a secret. He tried to ignore the feeling and went into the locker room to change for practice.

Chapter **19**

While Pichu was lacing up his cleats before the Westford game, he found himself whistling a tune. It was the theme song for the weekly televised soccer matches in Mexico. On Saturdays, after he was done fishing, he would hurry to the bar at the Hotel Palmas de Cortez. If the bar wasn't filled with gringos watching baseball or golf on TV, then the bartender, Esteban (himself a huge soccer fan) would switch to the match of the week. First they would hear the theme music. And they would all start clapping and cheering. He was getting that excited feeling of anticipation in his stomach as he thought about how his new strategy was working. Not only that, but he was now an actual member of the team.

"You won't be whistling two hours from now," Rev said.

"Why not?"

"Westford — that's why. They always kick our butts. They're the best in the league. Last time we played them they beat us 5–zip. Not only that, but they're a bunch of jerks. They hack you when the ref isn't looking, pull your shirt, throw elbows. They'll do anything to win."

Pete heard what Rev said and added, "That's because they know they can't lose."

"Anyone can lose," Pichu said.

"Not Westford," Pete said. "They have too much invested in their program. Those guys do whatever it takes to win."

When Pichu got out on the field, he saw that the stands were already half full. He heard his name and turned, searching the faces. In the first row of the bleachers he saw Christy jumping up and down excitedly and waving to him. He felt embarrassed that she was calling his name so loudly, for everyone to hear. But he was also pleased. He thought he should do something to thank her for coming. He took two short steps, jumped and turned a back flip. Looking back up at the stands he saw Christy clapping excitedly and telling her friends to watch him. She was very pretty, Pichu thought. And it was nice of her to come to the game to welcome him like this.

The crowd suddenly reacted to something. Pichu looked around and saw the Westford players running out onto the field. The day was cool, and each player wore an expensive warm-up uniform. They stretched for a few minutes then shed their warm-ups, revealing maroon and white shorts and shirts. The coach barked orders as the team ran drills in precise formation, running side to side, then jogging with their knees high in the air. Watching the Westford players, Pichu began to dislike them. But then he realized he only felt this way because of Rev's remarks. He forced himself to stop looking at them and begin his own warm-up.

A few minutes later Coach Connors yelled, "All right, guys, bring it in!"

Pichu turned and jogged back toward the USF bench. To one side, he saw Coach Jordan talking with Frasier. The coach had his hand on Frasier's shoulder, and Frasier's head was bowed. Pichu had a feeling he knew what had upset Frasier.

The players gathered around Coach Jordan.

"First game of the season," the coach said. "And they're throwing us right into the fire. Now I want you to forget all the past games with Westford and focus on what you do here, today. We have some new players on this team and each of you has, I'm sure, improved a lot over the summer. So you have to believe — really believe — that you can win this game."

The coach paused and looked at the players' faces. In the silence, Pichu heard cheering from the crowd. He looked around and saw Señor Vargas and the guys from the cafeteria walking into the stands. They were calling Pichu's name and cheering. Pichu waved back.

"Brought your own Mexican cheering section," Frasier sneered at Pichu. "That's real classy."

"Eyes here," the coach said sternly. He took a deep breath and said, "I've made a change to the lineup for today. Pichu is going to start at center forward."

Shields said, "Coach! What are you — "

Coach Jordan held up his hand. "Pichu is starting to work well with you and Moore and Rev. I think he can make things happen, if you give him a chance."

"Whatever," Moore said, trading a look with Frasier.

Pichu felt the coldness toward him. It brought back feelings from his first week here. But then he thought of his new approach to the game. He blocked out the negative thoughts and turned back to the coach.

"Okay, so here's the starting lineup." The coach began calling out names and the players ran onto the field and took their positions. Westford had the kickoff. Pichu waited at the top of the circle, watching the Westford players take their places. The Westford center forward was tall with long, straight black hair parted in the middle. He seemed very confident. His eyes slowly surveyed the USF team and he smiled coldly. Then his eyes found Pichu.

"You must be the ponga dude," he said.

The way he said it made the words sting. Anger sparked inside Pichu. He said, "No. I'm ponga boy."

"We've heard all about you," the center forward said. "We know how to deal with your type. We're gonna take you out."

"You can try," Pichu said. "But you won't succeed."

The center forward's lips curled into another slight smile. "I guess you don't understand English, little ponga dude. I said we're going to take you out. We got a fullback we call the Terminator." He smiled and walked away.

Two other Westford strikers came up and huddled together, talking softly. Pichu could tell by their secretive manner that they were planning a kickoff play. He saw them look at the halfbacks and then the wing. Pichu still felt angry, and there was so much energy in him he couldn't wait for the game to begin.

The referee called the two team captains in and gave them final instructions. He placed the ball down at the foot of the Westford center forward and backed away. He held up his arm, looked around to make sure everyone was ready.

And blew the whistle.

Pichu waited for the center to nudge the ball forward, then took off. He sprinted around the center of the field and straight for the right half-back. Sure enough, the ball was heeled to the halfback and he had a chance to intercept it. The ball was right there in front of him — but one stride out of reach. He lunged foot first and deflected the ball away from the halfback. Then he scrambled to his feet and retrieved the ball, hoping to find an open player on the wing. But no one was there.

Pichu dribbled through the defenders to the top of the penalty area. By now Moore had caught up and was even with the fullbacks, waiting for the pass. Pichu threaded the ball between defenders and put it on Moore's foot. Moore could have taken the left-footed one-touch shot but instead he trapped it and began dribbling. He beat the fullback and angled in on the goal. The fullback covering Pichu ran toward Moore to double team him, leaving Pichu wide open in the middle.

"Mira! Mira!" Pichu yelled, so excited he forgot to use English. "Look! I'm here!"

Moore glanced up and saw Pichu, but continued dribbling, trying to get open so he could take the shot himself.

"Right here!" Pichu yelled. "Pass, pass!"

Again Moore looked at him but didn't pass the ball. By now, there were three defenders on him. He faked left and tried to cut between two of them — and lost the ball. The fullback cleared the ball and Pichu started back upfield. As he ran, he sensed someone coming up from behind. He veered away, and a Westford fullback swept by close enough so that he felt the wind on his face.

"That's the last time you pull that crap," the fullback said. He had short red hair and freckles and was thick in the neck and shoulders. "I get one clear shot at you — you're out of the game."

Pichu jogged back to center field in time to see Pete, at fullback, challenge the Westford center-forward with the long black hair. The center dribbled casually to his left, looking for the chance to cut back and take the shot. He made his move. But Pete anticipated the play perfectly and stripped the ball. The center was left looking very foolish. A huge cheer went up from the stands. It seemed the fans were beginning to dare to hope that they had a chance of winning.

Pete passed off to another fullback, who cut back sharply and caught a Westford striker off balance. The fullback looked up, saw Pichu and sent a long high pass to him. A Westford fullback was closing fast but Pichu headed the ball up and over him. He spun around the fullback, who would have run right over him. Now the path on the edge of the field was open. Rev saw that Pichu was running down the wing, and he cut inside to fill the open position. Pichu dribbled right in at the goalie who had no choice but to come out to stop the charge. At the last second, Pichu flicked the ball with the outside of his left foot. Rev had one fullback on him but the defender was rushing in at an angle. Rev cut the ball back in the opposite direction, avoiding the fullback, and banged the ball into the back of the net.

There was a moment of stunned silence, as if the crowd couldn't believe what they saw. And then an enormous cheer went up from the crowd. Rev and Moore hugged each other, and the rest of the team ran in and mobbed them. Pichu jogged back to the center field alone. Looking back, he saw the red-haired Westford fullback glaring at him. The fullback pointed at him and then drew his finger across his throat.

As Rev ran back to his position on the wing, he gave Pichu a high five. "Dude, great pass," he said.

Westford's center forward seemed unshaken by the goal. He took the kickoff, passing to an inside striker. The ball came back to the center, and he began dribbling forward swiftly, fluidly. He beat the halfback, then the fullback and took a low, rising shot that Kevin blocked with a diving save. The ball trickled out of bounds. Westford set up for a cor-

ner kick. The kick was perfectly placed on the far post. A Westford forward headed the ball down. Kevin was there and punched the ball out.
It rebounded to the Westford center, who tapped it over a sliding fullback, then kicked it into the top of the nets. The goal had taken them
only two minutes.

The center forward unemotionally shook hands with his teammates
as they ran back to center field. They treated the goal as if it were routine. Watching this, the USF players began to feel that Westford could
score any time they wanted to.

The crowd was quiet as the players lined up for the kickoff. The ball
went to Pichu, who controlled it in the center of the field, looking for
an open player. Westford was very aggressive now, but Pichu was able
to avoid several players who challenged him. He began moving the ball
down field slowly, frustrating the other team. He passed off to Moore,
who took it to his wing. They passed skillfully, keeping the ball in
Westford's territory for a long time, looking for the shot. Finally, Shields
broke free and took a long shot that dipped sharply. The goalie almost
misjudged it but at the last second, he jumped high and arched back-
ward, tapping the ball over the goal post.

The near goal woke the crowd up. They began yelling and chanting.
The USF fans blew horns, stamped their feet and whistled. They sang
songs and waved flags. As the team lined up for the corner kick, Pichu
heard his name being called. He saw a dozen men filing into the stands
— it was the guys he had played soccer with that Sunday in the park.
They all still wore work clothes covered with white dust from a hard
day's work on construction sites. But they quickly got involved in the
game and began cheering and stamping their feet on the planks of the
bleachers.

The two teams battled evenly for the rest of the first half. Pichu
spent most of his time lurking just outside the penalty area, trying to
control the ball and draw defenders in on him. In one case, he threaded
a perfect pass to Shields, but the play was called offsides. All this time
Pichu had one eye on the Westford fullback who had threatened him.
Doing this cost him some concentration. But he had to do it. The fullback was always there, always looking for a way to hurt Pichu.
Whenever he had the chance, he slid in with his cleats aimed at Pichu's
shins. Once, the fullback hit him from behind just after he had passed
off the ball. Since the referee was following the play, he didn't see the
foul. Pichu was dazed, but he shook it off. Finally, the whistle blew to
end the first half with the score tied 1–1.

As soon as the second half started, Westford scored quickly on a direct kick that dipped over the wall of defenders and fooled Kevin. The USF players angrily responded with a charge of their own. Pichu knew that his teammates desperately wanted to win this game. It had taken them so much work just to get to this close. Now, to see the game slipping away was heartbreaking. They kept up steady pressure on the Westford defense. They rushed every player and fought for every loose ball. But the Westford players were fast and powerful. Every time they got the ball, they posed a threat to get another goal and put victory completely out of reach.

With just five minutes left in the game, Moore took a shot that was barely deflected by the Westford goalie. Setting up for the corner kick, Pichu positioned himself at the top of the penalty box and felt someone grab his shirt from behind. He turned to find the red-haired fullback holding him back as he tried to move into position.

"You're not going anywhere," the fullback growled, his freckled face looking blotched and angry.

Without thinking, Pichu kicked backwards and felt his heel connect with the fullback's shin just above the pad. There was a grunt of pain, and Pichu was free. The kick was taken, and the ball sailed right toward Pichu. In most cases, he would have headed it into the upper right corner of the nets. But for a moment he hesitated, still guided by his decision to set up his teammates. As the ball curved in on him he trapped it on his chest, dropped it to his feet and flicked a pass with the outside of his foot. The left wing was running in and was open for the shot. He fired the ball across the net, and it hit the right post. The ball bounced out and there was a mad scramble in front of the nets. Pichu expected to see a goal any second but suddenly the ball was cleared down field.

"Hey, ponga dude," the fullback called rushing him. "It's lights out for you, you little — " he threw a punch that Pichu ducked. The fullback threw another punch and came in fast. Pichu moved left and tripped the fullback as he went by. When the ref turned he saw Pichu standing over the fallen fullback. He blew his whistle and reached in his pocket for a yellow card.

"He's been trying to foul me all game," Pichu shouted at the ref.

The ref held the yellow card in his outstretched arm at Pichu, ignoring his protest. Pichu was sorry he had said anything. The ball was given to Westford and the fullback blasted a long kick down field. The center forward deflected the ball around the fullback and broke free. But the ball was too far ahead of him and Kevin, the goalie, raced out. Instead of catching the ball, he sent a long pass back to Rev. A fullback was closing in on Rev, so he headed the ball, deflecting it to Pichu's feet. It was a tough ball to handle but Pichu took it in the air, popping it over the defender's head, then raced around the fullback to touch the ball again before it even hit the ground.

People in the stands screamed with delight. Pichu sprinted toward the goal. His vision to the right was screened and he didn't see the red-haired fullback coming in hard. He ran right through Pichu, flattening him. But somehow, as Pichu fell, he pushed the ball to his left between defenders. The ball trickled toward the goal and wound up right on Moore's foot. With the goalie rushing out, Moore waited until the last second, then put the ball low to the left and into the nets.

The fans were screaming so loudly they almost couldn't hear the referee's whistle. He waved his arms and pointed at a spot at the top of the penalty area — he was saying that Moore was offsides. The goal didn't count.

The crowd groaned in agony and then booed. But the referee was insistent. He pulled the ball back and placed it on the ground. The Westford players took the kickoff and the USF players didn't even react — they were still in shock. Coach Jordan charged onto the field and chased the ref, protesting the call. Seconds later, Westford scored an easy goal as the USF fullbacks watched the chaos on the field. The referee pulled the ball back to center field but then glanced at his watch and blew the whistle. The game was over. Westford won 3–1.

The USF players milled around in shock. Some refused to shake hands with the Westford players. The jeering and booing from the crowd wouldn't stop.

Shields' face was a violent red and his eyes were filled with tears. "That was our game, man!" he yelled to no one in particular.

Moore said, "The ref should have called that hack job on Pichu. That fullback was on his butt the whole game."

The Westford players were filing back to the bus. The red-haired fullback yelled over, "Nice try, ponga dude," and laughed

Suddenly, Moore bolted toward the fullback. Pichu chased him, wanting to stop him. Moore charged the fullback and swung his fist. But the other players were ready for him, mobbing him and throwing punches. The two coaches rushed the fighting players and dragged them apart. Pichu was in the middle of all the players, trying to stop them from fighting. He turned and suddenly found himself face to face with the redheaded fullback. Pichu saw the angry freckled face break into a grin and a big fist was suddenly coming straight at him. Pichu ducked and he heard a mushy crunch and a shout of pain. Turning, he saw the Westford center forward doubled over, his hands covering his face and blood pouring through his fingers. Blood ran down his long black hair and dripped on the ground. The fullback had broken his own teammate's nose.

The coaches, referees and linesmen finally pulled apart the fighting players. The Westford team was put on the bus and it pulled away. Coach Jordan called the USF team together. The players were still upset, kicking the ground and complaining about the loss.

"All right, guys! That's enough of that!" the Coach said. "We had some bad breaks — and I've never seen worse officiating. But the fact remains, you all played one hell of a game. You showed yourselves and you showed them that you can play with the best. Now shake it off and hit the showers. And just remember — we play Westford again later in the year. Next time things will be different."

Everyone headed for the locker room. But Pichu saw someone in the stands he had to talk to. It was Humberto, dragging his black plastic bag and picking up trash, swaying lopsidedly as he moved. He heard Pichu coming and turned. A huge smile split his lumpy face in two.

"Outstanding!" Humberto said.

"But we lost," Pichu answered.

"Lost?" he said as if he didn't understand the word. "You had the lowest score, but you didn't lose. Besides, I saw you starting to play as part of a team this time. If you keep doing that, no one will beat you." He turned, sweeping his arm toward the empty stands. "And then these stands will shake like an earthquake. And the fans will cheer. And Humberto will do his dance. Rump-ta-dump-ta-dee..." He hummed a tune and danced in a circle. Pichu couldn't help laughing. And as he laughed, the tension and anger began to melt away.

"Ponga boy!"

Pichu turned and saw Rev running toward him.

"Party time, dude," Rev said, smiling in that way that Pichu didn't quite trust. "Get changed, we're leaving in 10 minutes."

"I need to practice," Pichu said.

"You need to party," Rev said, dragging him toward the locker room. Pichu turned back and saw Humberto picking up trash again, his shoulders hunched, humming softly to himself.

"Dude, you don't understand," Rev said, throwing his arm around Pichu's shoulders. "Christy's waiting for you." He pointed to the gate near the parking lot. Christy stood there with several other girls. Seeing Pichu look in her direction, she smiled and waved.

"See?" Rev said. "It's time to party-American style."

Chapter 20

"Y ou were so robbed," Christy said as she drove her BMW through the mountains near USF. She was driving very fast, and she spent much of her time looking at Pichu instead of watching the road. It made him nervous, but he didn't want to say anything. "I mean, Westford must have paid off that ref or something because you were so robbed," she said, looking at him again instead of the road.

"Where are we going?" Pichu asked. "I thought the party was in your dormitory."

"Change of plans, dude," Rev said. He was in the back seat with his arm around a girl named Stephanie. "My parents are out of town, so my house will be party central for the night. Here, here! Turn right here, Christy."

The car cornered so fast the tires squealed. "You are such a bad driver," Stephanie said to Christy. But then she laughed as if that was a good thing. Pichu wondered why she would do that. He found American girls to be very confusing.

It was almost dark now and they were climbing a winding road up a steep hill. The car's headlights shone on passing trees with long branches that stretched out over the road. Through the trees, Pichu could see the lights of large houses with big windows. Many of them were behind large metal gates. The car swerved again, then stopped in front of a pair of gates that blocked their path. Rev jumped out and pressed buttons on what looked like a telephone keypad. The big gates slowly swung open. Rev jumped back in the car and they drove down a long driveway and stopped in front of a big house.

Pichu stepped out and looked around. The driveway was filling with cars and he could hear loud music. The air was cool and moist with the sharp, clean smell of pine trees. From inside the house, he heard voices and laughter. He felt someone take his hand and found Christy smiling at him, pulling him into the house. Her touch sent a quiver of excitement through him.

"We're going to show you how we party in the good old U.S. of A.," she said, guiding him down a walk marked by lights in a very pretty way. Her fingernails dug into the back of his hand and made his skin tingle.

Inside, Pichu looked around in amazement. The ceilings were high with fans turning silently. Paintings hung on the walls, but they weren't pictures of Jesus or Mary or even any of the disciples like in Pichu's house. What was the purpose of having paintings if you didn't show religious figures? One picture over the fireplace showed tall mountains above an ocean in which whales were swimming underwater. He liked the whale pictures, and it reminded him of the paintings in the Hotel Palmas de Cortez that showed marlin striking the bait and jumping from the water.

"Come on, you!" Christy said, pulling him by the hand again. They went into the large kitchen where the counters were made from a stone that was smooth and cool to the touch. Two refrigerators were in the wall. Christy opened one as if it were her house. Cans of soft drinks and bottles of beer filled the shelves.

"I bet I know what you want," she said, handing him a bottle of Mexican beer. "Is that good?"

"Yes. Very good," he said. She looked at him and suddenly laughed.

"You're funny," she said. "So quiet and polite. That's a nice change from these animals."

"Hey! I'm not an animal," Rev said. He then let out an enormous burp, which made everyone laugh.

Christy opened the beer for Pichu and he took a small sip. Pichu and the other boys on the dock would sometimes share a beer if a fisherman accidentally left an unopened can in their cooler. He thought beer had a strange, bitter taste that was somehow more thirst-quenching than Coca-Cola. It didn't seem like it should be good — but it was very good. He knew his father didn't want him to drink beer, so most of the time he just avoided it. But now, he was still thirsty from the game. He took another sip, although he wouldn't drink much because he knew bad things could happen if you drank too much.

"Dude, try the punch," Rev said, standing next to a big bowl with a red drink that he was stirring.

"Oh, definitely," Christy said. "You have to try to the punch."

"What is it?" Pichu said, suspecting it might be a joke.

"Kool-Aid," Rev said. For some reason Christy thought this was very funny and laughed. Rev poured a glass and Pichu took a sip. It tasted sweet, like the kind of juice they served in the cafeteria at school when he was little. But it had a funny aftertaste. He put his beer to the side and decided to drink this punch instead.

"Good," Pichu said, smacking his lips.

"Very good," Christy said, and laughed again.

"Check it out," Rev said, pointing out through the kitchen window.

Pichu saw a swimming pool with steam rising from it. As he watched, Kevin, the goalie, jumped off the diving board and flipped in the air before making a huge splash. People standing around the pool cheered.

"Did you bring your suit?" Christy asked. "Even if you didn't you can still go swimming. I'll meet you in the pool."

Pichu was relieved to see that some of the players were wearing their boxers. He went outside carrying his glass and stood by the pool. He drank the rest of the Kool-Aid. Then, from behind, he felt strong, wet hands on him, pushing him toward the pool. It was Shields and Moore. "In ya go, Ponga Boy!" they said, laughing.

Pichu fought his way free and stood facing them. They were in their boxer shorts and dripping with water from the pool.

"You're getting in one way or the other," Moore said.

"No problem, dude," Pichu said. He was a little surprised to hear himself say this. And, for some reason, the people around him laughed. He set the glass down on a table. He removed his clothes until he was just standing in his boxers shorts. The music suddenly became much louder and he saw that Rev was inside the house placing the speakers next to the window so they faced the pool.

Moore and Shields tried to rush Pichu again but he said, "Wait! I want to show you a trick."

"A trick!" Moore yelled to everyone. "The ponga boy will do a trick for us."

Pichu went to the diving board and looked down at the water. Staring at the water, still moving with small waves, he forgot where he was. In his mind he was standing on the bow of his father's ponga boat looking down into the clear sea, feeling the waves moving beneath him. He saw the sardines and mackerel darting in the sunny water, and he heard his father's voice humming his song that never ended. But it had ended, Pichu realized, because the fish had gone and everything had changed. He was afraid to even think about that.

"Are you going to do the damn trick or not?" Frasier yelled. His angry voice woke Pichu out of his dream.

"Okay, boss," Pichu said. He had heard that nickname from Herman the German who used it when talking to the Americans. They seemed to like being called "Boss."

Pichu stepped off the diving board and began jogging around the pool, circling it. He was picking up speed, his feet smacking the wet cement.

"What kind of trick is that?" Frasier said.

By now Pichu was going full blast, rounding the last corner. He ran to the end of the pool, then turned sharply. He ran up onto the board, took a huge leap and traveled through the air upside down, his feet straight up in the air. It was the strangest, most impossible thing anyone had ever seen, like a flip without the tuck. Then, just before Pichu hit the water again, he spun around and splashed in, feet first.

Pichu sank to the bottom of the pool and lay there enjoying the silence. He knew what would happen next. He would stay here until they came to get him. It was what he did with Rudolfo and Angelina in the water beside the dock. It always scared them when he stayed down so long.

They should be coming any second now, Pichu thought, watching the surface of the water. Suddenly, there were explosions of air bubbles from all directions. He pushed off the bottom, found the ladder and pulled himself out of the pool. Moments later several surprised heads bobbed to the surface.

"What are you guys looking for?" Pichu asked.

They sputtered for a moment in anger, then began laughing. Christy had watched the whole thing from the side of the pool and was clapping with delight.

"You were so scared," she said to Frasier, still laughing. "And the whole time he's on the bottom of the pool like waiting for you guys to jump in."

Frasier's face darkened. "Funny joke there, ponga boy."

"Come on," Christy said, and pulled Pichu toward the pool. She was wearing a small black bikini that made him afraid to look at her. He wanted to look at her, but he was afraid she would think he was staring at her. Her hand was hot and he felt her fingernails again. They jumped into the pool and when he came to the surface and stood in the shallow end, she wrapped her arms around his neck. He had never been in the water with a girl like this before and his whole body felt funny. She was pushing her body against his, and he felt her bare legs against his. Her skin was so smooth and soft and he felt jumpy and weak inside.

"So Ponga Boy, what did you think of Westford?" Rev said. He was nearby in the pool with Stephanie. They were standing the same way Pichu was standing with Christy, holding Stephanie the same way he was holding Christy. He had a strange feeling of becoming like the other members of the team. He wondered if he might be mistaken for an American. He could lose his accent and learn to dress just like them. Then, they would all like him, even Frasier.

"We can beat Westford," Pichu said.

"Yeah, right. We were lucky to get one goal." Rev was kissing Stephanie. She pushed his long hair back from his forehead and kissed him as he talked. Christy did the same thing to Pichu, kissing him on his cheek, then lightly on his lips. His whole body was burning and he could hear blood in his ears. He was amazed that a girl could have such an effect on him.

The smell of cooking meat drifted across the pool. Bart was flipping hamburgers and putting them on buns. He was handing out plates of food. It made Pichu realize how hungry he was.

"Food! Yum!" Christy said. She dragged Pichu to the steps. She climbed out of the pool right in front of him. Pichu couldn't stop himself from watching as she rose out of the pool, the water running off her back and off the small black bikini bottom.

Pichu was about to climb up the ladder. But then he realized that if he did everyone see how excited he was. They would laugh at him. Christy turned and held out her hand to Pichu to pull him out.

"Well, come on!" she said, bending over. The black bikini top was loose and he forced himself to look away. "What are you waiting for?"

Pichu sunk back into the pool feeling like his face was on fire. "No. I just want to — " he couldn't think of what to say. "I want to swim," he said weakly.

"Okay, I'll come back in," she said.

"No! Go eat," he said. "I'll — I'll swim." He closed his eyes and sank under the water. Maybe the cold water would make him return to normal. Maybe he would have to spend the whole party in the pool. What could he think of that would help? He thought of the time he stepped on a piece of glass. Then he thought of the time he put a fishing hook through the web of skin between his thumb and forefinger. All his muscles tightened in response to this memory. There, that helped. Maybe he could get out of the pool soon. He tried to look everywhere except at the girls. They all wore swimsuits that showed everything. He had to stop this! He went back to thinking of that fishing hook. He remembered how his father took wire cutters out of his tool box and clipped off the barbed end of it and pulled it through with pliers. Then his mother poured tequila on the wound, and it made him jump around the kitchen in pain.

Pichu climbed out of the pool and hurried over to a stack of towels.

He dried off and knotted a towel around his waist. He turned around and Christy was there with a plate of food.

"What do you want to drink?" she asked. "How about a beer?"

"No. I want more Kool-Aid."

"One Kool-Aid coming up," she said.

After Pichu finished the burger and a few more glasses of Kool-Aid, he got into the hot tub with Christy. Rev and Shields were there with their girlfriends. Once again, he had that feeling that they were all alike. They were all on the same team. They all had girlfriends. It felt good to be included. But deep inside him, there was still a feeling that, while being the same, he was still different.

"Ponga thinks we can beat Westford," Rev said.

"Yeah? That would be sweet," Shields said. He reached behind his girlfriend and picked up a beer. Shields' voice was heavy and thick and his words slurred together. He was getting drunk. It was a good thing Pichu had decided to drink Kool-Aid.

Shields said, "So, genius, how we gonna beat Westford?"

"Score more goals," Pichu said.

"Yeah, I already figured that out," Shields said. "Who's gonna score them?"

"The Ponga Boy," Christy said, and kissed Pichu on the side of his mouth. "The Ponga Boy can do anything."

Rev said, "The Ponga Dude is a playmaker. Not a goal scorer."

"Hey!" Pichu said. "Don't call me that!" He was surprised to hear his voice sound so angry.

"Call you what?"

"Ponga dude. The Westford players called me that. I don't like it."

"What do you want to be called?"

"I'm Ponga Boy."

"Okay, dude. I'll call you Ponga Boy."

Everyone laughed. Pichu felt angry at first. But then he thought it was very funny too. He began laughing. And soon he couldn't stop. Then it was like he was hearing himself laughing at the other end of a tunnel. He got out of the hot tub and bumped into a girl dancing by herself. He saw the pool and felt the cold water might make him feel better. He dove in. But even lying on the bottom, it didn't seem quiet anymore. Something was wrong. He swam to the shallow end. Arms wrapped around him from behind. He heard Christy's voice and felt her breath on his ear.

"Are you trying to get away from me, Ponga Boy?"

He turned in her arms and hugged her. He kissed her. She murmured and pressed her body tight against him. He could feel her eager body through the thin suit. He had the feeling that he was both weak and very strong at the same time. His excitement returned, but he didn't care anymore.

"Let's go lie down," Christy said, her voice sounding very low.

"Towel," Pichu said. "I need a towel."

"We'll get you a towel and then we'll lie down," Christy said. "I think you had a little too much Kool-Aid."

They climbed out of the pool and Christy wrapped him in a big fluffy towel. Something she had said came back to him.

"Too much? But it's Kool-Aid."

"With grain alcohol in it," she said. "You can't taste the alcohol. But it sure does a number on you."

Pichu walked toward the house, hoping he could find a couch or a quiet corner to lie down in. Faces appeared in front of him, asking him questions. He heard himself answering. He heard himself laughing in a voice that didn't sound like his. He remembered doing another trick dive into the pool, and when he came up everyone was cheering. He heard the music and danced a funny dance that made everyone laugh. He kept telling Christy he had to lie down.

A long time passed, filled with little scenes he didn't understand. It was a little like watching someone else on TV and thinking, "They are acting really funny." Then there was a black space during which he didn't remember anything. Then things got quiet and he felt something soft under his feet. It was carpeting. He was in a dark hallway somewhere. A door opened and soft yellow light showed a bed. The bed was so large that there were already two people in it moving around under the covers. This would be a very good place to lie down, he thought. He wanted to lie down because he was very tired. He would just go to sleep and not disturb these people at all.

Pichu fell onto the bed and rolled over. A voice was calling him from far away. He looked up and saw Christy above him smiling, still wearing the little black bikini. She was always smiling at him. She was very polite and kind to him. His eyes closed. Her voice called him again. He opened his eyes. He saw that she was no longer wearing the bikini top. But she was still smiling. Smiling more than ever before.

Chapter 21

Pichu arrived at the church the next morning just as Mass was over. People were streaming out of the big front door and hurrying toward their cars. They looked peaceful and relieved, as if they had done their duty and could now move on with their lives. He wanted to feel that way too. He desperately needed to feel that way, but he had missed Mass. He was very disappointed. He would just have to go inside for a visitation. It was all he could do.

Early that morning he woke up in the big bed next to Christy. She was still asleep so he got up and found his clothes that were lying in a pile beside the pool. His mouth was dry, and no matter how much water he drank, it still felt chalky. Kevin stumbled out of one of the other bedrooms with his red curly hair flying in every direction. He drove Pichu back to campus, laughing about what a great party it was. Pichu said nothing. All he could think of was the terrible mistake he had made. Pichu went to his dormitory and took a long shower. He was planning to study but he couldn't concentrate and soon he found himself outside aimlessly walking. When Pichu spotted this church, his hopes rose. But now that Mass was over and he was walking into a church that was mostly empty. Two choirboys in their robes were picking up hymnals and joking with each other. Their voices echoed in the high-ceilinged sanctuary. They saw Pichu standing there and quietly went back to their duties.

Pichu made the sign of the cross and slid into a pew. This was an enormous church, so much bigger than the one he went to in Los Barriles. There, his church wasn't even finished being built yet. It had been like that ever since he could remember, with wheelbarrows and piles of sand and bricks beside the building. But the church was on a scenic spot on the mountainside overlooking the sea, and he could look out the window while the priest said Mass. He could see the line where the deep blue of the water met the light blue of the sky. And occasionally, an albatross would fly past, hanging on the sea breezes. When he was very young, he would watch the albatross and wonder what it was like to be able to fly.

Pichu abruptly returned to the present and was startled to find himself in this large, empty church in America. There was a kneeler in front of him, and Pichu folded it down with a bang that echoed in the silent church. He knelt. Leaning forward he closed his eyes. When he did this, he felt like the ground was moving underneath him. He was still so dizzy from the drink last night he was afraid he would fall over. But after a few moments, this feeling stopped and he was ready.

"Heavenly father, please hear my prayer," he whispered. Maybe if he sincerely apologized to God he would be forgiven for what he must have done with Christy. He waited for more words to come, but his mind was too chaotic to form sentences. Words floated through his mind: sin, forgiveness, sorrow, guilt. Guilt? Yes, guilt. He wondered if God would hear these random words. Or did they all have to fit together into neat sentences for God to understand what he was feeling? He waited, hoping to hear a prayer come from inside him that would take away the feeling of dread that weighed down on his soul. But nothing came. I can't even pray anymore, he thought.

Pichu knelt there for a very long time, struggling silently. If someone had stood nearby watching him, he would have noticed that his hands were clenched together so tightly that his knuckles were white. His shoulders were hunched and heaving. His breathing was hoarse. Anyone seeing him like this would have sensed the pain that filled his mind, his body and his soul. But no one was there to see him. The church was empty. And Sunday afternoon felt very, very lonely to Pichu.

Pichu left the church and drifted to the park, hoping to find a pickup soccer game to play in. Maybe that would help him forget what he had done. Once again he found the park filled with Mexican families eating picnic lunches and enjoying the sunny afternoon. There were many soccer games here and there played by young boys and girls. But on the bigger field, men were gathering. They kicked the ball back and forth and warmed up.

"Hola!" someone called to him. "Ponga Boy!"

He turned to see a man waving to him and smiling. He didn't recognize the man, and as he approached he heard him say to his friend, "He's the one I was telling you about. I saw him play against Westford. You have to come to the next game and see the amazing moves he has."

Pichu found his friends from Chihuahua, and they formed a team against the guys from Mexico City. At first, Pichu felt so sick he could barely dribble. The ball was like a dog that wouldn't obey and kept running away from him. The Mexico City team scored three quick goals and began to appear very confident. They even started toying with the Chihuahua players by doing fancy moves that were unnecessary but showed off their individual skills. The players on Pichu's team looked at him bewildered, wondering what had happened to his ability. He played on under the hot sun with his throat feeling like sandpaper. He had to leave the game many times to drink from a drinking fountain to quench his thirst. And once, he threw up behind some bushes.

Then, on a fast break, Pichu was about to attempt a shot when he saw movement to his right. A teammate was open at the far side of the goal. He flicked the ball with the outside of his right foot. The defender didn't expect this, and the ball squirted past him and lay right in front of the goal. The player saw a defender coming, cut the ball to avoid him, timed it perfectly, and fired a low shot into the corner.

The goal sparked the team's spirit, and they began to play evenly against the guys from Mexico City. Pichu fed them many passes that resulted in goals. Each time, the player who scored came to Pichu respectfully and thanked him as if he had given him a valuable gift. As the afternoon progressed, there were times when Pichu was so involved in playing the game that he forgot about the terrible thing he had done the night before. But when the memory of his actions came back, he felt worse than ever.

With Pichu's help, the guys from Chihuahua beat the Mexico City team once again. They gathered around a big ice chest and celebrated by drinking Cokes and reviewing some of the great plays. Each of the players found a way to bring up the subject of the goal he had scored and described it in detail, embellishing slightly. Eventually, the guys began drifting away. One of the players, seeing Pichu walking off alone, gave him a ride back to his dormitory in his pickup with a big steel toolbox bolted to the truck bed.

Climbing the stairs to his room, Pichu realized he was very tired. He also realized that, for short periods of time while playing soccer, he had not thought of Christy and what had happened last night. He was starting to feel a little better. But as he opened the door to his hallway, he saw Christy standing in front of his room waiting for him. She looked upset. Her eyes had circles under them, and she wore no makeup.

"I have a huge favor to ask you," Christy said. "Can we go into your room?"

Pichu hesitated. She saw his reaction and said, "Just to talk."

He opened the door and they went inside. She shut the door behind her and sat on his chair by the wooden desk. He sat on his bed, waiting for her to speak.

"I'm so embarrassed," she said, holding her face in her hands and resting her elbows on her knees.

Pichu dreaded what she was going to say. He even wondered if she was going to say she was pregnant. Or maybe she would accuse him of mistreating her. "Why?" Pichu finally asked.

"Everyone's talking about how I slept with you."

"Slept with you?" he asked. Pichu had never heard that expression before.

"Yeah, you know…" She said. "Everyone is saying that we had sex."

Pichu felt his heart sinking. Not only had he done something terrible, not only had he been untrue to Angelina, but now all his new friends here at the university knew about it.

"All my friends are asking me, 'What was it like?'" she said. "And all I'm thinking about is how embarrassed I am."

Pichu was trying to understand what she was saying. "You are embarrassed because we had sex?"

Christy was startled by his words. She was quiet for a moment, staring at him with her pretty dark eyes that searched his face in confusion.

"No," she said in a serious tone. "I'm not embarrassed because we had sex. I'm embarrassed because we didn't have sex."

"You mean — " Pichu started to say. But he didn't really know how to phrase it.

She nodded. "Right. Nothing happened. We were so drunk that we just passed out."

An incredible feeling of relief flooded through Pichu. He felt like he was waking up from the worst nightmare of his life. But maybe he misunderstood. He had to be sure.

"We didn't sleep together?" he asked. "We didn't have sex?"

"No. Don't you remember?"

The relief came in waves, rising from somewhere deep inside Pichu. He felt his whole body becoming wildly happy. He felt light, as if he wanted to run as fast as he could. But then he thought of something that still confused him.

"What is the favor that you wanted to ask me?"

"Please," she said. "Please don't tell people we didn't sleep together."

Pichu laughed in surprise. "Didn't?"

She saw his expression and seemed to understand his confusion.

"I know it must sound strange to you," she said. "But here, with my friends, we have a game. To have as many boyfriends as we can."

"That's not such a good game," Pichu said, feeling a little disgusted. It was hard to imagine what she was saying.

"But please don't tell people that we didn't sleep together. Okay?"

She smiled at him, her eyes pleading. Pichu felt angry. She had made him feel so terrible. Now she wanted him to say he had done something that he hadn't. He just couldn't understand this strange behavior at all.

"Please," she said again. She leaned toward him and took his hand. Suddenly, all the feelings of last night came back to him like angry electric shocks. His body was going in two directions at once. He was still feeling relief, but now the excitement started again. This was the strangest thing that ever happened to him.

It was very quiet in the dorm room. So quiet he heard the hand on the clock moving, ticking away the time. He glanced past Christy at the clock.

"Ayi!" he said, standing up. "I have to work! I'm late!"

Pichu took a T-shirt out of his drawer. He found his hairnet. When he turned back, Christy was blocking his way to the door.

"I'm really not a bad person," she said. "I hope we can still be friends."

She smiled at him and for a moment she looked younger, even a little like the girls in Pichu's school in Los Barriles.

"Yes. We can be friends," he said. "But now I have to go. Señor Vargas will be mad."

Pichu was reaching for the door knob when she kissed him on the cheek. The electricity shot through his body again. He looked at Christy. She was smiling at him and, for the first time, her smile seemed simple and honest.

He quickly opened the door and left.

Chapter 22

There were fish everywhere. Golden fish with bullet-shaped bodies. Long, silvery fish that flicked through the water like beams of sunlight. Menacing sharks that would suddenly appear out of the shadows and long eels that looked like ribbons of shiny black rubber.

Pichu stood in front of the huge tank at the Monterey Aquarium and stared in awe at all the fish. The other students from his class milled around him, talking and taking notes and reading the plaques on the walls. But Pichu stood there silently, turning in wonder and watching the fish move through the long strands of kelp. In another tank that rose and fell with the ocean outside, a sea otter appeared and came right up to the glass. He seemed to smile at Pichu like a clown entertaining children. With a flick of his tail he shot out of sight and then reappeared, lying on his back, riding the waves.

There was something in the sea otters' manner that made Pichu laugh. He wanted to dive in the water and chase the otters and swim in circles with them. He wanted to stay here near the water all afternoon. He had been in America for nearly three months now and he hadn't realized how much he missed the ocean. Being surrounded by fish was like being in a dream of abundance. It made him think of the waters off the coast of his village in Mexico. And it painfully reminded him of his father's ponga, which was probably lying unused on the beach while he worked on a boat owned by some big company.

The last time Pichu called home, his father didn't even come to the phone. Instead, his mother relayed the news. She said the fishing was still so poor that many of the boats didn't even go out during the day. She said Pichu's father was working for a fishing fleet in Cabo. He was gone for days, then back for a week when he slept all day. In the background, he heard his father's angry voice, shouting at Neto for waking him. His mother had taken a second job at the Super Mercado and sounded very tired, too. But she was quick to tell Pichu that the only way they had made the last payment on the boat was with the money he had sent. She thanked him profusely in a way that almost embarrassed him.

"Do you see anything that you recognize?" Professor Baca asked as he joined Pichu beside the large exhibit titled "The Pacific Ecosystem."

"Well, I…" The fish overwhelmed Pichu. He didn't know where to start. The professor misinterpreted his silence.

"You see that school of fish there, Pichu? Those are barracuda. It's a predatory fish that feeds mainly on the — "

"No, it's not," Pichu said, unable to contain himself. "That's wahoo. That over there, that's the barracuda. The wahoo travels in schools, but never more than 10 or 12. And when the sardines jump out of the water to escape, the wahoo and skipjack jump right after them. And then the water around looks like it's boiling. And if you are fishing in such a school, you can pull so many fish out of the water that your boat will sink."

Pichu turned to another tank and pointed out a different type of fish. "And that guy there, that's the rooster fish. We have many of them in our waters. The sport fishermen like to hook the roosterfish because it will put up a tough fight. But when they eat the roosterfish it tastes like plaster." He made a face as if spitting a sour mouthful. "Good fighting, bad eating is what they say. But the tuna will give a good fight and has a wonderful taste. My mother cuts it in steaks and my father puts it on the grill and cooks it on a very hot flame. When it is ready to serve, my brothers and I fight for the biggest piece."

Professor Baca had fallen silent during this enthusiastic speech. He watched Pichu's face as if peering through a window into his life.

"Pichu, let's go outside and watch the otters," the professor said. They moved out onto a deck that overlooked the otter tank. From here, they looked across the bay and could see moored boats swaying on the waves. The water was filled with whitecaps and the air was cool and carried the feeling that the seasons were changing.

Professor Baca leaned on a railing and looked out over the water. When he spoke, his voice was low and serious. Pichu had come to recognize that he used this voice whenever he gave advice. At first, Pichu thought the tone was a stern warning. But later he realized that Professor Baca's advice always carried concern and even love.

"I saw you play last week against Santa Cruz," he said, switching to Spanish. "I've never seen someone play with the freedom you do. I never know what you're going to do next. No wonder we're winning all our games this year."

"All except Westford."

"Yes, well, perhaps you will meet them again in finals."

"Did you play soccer when you were growing up in San Felipe?" Pichu asked. He tried to imagine the professor as a young boy, but it was difficult because he was always so serious and his hair was now streaked with gray.

"I tried to play," the professor said, smiling weakly. "I had no skill and the other boys teased me. So I returned to my books. And it was my books that brought me here. The boys who teased me, they are still in Mexico working in factories owned by American or Japanese companies. Meanwhile, I'm in America teaching college."

Professor Baca paused, suddenly uncomfortable. "All I'm saying is that you have something very special. I can see why you want to make a living playing soccer."

"A living?"

"You want to be a professional soccer player. Right?"

Pichu thought about it. "I don't know."

"I talked to Coach Jordan. He said scouts are coming to the next game from the MLS and even from a European league."

"Why?"

"They see your potential. They know you will get even better with the right training. If I were you, I would probably take that opportunity, too. But it also scares me to think of you going in that direction."

"Why?"

Professor Baca didn't answer for a long time. He stared into the distance as gulls cried and the wind swirled his hair around his serious face. Finally, he said, "I don't want you to lose your way."

"How could I do that?"

"In the world of professional sports, it happens all the time. Everything comes too easily. And then, one day you are thirty-five and you are too old to make the big plays. You're afraid of getting hurt and everyone forgets you. What do you do then?"

"I will be a fisherman, like my father."

"That would make you happy? After all the attention? After all the money and the women? You could go home and be a fisherman?"

"Yes," Pichu said, stubbornly. "I would be happy with that."

"And what if, when you are finally ready to fish, the fish are all gone?"

The question was like a slap across Pichu's face. A terrible picture flashed into his mind. It was the vision that haunted him whenever he thought of this subject. He saw the sea near his home completely empty, all the fish killed off. He pictured lifeless waves washing onto a barren shore. He turned away and looked at the tank inside the aquarium, teeming with fish. He felt something inside him that he didn't understand. It was as if a piece of something inside him broke loose and began to drift away.

"Excuse me," a new voice interrupted. "You're Pichu, aren't you?"

A student was approaching him, a young man holding a thin notepad.

"I'm Louis Carter. I work for the USF Bulletin. I just happened to see you here and wondered if you have time for a few questions?"

"About what?"

"About soccer, of course. You guys are really kicking butt now. My editor wants me to do an interview with you — where you're from and all that good stuff." The reporter had greasy black hair and talked very fast, laughing suddenly and for no reason.

"It'll only take a few seconds," the reporter added, laughing again.

"Yes. Of course," Pichu said.

Professor Baca turned away, shaking his head

"I'm sorry," Pichu said to the professor. "Can we continue this later?"

"Fine."

"I'll think about what you said."

"I hope you do."

Pichu moved off with the reporter beside him. The professor watched as they left.

"Tell me about the town you're from in Guatemala." the reporter said, holding his pen poised over the pad, ready to start writing.

"Mexico. I'm from Mexico," Pichu said. "It's a town called Los Barriles. It's on the tip of the Baja Peninsula. It's a beautiful place. Everyone who visits falls in love with it."

The reporter waited for Pichu to continue. But Pichu was lost in thought. Finally, he said, "I'll be there next week while everyone here is celebrating Thanksgiving. We don't have Thanksgiving in Mexico — but it will be a chance for me to go home for the first time in nearly three months."

The reporter smiled knowingly.

"I'll bet it'll be hard for you to go back. I mean, now that you've seen America and all, seen how good people can live. Hey, that might make an interesting follow-up story. I'll have to talk to you after you get back. But right now I want to ask you this: We've won the past eight games. One more game and we make it into the playoffs. What kind of odds do you give us to capture the title?"

The reporter's pen was hovered over the notepad as he waited for Pichu's answer. But Pichu was still thinking about what the reporter had said. For a moment, he saw his village from an American's point of view, and it seemed primitive. It was the first time he had thought of it this way and it scared him, as if he was becoming cut off from his home.

"The odds?" the reporter asked again. "What are the odds of being number one in the league?"

"We'll win it," Pichu said.

"Really?" the reporter asked, then began writing again.

"I promise you we will win it," Pichu said firmly. "Now excuse me, please. My friend is waiting for me."

Chapter 23

As the jet glided down the length of the Baja Peninsula, Pichu looked out the window, his eyes searching the landscape below for familiar landmarks. The landscape below looked more dry and sandy than he remembered. And he was amazed at how few houses and roads there were. Mostly he saw sandy mountains dotted with cactus and only a few buildings here and there, surrounded by junked cars and trucks. It looked very bright and hot outside. As the jet approached for landing, it was buffeted by gusts of wind that kicked up swirls of dust beside the runway.

Pichu stepped out into a blast of hot air under the midday sun. He felt the dry air sucking the moisture from his body. He pulled off his USF warmup jacket and tucked it into the grocery bag he carried. In the bag were gifts for his mother, his father and each of his brothers and sisters. As he had carefully selected each present, he imagined the screams of delight they would bring when unwrapped. He could hardly wait to hand them out. He continued walking toward the terminal, feeling the heat of the sun on his shoulders, right through his USF T-shirt. Why hadn't he ever noticed how powerful the sun was down here, even in November?

Pichu waited in a long line of people who were mainly American tourists. Many of them wore bright shirts and straw hats and spoke in loud voices, joking about the great time they would have drinking tequila, playing golf and lying on the beaches. Usually, these arriving tourists included groups of men carrying long tubes that contained fishing rods. This time, he saw no sport fishermen.

The area just behind the customs desk was a large tiled room through which the tourists hurried once their passports were stamped. They couldn't wait to get to the vans and buses and taxis that would carry them to their hotels in Cabo or to the villages along the East Cape of Baja Sur. Pichu couldn't help remembering the airport in San Francisco, where waiting families gathered to greet returning travelers with signs and balloons. The people who lived here in Mexico rarely went away, so there were no emotional reunions.

Pichu had almost reached the customs officer when he saw them coming. His family was rushing in through the entrance, all his brothers and sisters running and sliding across the tile floor, shouting and pushing each other. It was clear that they had just arrived and were hurrying to meet him. And here came his friends Rudolfo and Luis too! His mother walked behind them all, still wearing her maid's uniform. How had they all fit into the truck? They looked through the glass windows and saw Pichu. They tried to rush right past the guard but were stopped by a customs officer and severely scolded. They retreated and waited impatiently, jumping up and down for a better view of him and waving and calling to him.

Ayi! This customs officer is taking forever! Pichu thought. But finally his passport was stamped, and he picked up his bag and his suitcase. He hurried through the door, past the security guard and toward his family. He took in the sight of their faces, so happy and expectant, and knew the scene would stay in his mind like a photograph for a long time. And then they were on him, the little kids clinging to his legs and pulling his clothes and touching him while his mother and older sisters hugged him. Everyone was talking at once and his youngest brother, Luther, fell down and started to cry. Lucinda picked him up to comfort him and he jumped from her grasp into Pichu's arms and clung to him happily.

Through this turmoil, Pichu realized someone was missing. His father was not here. He was probably waiting outside in the truck.

"We saw you playing on TV!" Lucinda said.

"On TV? What TV?" Pichu asked, amazed.

"On the satellite TV at the hotel," Rudolfo said. "You were playing against a team that committed many fouls. They played dirty and tried to hurt you."

"That was Cal Berkeley," Pichu said. "But we won anyway. We are winning everything," he laughed. "We might go to the playoffs." He used the English word "playoffs" and Rudolfo looked puzzled. He translated it into Spanish.

For the first time, Pichu looked closely at his mother. She was wearing bright red lipstick, something she never did. Her graying hair was neatly combed and held back by a silver barrette. Suddenly it struck Pichu that she had tried to make herself look good. For him! What a strange thing to do. Despite the red lipstick she looked tired and older than he ever remembered. But then she smiled and hugged him again saying, You are too thin! And when she smiled and laughed, all the negative thoughts were driven from Pichu's mind.

"Your father wanted to be here, Pichu," his mother said. "He tried so hard to convince his boss to let him work a different shift so he could be here to greet you. But his boss a chilango — you know how they are in Mexico City. He is very mean and would not allow it."

They were all walking through the terminal now, his sisters holding his hands, the whole group moving together like a noisy parade. Pichu noticed with embarrassment that the American tourists were looking at him and his family. They seemed to have expressions of amusement and what he thought was disapproval.

"Why does Papa have to work for the fisheries?" Pichu asked. But then he regretted asking it because he was afraid of the answer.

"The fishing is still very poor," his mother said. "The tourists have learned that the fish are scarce." She forced herself to brighten up. "But we still have the beaches. Families come now for the swimming and to lie in the sun. They like to get tanned."

"So they look dark like us," Neto said and laughed. "They want to be Mexicans, too."

"Shut up," his sister said. "They do not."

Rudolfo opened the door to the parking lot and said to Pichu, "Look who is here!"

Herman the German stood beside the large hotel van with a big smile on his face. So that's how so many people were able to come to greet me, Pichu realized.

"Pichu! You came back!" Herman said. He was wearing wraparound sunglasses and trying to look very macho.

"Yes," Pichu said. "And do you know why I came back?"

"To brag about your American girlfriends?"

"No," he said. "I came back to bark."

"Like the dog from Tijuana! Right!" Herman the German laughed.

Then, at the same time, Herman and Pichu howled like dogs. "Owwwuuuu!!" And then they laughed some more.

Chapter 24

All the way home, Pichu watched his surroundings as if seeing them for the first time. Where were the lawns with the cool green grass? Why were the houses here so badly painted and falling down? Why did they let the dogs roam all over the place? Why were the roads so narrow and badly paved? At one point, Herman had to brake sharply for a herd of goats crossing the road. Pichu could hardly believe how different everything looked.

But by the time he got back to his house on the hill overlooking the water, with the long adobe wall running down the mountainside, things seemed familiar. It was home to him again. Just home.

Pichu looked around, hoping to see his father's truck. But his spot in the dirt driveway was empty. A brown stain in the tan soil showed that he hadn't yet fixed the leak from the oil pan.

"When will Papa come home?" Pichu asked.

"He tried very hard to change to another boat," his mother said. "But they said they would fire him if he didn't take the boat they assigned him to."

"Boat?" Pichu asked. "I thought he worked in a fishery in Cabo."

"He fishes on a commercial boat," his mother said. "He didn't want me to tell you. But I knew you would find out sooner or later. Please try to understand, Pichu."

They all went into the house and as soon as Pichu crossed through the doorway, it hit him: the smell of fresh-cooked tortillas still lingered from the morning meal. He inhaled deeply and let the smell and all it meant sink deep inside him. Pichu's mother saw his reaction and said, "I've cooked a special dinner for you. Many guests will come tonight."

"But I'm hungry now," Pichu said. "I want a tortilla."

His mother smiled and looked pleased. "I guess one tortilla wouldn't hurt anything."

"With melted cheese and salsa," Pichu said. But as soon as he said it, his brothers and sisters yelled, "Me, too! One for me, too!"

Luther was pulling at the bag that Pichu had carefully guarded. Its side ripped open and the gifts began to spill out, little tissue paper bundles held together by Scotch tape. They all began to grab for the presents.

"Hey! No fighting! I got something for everyone," Pichu announced. He began handing out the little bundles, starting with the youngest of the children and working his way up. There were unusual-looking toys that could only be purchased in America. And comic books and magazines. Lots of candy and treats. The children drifted off to play with their presents. When Pichu looked up, his mother held a plate of food.

"Here is a little snack for you. I hope it will be enough to hold you until tonight."

The plate was enough for an entire meal. Pichu selected the tortilla first. He rolled it up and sank his teeth into it, savoring its warmth, and the soft, moist texture. It was every bit as good as he remembered. As he devoured it, he saw his mother watching him with a satisfied look. And, seeing her, he understood why he had missed her cooking so much. She made this food with her own hands and with the love she felt for all her children. The tortillas he had eaten in America might have been just as good. But since she hadn't made them, they would never taste like this.

"I brought a present for you, too," Pichu said. He took out a flat item wrapped in tissue paper. She carefully opened the paper and found a silk blouse with a floral pattern. Her fingers touched it with great care. "I don't know if I can wear it," she said, blinking rapidly.

"Why?" he asked, disappointed.

"It is too beautiful to wear in this little town where the people are so simple. Maybe someday, if your father takes me to a restaurant in La Paz, then I will wear it."

"Mama, I want you to wear it tonight at dinner, for the party."

"But what if something spills on it?"

"You can wash it. Please, wear it tonight."

The house seemed suddenly quiet with only the distant sounds of his brothers and sisters playing outside. Pichu looked through the doorway at the wall that separated his house from Angelina's. His mother read his mind.

"I think perhaps that Angelina will be home from school," she said. "Why don't you go and say hello to her?"

Pichu reached into the bag and took out one of the last gifts. This one was not held together by scotch tape. It was a silver gift box with a beautiful ribbon and bow. "Nordstrom" was written on the box. He walked outside and found that the heavy earthen flowerpot was still in the same place. Holding the present carefully in one hand, he took two quick steps, sprang off the flowerpot, and landed on top of the wall. He sat with his legs dangling over the wall and looked down into Angelina's back patio. He could see Angelina sitting at the kitchen table, a soft drink can in front of her. He whistled and she turned and saw him still sitting up on the wall in the spot where he always sat. She gave a surprised scream of delight. Her face lit up and she ran outside. He jumped down off the wall and caught her in his arms.

"You're back!" she said, pressing her face into his shoulder and squeezing him tight. "You came back! I've been waiting and waiting."

"Of course I'm back," he said. "Every letter I wrote you I said I'd be back?"

"Well, you know..." she said.

"No. I don't know."

"Everyone said you wouldn't want to come back because America is so much better than our little village. And the women in America are so tall and beautiful with blond hair."

"That's all true," he said. "But I came back anyway."

She held up her fist as if she was going to punch him and waved it in his face. He saw her fierceness and pretended to be afraid.

"If any of those American girls tries to touch you, I will knock their pretty little heads off," she said.

Pichu wanted to laugh at this. But then he thought of that time when he had acted so badly with the girl named Christy. He was afraid she would somehow sense his guilt. To cover his reaction he brought out the silver gift box and handed it to her.

"Here is something that I bought for you in America," Pichu said.

She looked at the box and slowly read the label. "Nordstrom. They have many Germans in America?" she asked.

"Nordstrom's is the best store in America," Pichu said. "It only has things of the highest quality. And the sales people never even try to cheat you."

She gently untied the ribbon and opened the lid. Lying on a bed of cotton was a beautiful necklace. It was made of a fine mesh of silver, intricately woven, holding sapphires and pearls. It had cost Pichu an entire week's paycheck from the cafeteria.

"I've never seen anything like this," she said, hugging him. "I'll wear it tonight. We are having a big party for you, and I want everyone to see it. Now, you have to go because I want to change into different clothes. These are my school things and they are too plain."

They didn't look too plain at all to Pichu. She looked just the way he had remembered her when he felt lonely and forgotten, lying on his bed in his dormitory room in America. She looked just the way he pictured her as he walked around campus dreaming about her. And now she was standing right in front of him. He just wanted to keep staring at her and telling himself she was really here in flesh and blood, her voice like music. But she was getting impatient with him now, pretending to get angry, and looking so beautiful as she did. She shoved him roughly and he stumbled backwards, laughing.

"Now go," she said. "Go and I will see you at dinner."

Pichu jumped up and landed on top of the wall. He turned to look at her and found her standing below him, her face upturned.

"I saw you on TV," she said. "We all gathered in the bar at the hotel and Esteban found the game on satellite TV. Everyone is saying you will be the next soccer superstar."

"I don't know about that," he said.

"They are saying you will be as big as Pelé," she said, looking at him in a different way.

"I'm only a college soccer player," he said, shrugging and feeling a little strange about the way she was acting.

"I'll see you at dinner," she said. Then she smiled again and added, "Superstar."

Chapter 25

Friends and relatives began arriving for Pichu's party long before dinnertime. They came on foot or in cars or in pickup trucks with the children riding in the bed and dogs trotting along behind. The dogs met dogs from other families, and there was growling and some fighting out among the cactus. Soon, they returned, licking their wounds with their differences settled, and found comfortable places in the dust to lie down. Inside Pichu's house, it became very crowded and it was noisy with many excited voices and much laughter. The musicians from the mariachi band that played at the hotel heard about Pichu's return. They stopped by the house to play some of their most requested songs. Ricardo, the guitar player with a long, sad face, drew out the last note of El Rey in a comical way that made everyone laugh.

Soon, the house was completely filled with people who had come to see Pichu and hear about his experiences in America. Everyone was there except Pichu's father. Every time a car pulled into the driveway, Pichu thought it might be his father, but it was just another family joining the party. Angelina hadn't arrived yet either. But Angelina's mother was there, and she told Pichu that her daughter was still at home getting dressed.

"She spends too much time in front of the mirror," Angelina's mother said, rolling her eyes. "'But mama,' she says, 'Pichu has been to America now. I must make myself beautiful.' I tell her, 'You are beautiful! Come away from that mirror.' But she doesn't listen to me." She shook her head sadly. "She will be here soon. And then you will see what I mean."

The men from the dock came to visit Pichu but they were reluctant to enter the house. Instead, they gathered out in the yard, where they could slouch against the wall smoking cigarettes and drinking bottles of Corona with their thumbs hooked in their belt loops. Pichu joined them and soon there were many questions about soccer and about America and his new life at the university.

"Is it true that in America there are almost as many girls in college as there are boys?" asked a man named Ramon. He refueled the boats before they set out to sea. He was faster than any of the workers on the dock, performing his duties expertly and rarely sharing in the jokes.

"That is true," Pichu said. "The classes are filled with the girls. And each of them has a cellular phone that they talk on constantly."

"Why do they need to call to their mothers so often?" Ramon asked, bewildered.

"Their mothers?" Pichu laughed. "No. They call boys. Or other girls. They talk to anyone who will answer their phone. And they talk constantly."

"I heard that American girls are very easy to kiss," Herman the German said, grinning and shuffling his feet excitedly. "My cousin went to America, and he said the women wear clothes that you can see right through."

All the men laughed, but then they quickly looked to Pichu to see if this could possibly be true. He glanced around to see if Angelina was coming but she still wasn't anywhere to be seen.

"The girls in America are very different than Mexican girls," Pichu said. "They wear shirts that are so short and you can see their bellies. Then the pants are very low, to here." He held his hand on his hips. "So that you can see the tattoos on their hips."

"Tattoos?" one man asked. "Girls have tattoos?"

"That's not all. Their bodies are different, too," Pichu said.

"Oh. Now you are making this up!" Herman said. But then he excitedly added, "Go on. Tell us more."

"They are very big up top," Pichu said, using his hands to illustrate his words. He let the meaning of this sink in. "They wear special underwear to make them look very, very big."

The men looked at each other, a little confused.

"How big?" Herman the German asked.

"Very big," Pichu said, using his hands again to emphasize what he was saying. "But it looks so unnatural. And some of the girls have eaten too many McDonalds hamburgers and there is fat on their bellies that moves when they walk."

The men were all laughing. Pichu began walking back and forth imitating a typical American girl.

"So they have their pants too low and their shirt too high and their bellies are hanging out. They have so much makeup on that you can't even see their faces. And they walk around with their phone to their ear saying, 'Hey! What's happening? What's happening?' And they walk like

this and have padding here. 'Hey! What's happening?' Pichu spoke in a
high voice, imitating the girls he was describing, pretending he was on
high heels.

And as he did so, he turned in a circle and saw that Angelina was
standing there on the walkway, watching him. She had heard everything. And she was dressed in the outfit that he had just described —
high heels, low pants with a tight white top that left her navel exposed.
Her beautiful face was hidden with a thick coating of makeup and her
eyes were outlined in black. And her shape was different, too. Her chest
was unnaturally large. Pichu saw her expression and realized she had
heard his entire speech. She was crushed. She turned and ran back
toward her house.

Pichu was horrified by what he had done. The men around him fell
silent and looked away, embarrassed, realizing they had, in a way, helped
cause this terrible situation. But they were completely unable to help
make it better. Pichu ran after Angelina and caught up with her in her
kitchen. He grabbed her arm and turned her around to face him.

"Why did you do this?" Pichu asked, looking at her beautiful features all covered with makeup. She hid her face behind her hands.

She couldn't look him in the eye. He felt a sickening lump in his
throat, as if he was being forced to swallow something that wouldn't go
down. He tried to touch her face but she slapped his hand and struggled
to get away.

"Why would you do this to yourself?" he asked again.

"You already know."

"No I don't."

She began to sob. And through her tears he heard her say, "For you
— I did it for you."

"For me?"

"It's the way you want me to look now."

"What way is that?"

"American." She looked up at him from under long false eyelashes.
"I read the magazines. I watched TV. All the time I was thinking, 'If only
I could look like that, maybe Pichu would come back to me.' I want you
to still like me so that maybe someday, you will not need to stay in
America. Maybe someday, you will come home to stay."

Pichu looked at her again, at the face he loved, now grotesquely
painted. He felt a disturbing blend of emotions, disgust and pity and
love, all at the same time. But then he began to laugh — not because it
was funny, but because it was such a shock. She looked hurt by his
laughter so he quickly hugged her and said, "I'm sorry, Angie. I'm

laughing because — because this isn't what I want at all. Everyone I see in America is trying to be someone else."

"What do you want, then?"

"I want you. Just as you really are."

"Truly?"

He didn't answer. Instead, he hugged her and rocked her in his arms. And she cried softly, but happily and with relief. The tears ran down her face, through the hideous makeup, and fell in black drops on the white top. They held each other for a long time just letting their togetherness heal what the words could not. Eventually, they became aware of laughing and they turned to see a line of little boys and girls standing outside, watching them. Pichu saw that one of them was his little brother Luther, who was giggling and pointing at them.

"Why are you spying on us?" Pichu yelled at him.

"We're watching you do kissy kissy," Luther said, smacking his lips. Pichu dove for his little brother but Luther was too quick and he ducked under a table out of reach. He was going to be very fast, Pichu realized. As the chase continued, Angelina disappeared into her room.

A few minutes later she returned wearing a simple blue blouse with the necklace Pichu had given her. The makeup was gone from her face and the shape of her body was once again her own. Her complexion was radiant, shining with youth and beauty, and she walked easily in flat sandals. Once again, Pichu thought, she is the girl that he loves.

They stepped back outside into the warm night and were about to return to the party when they found their feet taking a different path. They walked down the hillside and kicked off their sandals and worked their toes into the sand that was still warm from the day's sun. They stopped many times and kissed, and Pichu felt his pent up loneliness flowing out of him and disappearing. Angelina's embarrassment was forgotten and, in between kisses, she told Pichu every single thought that had gone through her mind since he had left three months ago. He laughed at her descriptions and kissed her lips even as she continued talking and finally she stopped talking and their kisses became long and deep.

They reached the edge of the water, where the sand sloped down into the sea. They stretched out with their feet touching the warm water as the waves came in. Angelina sensed that Pichu had been through a lot while he was away in America. So she stopped talking and waited quietly, until he began to speak.

"As more people have heard of me and my soccer playing, I've noticed people want to know what I'm thinking," Pichu said. "They assume I want to be rich and famous. They think I like American styles and sexy girls and all those things. But this isn't true. Instead, I spend most of my time thinking of you, or my friends, or my family, or my mother's cooking. I think of the smells of our village and how much I miss my brothers and sisters. I think about the fish and the danger to our way of life here. Yes, I've been given the gift of athleticism and I am not afraid of it. But I am still the same person in my heart."

Angelina knew that he wasn't done talking. He seemed to be struggling within himself, so she held his hand tightly and pressed close to him. She looked at his face and saw him staring into the sea as if it would give him the answers he was searching for.

"I need you to believe what I tell you. I need to know that you see me as I am — not as you want me to be. I need you as my anchor to keep me from floating away, because otherwise, the loneliness is too much. I do not want to lose my way. But I know that if we are together, and that if I have your love, there is nothing that I can't handle."

He turned to her for an answer. She felt that no words could describe what she was feeling so she just held him. And then they kissed, and it was complete. Or nearly complete. There was something still between them and they both felt it. They drew apart and looked at each other. Then she realized what it was — she hadn't removed the thick lipstick she had been wearing. She dipped her hand in the salt water and washed it off, laughing. Then they kissed again and they were touching more completely than ever before. Pichu felt energy and happiness flow through him as if he were once again connected to the entire world.

They knew they had to return to the party, so they slowly walked back up the hill. When they reached Pichu's house and walked back inside, they found the gathering had become very noisy. The mariachi band was playing a lively ballad about a bandito who was very handsome and had many girlfriends. When Pichu and Angelina entered holding hands, with their faces flushed, the mariachis quickly switched to a romantic song. Everyone clapped at the site of this striking young couple. Angelina was shy and hid her face behind her hands. But Pichu proudly gazed around him at the faces of all his friends and felt happiness flooding through his body as he realized he was in just the right place. Soon, plates of food began appear, heaped with all of his mother's best cooking. Everyone ate many helpings and afterwards they groaned and held their stomachs, shaking their heads. Finally, they began to leave, saying their goodbyes to Pichu and wishing him luck with the rest of his soccer games and promising to watch him, if they could, on satellite TV. Pichu's brothers and sisters grew sleepy and curled up in their beds. And soon the house was quiet.

Pichu walked Angelina back home. They hesitated, holding hands, not wanting to be separate even for the few hours until the next day. But it was late and they knew they had to sleep. After one last lingering kiss, she disappeared into her house.

When Pichu returned to his house, his mother still stacking the dishes and cleaning up. The house was quiet, and the village around the house was quiet, too.

"When will Papa be home?" Pichu asked, drying the dishes.

"I never know anymore," she answered. "You should go to bed. He will probably come in during the night."

"I want to wait up for him," Pichu said.

"You might be waiting a very long time," she said. She folded the dishcloth and hung it on the handle of the stove, the way she always did. "Pichu, go to bed. You will see him in the morning. In the morning, everything will be better."

"Good night," Pichu said, hugging his mother. "I'll turn in soon."

She smiled and touched his cheek and said, "It's so good to have you home." Then she walked down the hallway to her room.

Pichu found himself alone in his house in the still of the night. He strained his ears for the familiar sound of his father's truck coming down the road. But he heard nothing except the desert wind and, faintly, the surf on the beach. He was very tired but he was determined to wait up for his father. Of course, it wouldn't hurt if he lay down on the couch for a few minutes. Maybe he could rest a little without falling asleep, he thought. Stretching out, he thought how good it felt to lie down after his long trip and the excitement of the party. It even felt good to close his eyes for a moment or two. If his father came home now, he would understand and not be offended. His father always understood, Pichu thought, as he smiled slightly and then drifted off to sleep.

ichu woke up with a start and found his father sitting in the chair across from him, watching him sleep. He had no idea how long he had been asleep. His father was still dressed in his work clothes, his dark blue baseball cap pushed back on his head. The smell of fish clung to him and filled the room. Normally, it was a familiar, comforting smell. But now it was troubling. His father looked very tired and there was more gray in his hair and his mustache than Pichu remembered. He had aged alarmingly since Pichu saw him last.

"Papa," Pichu said, sitting up quickly. "I — I wanted to wait up but — "

His father nodded and held up his hand as if to say that it was okay.

"I missed your party," his father said. "Was is good?"

"Everyone was here," Pichu said. But then he realized that might make his father feel bad so he added. "We missed you."

"I tried to change boats. I told el jefe it was an important day, that my son was returning from America," his father said bitterly. "But he is from Mexico City. He didn't give a damn."

Pichu was a little shocked to hear his father swear. His father had never sworn in his presence before. His father was upset. Pichu wondered if he had done something wrong.

"Come with me," his father suddenly said. "We must talk."

"Where are we going?"

"Follow me."

Pichu hurried after his father as he walked out the front door. The night sky had paled in the east and the day would be coming soon. It reminded Pichu of all the times they had left at this hour to fish. Was that where they were heading? Pichu heard the door of his father's truck groan in protest. He quickly walked around and climbed into the passenger seat. They drove down the bumpy dirt road and soon they were rolling out onto the hard-packed sand on the beach by the pier. Pichu's father stopped the truck next to their ponga boat, lying tilted on its hull in the sand.

"It's been a long time since I took the boat out," his father said. "With you here it would seem wrong if we did not spend time together on the water. Even if we can't fish, at least we can be together on the water again."

Working together, they used the pickup to push the heavy ponga boat into the water. His father tilted the motor into the water and pulled the starting cord several times. The engine coughed but did not catch.

"Water in the gas line," he muttered, pulling the cord over and over again. Finally, the engine caught and they picked up speed. Soon, they were skimming across the waves. Pichu knew where his father was heading — to their favorite spot near the blowhole. It was where they always caught the most fish. As they approached the rocky outcropping, Pichu felt his father cut back the engine. They glided to a stop and the motor died. His father instinctively turned the bow into the waves to hold their place on the sea. Soon, the only sound was the water lapping against the sides of the ponga boat.

Suddenly, Pichu remembered that he had brought something for his father.

"I brought everyone a gift from America," Pichu said. "But the gift I have for you is different."

"You didn't have to get me anything," his father said. But he glanced up curiously to see what it was.

Pichu reached into his back pocket and pulled out the folded newspaper. He handed it to his father. The paper was turned to an article that showed a photograph of Pichu in his soccer uniform with his arms folded across his chest and his foot up on a ball.

"My son's picture in the newspaper," his father said. "This is indeed a great gift."

"No, that is not the gift. Look, right here." He pointed at a sentence that told how Pichu fished with his father every morning. He read it once in English. Then he translated it into Spanish so his father could understand it. He showed his father how his name was clearly printed in the newspaper. It was even spelled correctly and his nickname, Chuy, was in quotation marks.

"Your name is in an American newspaper," Pichu said. He sat back and watched his father, hoping it would cheer him up. His father studied the words closely. The bushy black mustache, streaked with gray, twitched as he concentrated, trying to grasp the meaning of this important event. He softly spoke his name as he touched the words on the paper. Finally he looked up.

"I never thought I would live to see such an amazing thing," he said. "I can hardly believe it."

"You must believe it," Pichu said. "I am in America playing soccer because of you. You gave me the opportunity to do this thing. And I had to let everyone know that."

His father's expression showed his pride. But then Pichu saw the troubled look return. The sun was up in the sky now and Pichu could see his father's face better, could see the dark circles under his eyes, the lines in his forehead under the hat visor.

"What is it, Papa?" Pichu finally asked in desperation. "Why do you look so sad?"

"I have a terrible confession to make to you," his father said with a long, ragged sigh. "I know you will not like this but I must tell you so that I can feel honest again."

"I know you are working for a commercial fishing boat," Pichu said. "I understand that you must work to feed our family."

"That's not all," his father said. "The company I work for, they use the long lines."

Pichu was not prepared for that. It had never occurred to him that his father would work for such a company.

"But Papa — " he began.

"We sail out in the middle of the night, and play out a line that is two miles long." His father looked away and spoke rapidly, unburdening himself. "We travel for more than one hundred miles, dragging the line behind us. Every five feet there is a hook with bait on it. It is like thousands of people fishing all at once. And then, when we have traveled far enough, we pull in the line. It comes in very fast and we have to look out for the fish and the flying hooks. And what the line brings up is like watching the earth split open. It is like hell, Pichu. The line drags in everything — tuna and dorado, of course, but also many other things they never intended to catch and fish that they don't even want. It brings in sharks and rays and even birds. But it is the dolphin who are the most tragic. They come up thrashing and screaming. The first time it happened I wanted to unhook the dolphin and throw it back, so it would live. But el jefe forbids it. 'There is no time for that!' he shouts at me. And so the dolphin lie on the decks, screaming in agony as they die. And when their screams fill my head and I can't stand it anymore, I turn and club them to death. So that at least they won't suffer anymore."

His father took a deep breath and turned to Pichu: "These people who own the company, they have no respect for the sea. They are raping the sea and destroying everything in it."

Pichu watched his father in silence. He could feel the struggle inside him, a powerful force tearing him into pieces.

"You should stop!" Pichu said. "You should quit your job! Papa, please. Promise me you will quit."

"I want to," his father said. "But we need money. I have a payment due on this boat and I cannot miss it."

"Isn't the money I send you enough?"

"It is helping, thank you," his father said. "But I need more, for the boat. One more shift — that is all I will work. It is all I can stand. After what I've seen, I don't care if I never fish again. I'll — I'll work in a factory or — "

The words hit Pichu full force. He felt himself beginning to speak, and he was amazed at the words he heard coming from his mouth.

"Papa, now you listen to me," Pichu said. "You gave me advice before I left for America. Your words guided me even though you weren't there. Now I have advice for you."

His father looked at him, surprised, so Pichu added, "Yes, the son will give the father advice."

Pichu's father sat back in amazement. But he listened.

"You are a great father and a good man. Despite this horror you have seen, you are still a good man. But you are also a stubborn man. And I want you to believe what I say and to act on it. You must not think of yourself as a man who has to work for a boss. No. You are an independent fisherman. You were born to be a fisherman. That is what God created you to be. And you are not just an ordinary fisherman. You are a fisherman who owns his own ponga boat."

Pichu paused to let his words sink in. Then he continued in the same firm tone: "And this, more than anything else, you must believe: You will fish for yourself again. In the mornings you will be the first with your ponga in the water. You will catch the best fish and you will be the first to sell them at the highest prices. And you will say goodbye to the commercial fishing boats forever. That is my promise to you."

During this speech Pichu saw his father's eyes grow sharp as if he were seeing the things that Pichu was describing. He sat up and his strong shoulders straightened. His muscular hands once again touched the magic newspaper from America, as if it were proof that what Pichu said was true.

"Will you remember what I have said?" Pichu asked.

"I will," his father said.

"And will you believe it?" Pichu asked.

His father's mustache twitched again as he struggled with the concept. The words were slow in coming. But when he finally spoke, there was conviction behind them. He said, "I will believe that I will fish for myself again, from my own ponga. Yes, I believe that this can be true."

They sat there in silence for some time, letting this vision of the future sink in. Slowly — very slowly — Pichu saw his father's expression change. And, once more, he saw the man who had raised him. He saw his father again.

Chapter 27

When Pichu flew back to San Francisco and returned to school, he knew he had to mentally prepare for the final game of the regular season against the University of Santa Cruz. It would be played at the stadium in Santa Cruz on a Saturday night in early December. USF needed a win, not just a tie, to face Westford in the finals. Westford was virtually assured a spot in the tournament, because its final game was against Chico State, and everyone assumed Westford would easily win.

Riding the bus to the big game at Santa Cruz, Pichu and his teammates were very quiet. They seemed to be sharing one thought — how everything had come down to this one game. Pichu looked around at the solemn faces as the bus bumped along the winding mountain road to Santa Cruz. The engine groaned, and the brakes hissed as the bus navigated the sharp turns. Then, as they swung around a bend on the steep descent, they could see the city below them. The sparkling lights abruptly ended at the ocean, dark and mysterious in the distance.

The driver parked on a side street near the stadium, and the players began getting off the bus, carrying duffle bags over their shoulders. As Pichu walked down the steps to the street, he saw a line of old cars and pickups pulling into the stadium parking lot. One of the cars beeped and arms jutted out of its open windows, waving enthusiastically.

"Pichu! Hola, Pichu!" voices cried. Pichu went over to the car and looked inside. It was a car full of the guys he played soccer with in the park on Sunday afternoons.

"What are you guys doing here?" Pichu asked, surprised.

"We came to see you beat Santa Cruz," one of the guys answered.

"Ayi!" Pichu said. "Santa Cruz is tough. And their defense is the best in the league. If they had a goal scorer, they would be the top team."

"You will dance your way through all their defenders," a man in the backseat said, pumping his fist.

"Hey, Pichu!" Coach Connors called to him. "You can sign autographs later. Get your butt in the locker room!"

"All right," Pichu said to his friends. "Thanks for coming."

"USF! USF!" they all chanted as he walked away.

Pichu walked to the locker room feeling the nervousness in his stomach building. It was a feeling he had learned to accept because he knew it would give him the energy he needed for the long game. His hand was on the doorknob when something stopped him. He felt a strange presence nearby and turned. There, by the grandstands was a short, round man. It was Humberto. He was calmly watching Pichu — not trying to attract his attention at all, just calmly watching. Pichu smiled and waved at the odd little man who always materialized so mysteriously. Humberto returned his greeting with a formal bow. He then turned and dissolved into the swirling crowd.

It was quiet in the locker room as the players dressed. They waited until everyone was ready, then they jogged out onto the field. Coach Jordan called to Pichu and motioned for him to come to the sidelines. The Coach was wearing a dark red windbreaker and holding his clipboard under one arm. His glasses gleamed under the stadium lights and Pichu saw that he had an amused smile on his face.

"You've become quite a popular attraction," the coach said.

"What do you mean?"

"I think you brought in most of these people, didn't you?" The coach gestured to the stands. As Pichu turned to look, a sea of arms began waving and hundreds of voices called out encouragement and praise in Spanish. In the crowd, Pichu recognized some of the faces of his soccer-playing friends from the park and the workers from the kitchen. They had brought their friends and families, and they were all calling his name.

"These aren't exactly the fans we're used to having," Coach Jordan said, smiling. "But we're happy to have their support. Very happy." Then he dropped his voice and spoke more seriously. "I feel I should tell you this, too… There are several scouts here."

"Scouts?" Pichu knew the word but not in this context.

"Scouting agents. They want to watch you play, and they might offer you a position on a professional team. A rep from the MLS is here, and so is a scout from an Italian team. Europe — that's where the big money is." He paused and looked closely at Pichu, his eyes were probing deep inside him.

"So, good luck tonight," the coach said.

"Thanks, Coach." Pichu was about to jog onto the field, but turned to look at the coach. "Thank you for believing in me."

The coach nodded, and Pichu ran out to join his teammates.

The first half ended without any goals, even though there were many close calls. For most of the time, the ball was in Santa Cruz's end of the field. Pichu was double-teamed any time he was near the penalty box, leaving either Moore or Shields wide open. But when Pichu fed them the ball they weren't able to convert the pass into a goal. Often, they were too eager, leaning back on the shot and launching it over the goal and into the stands. Or they mis-kicked the ball and it bounced harmlessly into the arms of the goalkeeper. Once, in desperation, Shields took a long shot that hugged the ground and then rose dangerously. But the goalie saw it clearly the whole way and made a spectacular diving save, catching the ball and hugging it to his chest before he slammed to the ground. This deflated the USF strikers and left them feeling that even their best effort wasn't good enough for a goal.

At the beginning of the second half, the Santa Cruz players's confidence seemed to have grown. Time after time, they penetrated deep into USF's end of the field. Their shots grew more dangerous, and the USF fullbacks struggled to stop them. At the thirty-five minute mark, Pete was preparing to clear the ball but didn't see the Santa Cruz striker sprinting in from behind him. The striker stripped the ball, worked it back into the corner and sent a long cross all the way across the mouth of the goal. It looked like it would sail harmlessly over everyone. But suddenly, the wing jumped high and headed it beautifully. It arched over the goalie's head at an impossible angle and dropped in for a goal.

The stadium exploded with cheers, horns and the noise of the inflatable thunder bats being pounded together. Pichu watched the Santa Cruz players congratulating each other and returning for the kickoff, looking confident and eager for another goal to seal the victory. Pichu had a terrible feeling, and he sensed his teammates' discouragement. They were arguing about who had been out of position and whose fault the goal was. Coach Jordan was yelling at them from the sidelines. Pichu knew that the game — and the season — could be lost right here, unless he could get something started.

The teams lined up for the kickoff. The referee blew the whistle and waited. But Pichu refused to touch the ball. His team wasn't ready. They were still arguing about the goal. The referee waited. The crowd grew quiet. Then, whistles and boos erupted. Everyone seemed to wonder what was happening.

"What are you waiting for?" Moore asked Pichu desperately. He was crouched like a sprinter ready for a race. The stadium lights caught droplets of sweat as they fell from the tips of his curly blond hair.

"What are you waiting for?" he asked again.

"I'm waiting for you," Pichu said. "Are you ready?"

"I'm ready! Kick the damn ball!"

"No," Pichu said. "Are you really ready?"

Moore looked startled, as if Pichu had slapped him. But he seemed to understand. He calmly answered, "Okay. Yes. I'm ready now."

The referee ran toward them, "What's going on? I blew the whistle."

"We are ready now," Pichu said and tapped the ball forward so it rolled in front of Moore. Pichu waited for the Santa Cruz strikers to crash in on Moore. As they came at a sprint, he dodged between them and into the open. Moore fed Pichu the ball and he controlled it, moving forward through the halfbacks. He had three defenders on him now as he cruised toward the penalty area. His touches and fakes had an odd, relaxed pace that threw off the defender's tempo. As they slid in to strip the ball away, it seemed to disappear as if in a magic trick. Frustrated, they tried to take out Pichu, going for his body. But he twisted and turned, always one step ahead of them. He used a series of body fakes and deft touches, playing the ball off the ground most of the time. He kept the ball moving with his feet, knees, thighs and chest, working it with quick motions that left the defenders paralyzed. Now he was in the penalty area, still in full possession of the ball for what seemed like an impossibly long time.

The stadium grew very quiet as everyone waited to see what would happen. The only noise was the shouts of the defenders as they frantically tried to stop Pichu. He looked up and saw that the fullback guarding Rev was about to be drawn toward Pichu. He waited until the fullback had just shifted his weight and couldn't turn back. Pichu threaded a pass to Rev, who was almost at the post. The goalie had seen the play developing and cut the angle. Rev chipped the ball over the charging goalie. Moore was there and headed the ball into the nets.

There was a stunned moment of silence and then the other side of the stadium erupted in wild celebration with cheers and the sound of horns. Pichu heard many voices calling his name and saw the guys from his Sunday game waving and yelling. As he jogged back to the center, Rev called over to Pichu, "Dude, that was unbelievable!"

Pichu heard his name being called from the bench. He looked over and saw Coach Jordan tapping his watch, gesturing that they had only five minutes left to play. Santa Cruz kicked off and the striker dribbled the ball rather than passing off to the halfbacks as Pichu expected. That left him far up field while the ball was being worked into the USF penalty box. The ball was passed out to the wing, then crossed in front of

USF's goal. Pichu held his breath as the ball seemed to hang in the air for an eternity. It was dropping toward the center, who was wide open. At the last second, it was deflected by the goalie, who landed on the field in a heap. The loose ball was pounded by another Santa Cruz player and sailed toward the nets for what looked like a certain goal. But Pete had seen that the goalie was down and ran in to stand in the open net. He saw the ball flying toward him and cleared it with a spectacular diving header.

A USF halfback controlled the ball and dribbled it up the field. Coach Jordan was shouting to his players and pointing to his watch again. Pichu looked over and saw the referee looking at his own watch and putting the whistle in his mouth. Pichu stayed even with the fullbacks so he wouldn't be offsides. The halfback sent the ball all the way across the field to the left wing, who was just barely able to get a foot on it. The ball trickled toward end line. Pichu accelerated past the fullbacks and gained possession of the loose ball. He looked around and found he was alone — all the defenders were waiting for him to cross the ball. Moore and Shields were hovering just outside the penalty area, ready to crash in and try to score.

Pichu's mind became very calm. He was alone. Unchallenged. He began dribbling toward the goal. Still no one came out to pick him up. It was just him and the goalie. Pichu knew he could beat him with a low bending shot. But that wasn't the strategy that had gotten them this far. A flicker of confusion ran through his mind and body. And in that second of hesitation he lost the opportunity to shoot. A defender lunged in and blocked his path. Pichu hooked a low pass to a halfback at the top of the penalty area, who was sprinting in. The ball exploded off his foot and hit the underside of the crossbar. It bounced straight down, then high in the air. The goalie and all the players converged on the ball, and it disappeared under a pile of bodies. The whistle blew, and the referee ran in to see what had happened. As the players slowly got to their feet, the goalie was revealed lying on the bottom of the heap, the ball underneath him.

The referee blew the whistle and waved his hands — the game was over with a 1–1 tie. The season was finished. USF wouldn't play Westford again. The USF players stood in the field, under the lights looking stunned. Some of them fell down on the ground and lay motionless. Others held their heads in their hands, tears streaming down their faces. Coach Jordan walked out onto the field, his face somber. He looked at Pichu with a sharp accusing expression.

"You had the chance," he said gesturing at the now open goal. "Why didn't you just shoot?"

Before Pichu could respond, Coach Jordan turned away and put his arm around Shields, then Moore. The three of them talked softly as they walked off the field. Half of the stadium was quietly drifting away while the other half was wildly celebrating.

Pichu heard a commotion and saw Coach Connors talking on his cellular phone on the sidelines. He suddenly began jumping up and down excitedly.

"Are you sure?" he was yelling into the phone. "Are you sure! Oh my God! That's unbelievable!" He ran toward the players, the phone still in his hand. "Westford lost to Chico State!"

"What?" Coach Jordan said.

"I don't believe it," the assistant coach was saying. "Westford lost to Chico. We're in the playoffs!"

Pichu watched as the news spread among his teammates. It was as if they were returning from the dead. They rose from the ground, then hugged each other and ran around, waving their shirts over their heads.

"What happened?" someone yelled in Spanish from the stands. Pichu looked up and saw Humberto leaning toward him over the railing.

"Westford lost tonight!" Pichu yelled. "We're in the playoffs!"

"Amazing!" Humberto said. Then, slowly, almost seriously, he began dancing, singing rumpty-dumpty-rumpty-doo, bouncing up and down and turning around in circles.

Pichu watched him dance and began to laugh. Humberto saw him laughing but kept dancing with the serious expression on his face. Then he winked at Pichu and smiled. "This isn't the last time you will see my victory dance."

Chapter 28

So after living the good life as a college student at the University of San Francisco, this soccer phenom has a goal that many would consider, well, unusual — " the reporter turned to Pichu and she held out the microphone as she waited for his comment.

"I want to be a fisherman," Pichu said.

The reporter smiled, shaking her head in amused disbelief. "That's it? You want to go fishing?"

"No. I want to be a fisherman," Pichu corrected her. "But in my studies I've learned that this way of life might be threatened. So I've decided to — "

"Isn't that how you got your nickname?" she said, cutting him off. "Ponga Boy? Tell us about that."

"We fish from a ponga boat, which is owned by my father. So in Mexico, they call to me by saying 'Hey, Ponga Boy!'"

"Amazing. But even more amazing is the fact that despite being the top player, you haven't scored a goal the entire season — yet your team has scored many upset wins. So, you're basically a playmaker — is that it?"

She turned the microphone to Pichu. "It doesn't matter who puts the ball in the nets," he said. "It's the goal that counts."

"And your goal will be to beat Westford in the NCAA finals tomorrow. Good luck, Ponga Boy. Now let's see that famous — what do you call it — cross? Guys?" she called to Moore, Rev and Shields, who had been standing nearby, watching the interview. "Guys, can you help us out?"

Pichu jogged toward the sidelines. It was night, and the stadium was empty, with the bright lights shining down on the nearly empty field. He took a soccer ball and crossed it with his left foot so it curled away from the goal. It was too high for Shields to reach but Moore raced in, jumped high and headed the ball into the net.

The reporter turned back to the camera, "Now that's a winning combination. Reporting live from the USF campus, this is Alice Lepinski, Channel 7 News."

The light on the camera died. The reporter thanked Pichu and the news team packed up their camera equipment and began heading back toward their waiting van. As Pichu, Moore and Shields continued practicing with Rev, an odd figure appeared by the side of the field. It was Humberto. He stood there jingling a ring of keys and clearing his throat loudly. He watched the players kicking it back and forth and cleared his throat several times. He seemed to be deep in thought. Several more times he looked as if he was about to speak but then changed his mind. But finally, his eyes grew firm with conviction and he spoke.

"Can I have your attention, please?" Humberto said to the soccer players using a loud and commanding voice.

They all stopped, surprised. Moore stood poised with his foot on top of the ball. "You closing up or something?"

"No sir. I'm offering you a way to beat Westford tomorrow."

"Right, a chalk talk with X's and O's," Shields said. "Got it. Don't need it. Thanks."

Moor and Shields went back to dribbling again, ignoring the peculiar little man. Humberto spoke again more forcefully.

"I need your attention here! Now!"

They turned toward Humberto, annoyed. Moore seemed about to say something but Pichu held up his hand.

"Yes, Humberto. What do you want to say?"

"It is true that Pichu is an excellent playmaker. That is what has gotten your team into the playoffs. But his real talent is as a goal scorer."

Moore held Humberto in his gaze for a moment, then said, "Man, you don't know what you're talking about."

Humberto smiled slowly. "Pichu?"

They slowly turned to look at Pichu but he said nothing.

"Yeah, right," Shields said. "If you're such a great shooter, why haven't you scored all season?"

"I wanted to set you up."

Moore said, "You're saying you could have scored any time, but instead you set us up?"

"That's right."

"Why?"

"So that you would accept me," Pichu explained. "In the beginning, all of you hated me. If I touched the ball, you shoved me to the ground. If I was open, you ignored me. If I attempted a shot, you yelled insults at me. It was only after I began giving you goals that you accepted me. Now I'm asking you to set me up. So we can win."

Moore considered this, then shook his head. "Sorry, man. I don't buy it. Besides, Westford's fullbacks are too tall. You'll never get a header. That means you have to shoot from outside and that's too tough. Their goalie is All American."

Humberto began laughing. "Too tall? Pichu, tell them."

Pichu held his hand way up above his head. "If you give me this ball — a ball right here — I can score every time." He moved his hand to head level. "Or if you give me a ball right here, I can also score." He held his hand at chest level. "Or here. Or here or here."

They laughed in amazement at what he was suggesting.

"And I can score the goal with my right or left foot," Pichu added.

"Dude," Rev said. "Dude, seriously, that's impossible."

"I've seen him here late at night," Humberto countered. "Practicing with the player they call Pete. I know what he can do. Show them."

Shields shook his head. "Sorry, man, I don't have time to waste on this. I got to get some sleep. I'll see you in the morning."

"I'll make you a bet," Pichu said.

Shields stopped. "How much?"

"Three Cokes. And one Snickers bar."

"Each?" Moore asked.

"Yes, if you want," Pichu said. "All you have to do is feed me the ball — up here."

"Way up there? Yeah, okay," Rev said. Then to the others he said, "Easiest bet I'll ever win."

Rev took a ball and dribbled to the sidelines. Pichu turned to Moore and said, "Go ahead, play goal. If you stop the shot, I lose the bet."

Moore took his place in goal. He stood with his hands on his hips, obviously not expecting much of a threat.

"Where do you want the ball?" Rev called.

Pichu extended his hand as high as it would go. "Right there."

"You're dreamin', dude. But, okay, here goes."

Pichu stood with his back to the goal. As Rev backed up to take the kick, Pichu began running in a tight half circle. Rev lofted the ball perfectly, placing it right in front of the goal so that it seemed to hang in the air. Pichu turned hard. For an instant, he was suspended, fully upside down. Then one leg shot out, and he made solid contact with the ball. It flew into the lower right corner of the net before Moore could even begin to react. Pichu completed the flip and dropped easily to his feet.

The three players were absolutely silent, gaping at each other, stunned. Then they heard a strange noise. It was soft at first, but it grew slowly. They realized Humberto was laughing. It was a contagiously funny, growling laugh. And it grew and grew until it seemed to fill the stadium.

"Oh yes, my young friend!" Humberto said, wiping tears from his eyes. "That was excellent. Oh yes, indeed."

"That was dumb luck!" Shields said.

"No," said Humberto, suddenly seriously. "That is not just a good goal, or even a great goal. In Spanish there is a special word to describe such a goal. We call it 'golazo.' It is a thing of beauty — it is a master-work."

"Bet you can't do it again," Moore said, still in the goal. But this time he crouched low, ready to block the shot.

"There can be two of you in the goal if you like," Pichu said.

Shields moved into position so there were now two goalkeepers.

"Put this one here," Pichu said, holding his hand at head level.

Rev crossed the ball. Again, Pichu did his wind up run, turning in a sharp semicircle. This time he was sideways above the ground. When he hit the ball, it made a clean, sharp smack and found the upper center of the net between the two goalies. They didn't even have time to move to stop the shot when it was already in the back of the nets.

"Golazo!" Humberto shouted.

"Dude," Rev said softly. "That was unreal. Un-real."

Humberto danced in circles. "Golazo! Golazo! Golazo!"

"Now I'll do it from the other side," Pichu said.

Rev went to the other side of the field and crossed the ball. Pichu took this shot left-footed. This ball struck the inside corner of the goal post and bounced in. The three players were silent.

Finally, Rev spoke. "Looks like we owe you some Cokes."

"And a Snickers bar," Pichu reminded them.

Humberto ambled up to them, beaming. "You see? The Ponga Boy defies gravity."

"I guess so," Moore said. "I mean, I don't know how you do it."

"Now," said Humberto, "it is time for you to see the ultimate weapon."

"There's more?" Shields asked. But his tone was no longer skeptical.

Humberto said, "It is the ultimate. I call it the Unstoppable Shot."

"We're gonna need one of those if we're going to beat Westford," Moore said. "Bring it on."

Pichu nodded. "I will. But first I need your help. On all these shots I need your help. But on this last shot, I need help from two of you. One to kick the ball and the other to fire me into the air."

"What?" they all asked.

"Please," Humberto said. "Allow me. I would be honored to have the ponga boy's cleats in my back."

Humberto crouched with his back to the goal. Rev had gone to the side of the field again.

"Where do you want this one?" he called.

"There," Pichu said, his finger indicating a spot about ten feet above his head.

"Okay. Here it comes."

Rev backed up to take the kick. Pichu started with his back to the goal. He ran away from the goal and planted one foot on Humberto's back just as Humberto was standing up. Pichu flew up into the air, flipping upside down as he did. At the top of his arch, he kicked the ball so it angled sharply down into the nets. Pichu completed the flip and landed on his feet.

Humberto was still bent over, struggling to rise and grunting as he did so, when he said, "No goalie on earth can stop that shot. The angle, the power — it's the Unstoppable Shot. Forget it."

Pichu helped Humberto to his feet. They stood facing Rev, Moore and Shields. The American players were looking at Pichu with a different expression. Finally, Rev spoke.

"Dude, we owe you an apology."

"Big time," Moore added. "We had no idea you could do any of this."

"Why didn't you give me a chance to show you?" Pichu asked. He didn't want to complain, but...

There was no answer to his question. So they stood there in silence for a few moments, letting the change settle in and adjusting to the new way that things would be.

"We're sorry," Moore said and the others mumbled their apologies, too, saying, "Yeah, sorry man."

"I'm thirsty," Pichu said. "I want two Cokes — one for me and one for my friend here," he put his arm around Humberto. "You three can divide the Snickers bar."

As they walked off the field, Moore said, "How in the world did you ever come up with that shot?"

"Well, in my village," Pichu said, "they have a rock formation called La Bufadoro — the blowhole. The waves flow in there and go shooting into the air. One day something very funny happened...."

The stadium lights cut off one by one as the four players walked through the gate together and back toward campus. Humberto stayed behind, closing up the stadium and watching them leave. Pichu turned and waved to him. He waved back, then pulled the lever to the last set of lights and brought darkness to the field.

Chapter 29

There was a severe labor shortage in the San Francisco area on the day of the final game between USF and Westford. The street corners where day laborers from Mexico usually waited to get pick-up jobs were empty. There was even a story told about four guys who mistakenly thought the big game, featuring their favorite player, Ponga Boy, was to be held the next day. They climbed into the back of a truck and headed for a job cleaning gutters at an industrial park. But as they passed an intersection, some soccer fans yelled out to them that the game would be starting soon and they would be crazy to miss it. At the next intersection, they jumped out of the bed of the pickup and ran off, eventually making their way to the Westford stadium where the crowds were already gathering.

By noon, the stadium parking lot was jammed solid. And still the cars kept coming. But instead of shiny new BMWs and Acuras, the lot was filled with pickups and old station wagons with entire families packed inside. Instead of the usual smell of hot dogs, the air was filled with the smell of fresh corn tortillas and chorizos. The normal rap and hip-hop music was replaced by wailing trumpets playing mariachi music.

By 1 p.m., the streets around the stadium had turned into parking lots. Soccer fans abandoned their cars in the middle of the street and continued to the stadium on foot. Once inside, they filled all the seats. Then they filled the infield area around the track. And then they tried to stand in the aisles. An announcement was made that the game would not be played until the aisles were cleared.

Deep underneath the stadium bleachers, the USF team dressed in silence. The players pulled on their uniforms and closely followed their own private rituals. Some wore dirty socks they considered to be lucky. Others wore their shirts either tucked in or untucked according to what had brought them luck in the past. Other players tied their cleats three times and put the knot on the side of their foot so they could take more

accurate shots. Still other players discarded superstition and ritualiza-
tion in favor of religion. Pichu was one of these players.

Pichu knelt and rested his head on the cool metal of his locker door.
He prayed simply and honestly, asking that he might be allowed to play
at the highest level of his ability. He prayed to make full use of the gift
of athleticism that God had given him. And finally, he said a special
prayer that his actions that day would make his family proud of him. He
knew that his father, his family, and the entire town of Los Barriles,
would be crowded into the bar at the Hotel Palmas de Cortez to watch
the game on satellite TV. When he got a goal, he would make the sign
he always did after he scored when he had played games in the little stadium where as he grew up. It was a simple gesture, but he knew that
when he did it, they would know that the goal was dedicated to the people of his hometown.

When Pichu was finished praying, he rose and started to leave. He
found Coach Jordan standing nearby, waiting to talk with him. The
coach turned to the rest of the team and said, "Okay, guys. Go ahead
out and get warmed up. I'll be out in a few seconds. I need to talk to
Pichu first."

The players filed past them, bumping fists with Pichu or giving him
high fives. Finally, Pichu was alone in the locker room with Coach
Jordan.

"Pichu," the coach said. "I don't know what you're feeling right
now. But I can tell you, I'm pretty darn nervous. We've come a long way
this season — much farther than I ever thought. But before we play this
game and whatever the outcome of it is, I want you to know something."

"Yes, Coach?"

"I want to thank you. For one thing, I think you saved my job, and
maybe even the soccer program here at USF. But I also want to thank
you for teaching me how to do my job better."

"How did I do that?"

"By being yourself. You played unselfishly. You played hard. You
never complained. I began to look around at the other players on the
team and I wondered why their attitudes couldn't be like yours. I had
accepted a lot of poor behavior that I shouldn't have tolerated. I won't
make that mistake again."

Pichu nodded. "Coach, I — "

"Please, I need to say these things. I've had some sleepless nights
about this. So I just need to say them."

"Okay," Pichu nodded. "I will remember what you've said."

The coach took off his glasses and wiped them with his thumb. He sniffed once and said, "Now, on a more practical level I have something to tell you. I heard through a source that Westford doesn't consider you a scoring threat. They believe you will try to draw in defenders so Moore, Shields and Revinski can shoot. You know what this means?"

"I'll be open."

"Exactly. I want you to shoot whenever you get the chance," the coach said. "I want you to score as soon as you can. That's very important. I don't want to get in a hole and have to dig our way out. If we can score early and send a message to them — and to our guys that we're for real — then we can win this game. Okay?"

"Okay, Coach," Pichu said.

Coach Jordan smiled and put his hand on Pichu's shoulder. "Let's go play soccer."

They walked out together. As they pushed the locker room door open, Pichu saw that it was a cool sunny day. But the clouds were moving quickly, blown over the tops of the mountains that separated them from the Pacific. He felt rain in the air.

They paused at the entrance to the field. Pichu looked out and saw the packed stadium.

"Well, this is it," Coach Jordan said. "Better get your butt out there and warm up."

Pichu sprinted out onto the field. As he appeared, the crowd spotted him and a cheer began to build. It spread across the stadium until half the crowd was standing, shouting and waving wildly. The sight and sound of all the fans filled Pichu with excitement and energy beyond anything he had ever felt. It was like a giant wave was picking him up and pushing him forward to his destiny.

Chapter 30

"T his has been the wildest 40 minutes of soccer I can ever remember watching," the TV announcer said as the clock ticked away the minutes of the first half. "Westford University, the perennial powerhouse of NCAA soccer, is throwing everything they can at USF. And USF is answering right back. I can't believe what I'm seeing here today."

The second announcer jumped in. "That's right. And much of the excitement has revolved around this dynamic new talent they call 'Ponga Boy' a young man from Los Barriles, Mexico. He has transformed this underdog team and turned the championship into a David and Goliath story. They say the Ponga Boy has a seventh sense about soccer — if a defender can think of a hundred ways he might make a play, Ponga Boy will choose the hundred — and-first way to do it."

It had all started 45 minutes earlier when the two teams tried to take the field. The players had to run through a battery of news photographers, TV cameras and reporters. The rivalry had caught the attention of the media and a last-minute decision was made to broadcast the match on network television. Then, the overflow crowd blocked the fire exits. When the announcer threatened to cancel the game if the fans didn't clear the aisles, it appeared that a full-scale riot would erupt. Finally, fearing the greater danger of a riot, the officials let the game begin.

Within a minute of the kickoff, Pichu sent a long, high pass to Rev that floated toward him at an angle. Seeing a defenseman rushing in to cover him, Rev deflected the ball softly off his chest and popped it over the defender's head. It rolled toward the goalie, who seemed certain to clear the ball. But Rev put on an incredible burst of speed and reached the ball and took a shot. The ball was blocked by the goalie and it ricocheted between them, then popped loose and bounced slowly toward the wide-open goal. The Westford fullbacks sprinted desperately but Rev was there first and placed a long shot perfectly in the center of the open nets for a goal. The roar from the crowd seemed to roll like thunder off the nearby mountains and shake the entire area.

Running back to center field, Rev looked over at Pichu and pumped his fist. "We can win this game!" he shouted. "We can win it!"

But only minutes later, the Westford center with the black hair, who had broken his nose in the earlier game, scored on a rebound from a direct kick. The tie lasted only five more minutes when Moore, trying to head a ball, missed it entirely. However, the Westford goalie, expecting the header, was wrong footed and couldn't even dive for the ball. It flew past him on the right and into the goal. Moments later, Pete clipped a Westford striker from behind who went down, rolling in agony, and drew a penalty kick. The Westford player, who had seemed gravely injured just moments before, jumped to his feet and drilled the ball into the upper right corner, tying the score at 2–2.

The two teams seemed absolutely evenly matched. Each time one appeared to have the upper hand, the other team would perform a play that was even more amazing. Little of the game was fought in the center of the field. Instead, it was one long series of headlong charges and scoring threats. The players were, as the TV announcers said, "playing with all their hearts and souls, fighting to capture the championship."

Throughout the first half, the Westford fullback with the red hair and freckled face was constantly harassing Pichu. He was broad-shouldered with a thick neck and small dark eyes under a heavy brow. His thighs and calves were corded with muscle and he was lightning fast, matching Pichu step for step on break-aways. "It's payback time," he told Pichu as soon as they were near each other on the field. "You're not leaving this game in one piece."

Pichu tried to ignore him. But the threats, and the fullback's constant shoving, elbowing and shirt-pulling took its toll. Pichu hurried his passes and they lost their pinpoint accuracy. He steered clear of the center of the field and avoided going one on one against the fullback. The strikers began to notice this and at one point, Rev called over to Pichu: "Dude, I can't give you the ball to score unless you're in scoring position!"

Pichu waved to Rev in acknowledgement. But the next time he got the ball, the red haired fullback was on him, hitting him hard from behind and sending him sprawling. Pichu lay on the ground, dazed, until he felt a hand helping him up. It was the fullback, who easily yanked him to his feet, his mean little eyes close to Pichu's face, and hissed, "Next time, you'll leave on a stretcher, ponga dude."

Pichu had to do something about the fullback's cheap shots. He thought of hitting him in the same way, but then he decided it would be better to draw a foul. Maybe he could get the fullback red-carded and thrown out of the game. At the next opportunity, he brought the ball slowly down the center of the field, trying to draw the fullback in. He saw the fullback coming in hard, with a slide tackle, his cleats aiming knee-high. Pichu jumped straight up, out of harm's way, but instead of leaping over him and landing on his feet, he fell forward, driving his knees into the sliding fullback's solar plexus as he landed on top of him. Not only did that leave the fullback gasping for air, rolling in agony on the field, but the foul went against Westford. Pichu extended a hand to the injured fullback, but he refused to take it, spitting obscenities at him as he struggled to breathe.

A few minutes later the referee blew the whistle and the half ended in a 2–2 tie.

The second half began with two quick goals by Westford. The first was on a fast break where the USF fullbacks thought the referee was about to call offsides and therefore didn't challenge a Westford player who had the ball on a fast break. But when the whistle didn't blow, it was too late to react, and the ball was in the net. The second goal came moments later on a corner kick when the black haired striker jumped high to head the crossed ball. He angled it down under the arm of the diving goalie and into the net. Right after the kickoff, Moore sent a long leading pass to Shields, who was sprinting between the defenders. Shields was sprinting flat out when the red haired fullback blindside him with his knees high, driving them into his ribs. Shields went down in a heap and rolled around in agony. He was led off the field and Frasier was brought in to fill his position.

With the score 4–2 in Westford's favor and the injured starter on the sidelines, Pichu noticed the stadium grow very quiet. It seemed as if the joy and energy had drained out of the crowd. He looked around and saw the other USF players moving sluggishly with their heads bowed and shoulders slumped. To make matters worse, dark clouds blew in from the Pacific and a cold rain began to fall. The rain and the defeated attitude of the USF players seemed to spell defeat. Even the announcers in the press booth noticed the change in the USF team: "Well, it looks as if the fight has gone out of this team. A lot of people came here to cheer on the underdog, but I guess an upset was just too good to be true."

While these negative predictions were beaming out on the airwaves, a different story was unfolding on the field because Pichu had made an amazing discovery.

After the kickoff, Pichu was dribbling the ball when he realized the rain had wet the grass just enough to make the footing slick and cause the ball to skip unpredictably. It was enough to throw off the timing of all the other players. But, now the ball was behaving just like it did on the concrete surface of Pichu's little stadium in Los Barriles. After a few steps, Pichu's whole manner changed. He seemed to become more relaxed and yet completely energized at the same time. He went into another gear and began playing his own game for the very first time outside of Los Barriles. He wasn't any faster, but his movements were tighter, more precise and unpredictable. He made so many touches on the ball, so quickly and expertly, that the defenders melted away in a blur.

Pichu dribbled down the right side of the field and passed to Rev who pushed the ball right back to him in a give-and-go play. Pichu beat another halfback, then a fullback, then found himself at the top right corner of the penalty area. The red-haired fullback charged in but Pichu faked, beat him and continued toward the goal. The fullback recovered, turned, and was matching him stride for stride, blocking a clear shot at the goal. But then Pichu did something no one would ever forget. He chose his moment perfectly, waiting until the fullback's legs were spread in mid-stride. Without any warning, he fired a shot that went right between the fullback's legs and hugged the grass as it sailed across the field. The ball rose with a slight backspin, just missed the outstretched fingers of the diving goalie, and hit the far post. The ball bounced into the back of the goal. The goal left USF trailing by only one point, 3–4.

The crowd took a second to realize what had just happened. But then they all woke up at the same time. The crowd's reaction was not a cheer — it was an incredible explosion. Twenty thousand people simultaneously screamed in astonishment and joy. On the field, the players were equally stunned. They watched as Pichu dropped to one knee and made the sign of the cross. Then he looked for the TV camera and faced it. He touched his heart twice with his right fist, then pointed at the camera.

"We understand that gesture has a special significance," the TV announcer said. "Apparently, whenever Pichu scored a goal when he was playing in the Mexican leagues, he would dedicate it to his family and his friends by touching his heart and then pointing at them in the stands."

"Wouldn't it be amazing if they could see him today?" the other announcer said. "We believe this game is being picked up on satellite TV and is being shown in his home town — if they have TV there."

Actually, that prediction was correct. The game was being shown on satellite TV, translated into Spanish. Pichu's friends and family were gathered around the big screen in the bar at the Hotel Palmas de Cortez along with just about everyone else in the village. Chucky, the owner of the hotel, had closed the bar for the afternoon. Several Americans came by and were annoyed that they couldn't watch the 49'ers football game. But when they learned that a local boy was playing in this championship game, they ordered beers and sat down to watch. Soon, they too were caught up in the game and were cheering as much as anyone else.

Back in the stadium, the misting rain blew out quickly, and the afternoon sun began to break through the clouds here and there. And with the sunlight came hope that USF might get a miraculous goal and even the score in the game's final minutes. The two teams battled on, Westford still leading by one goal. There were heartbreaking opportunities that were missed and heroic saves by the goalies and defenders. The players were beyond exhaustion and reaching into deeper levels of energy, playing with sheer will power. The crowd became frantic as the final moments of the game ticked away.

With only three minutes to go, Pichu had the ball at the top of the penalty box. As the defenders closed in on him, he pushed a neat pass to Rev, who was in the clear. Rev trapped the ball and was about to shoot when the red haired fullback, realizing that this was almost a certain goal, hit Rev from behind so hard that Pichu heard a bone-on-bone crack. Rev went down in a heap and rolled on the grass holding his right knee. The team trainer and Connors, the assistant coach, raced over and knelt beside Rev. Pichu leaned in and saw Rev's face twisted in anger and pain.

"That bastard!" Rev said. "That goal was mine! It was in the nets!"

Pichu saw the trainer probe Rev's knee and shoot a dark look at Coach Connor.

"Let me up," Rev said. "I'm okay."

"You're out," the trainer said.

"I'm telling you, I'm okay," Rev pleaded.

"No way," the trainer said, shaking his head. "Pichu, help me get him off the field."

Pichu threw Rev's arm around his shoulder and, with the trainer, lifted him to his feet. The crowd cheered for the injured player as they headed for the sidelines. As they passed the Westford fullback who committed the foul, Pichu heard him talking to the black-haired striker. "Two down and one to go," the fullback said. The black haired striker laughed and sneered at Pichu.

Rev turned to Pichu, tears of pain in his eyes. "You've got to get him, Pichu. Promise me you'll take him out."

Pichu felt something stirring inside him, something ugly and dark that didn't seem to belong to him. But the feeling took hold of him and started to build. He lowered Rev onto the bench and the trainer put an ice pack on his knee. Pichu saw Coach Jordan speak to Pete, who jumped up and began to strip off his warm up suit. Pichu, about to run back in, felt a hand on his arm. Rev was clinging to him desperately.

"Get him, Pichu," Rev said, his face shiny with tears. "Get that bastard — for me and Shields. And for your team."

Pichu jogged back onto the field, staring at the fullback. He saw himself taking him down with a quick flurry of punches. Or maybe he would slide into his knees and ruin him for life. It was what the fullback deserved, so he would have to do it to get even for his friend. Pichu felt his hands balling into fists by his side. He began walking toward the Westford fullback, not even sure what he was going to do. He was closing on him a step at a time. This would feel so good, so right, he thought. The fullback looked at Pichu coming and saw the look on his face.

"What?" the fullback mocked. "You want to fight now? Okay. Come on. Come on, Ponga Dude, fight like a man."

The words stopped Pichu. Something from long ago came back to him and broke the spell. He stopped, staring at the fullback, realizing that all he had to do was throw one punch and everything would be ruined. The referee would wave the red card in his face and he would be sent out of the game. The fullback seemed disappointed Pichu wasn't attacking him.

"What're you looking at?" the fullback snarled at Pichu.

"I'm looking at a loser," Pichu calmly answered and took his position.

Frasier was now in Shields' position while Pete was on the wing. The foul had brought an indirect kick just outside the penalty box. Pichu saw the red haired fullback to his left, ready to crash in and challenge him. He looked for one of his teammates to pass to. No one was open. And yet, there was a spot right in front of the goal that was clear. If only he had the ball there, he knew he could shoot and score. The red haired fullback turned away for a second to check his position. Pichu saw an inviting target and couldn't resist.

The referee blew his whistle.

Pichu ran toward the ball.

The red haired fullback was taken by surprise by the whistle and still had his back turned to Pichu. With a short, quick pass, Pichu kicked the ball right at the fullback's butt. It spanked him hard and rebounded right into the open area Pichu had selected. He threaded his way through defenders to the loose ball then fired it low and hard. It was a real rocket that was in the net before the goalie could even react. The score was tied at 4–4!

The crowd reacted with a mixture of surprise, joy and laughter. Long after the applause died, pockets of hysterical laughter still broke out and built back into wild cheering. Meanwhile, on the field, the USF players piled onto Pichu, mobbing him with high fives, chest bumps and hugs. When Pichu finally got free, he turned to Rev on the sidelines and pointed at him, as if to say, "I took care of the fullback for you."

The teams lined up for the kickoff but the crowd wouldn't settle down — they were still celebrating the incredible goal. Up in the broadcast booth, as the goal was being replayed, one announced turned to the other and said, "You don't think he actually did that on purpose, do you?"

"It sure looks like he did," the other announcer said. "I'm beginning to wonder if there is anything this amazing young player can't do."

The referee finally had to ignore the celebrating crowd and he blew the whistle for the kickoff. The humiliating goal seemed to infuriate the Westford team and fill them with more energy and conviction. They began pressing continually and, a short time later, narrowly missed a long shot that the goalie didn't even dive for. Luckily, it sailed just wide of the post. It seemed that either the game would go into overtime or Westford would squeeze in a quick goal before the end of play to steal the victory. Seeing this, Pichu ran back to play defense whenever he could. At one point, as he neared the penalty area, Bart saw him coming and was able to punch the ball clear so that it landed at Pichu's feet. Pichu beat one Westford striker and fed a long pass to Pete on the wing, then sprinted down the field. Pete saw Pichu coming and pushed the ball back to him at midfield.

"We're in injury time now," the TV announcer told the listening audience. "No one except the referee knows exactly how much time is left. But it can't be more than a minute or two."

Pichu saw the referee glance at his watch and began to move urgently, the slippery grass still evoking memories of his hometown soccer field. After he beat the strikers and then the halfbacks, the fullbacks were afraid to challenge him. Instead, they dropped back, simply trying to contain him. But once he was approaching the penalty area, the red-haired fullback came at him hard and fast and went for his body, trying to take him down. Pichu was nearly knocked off balance but he somehow stayed on his feet, kept going, working into position for a shot. Then, just as he was about to shoot, the fullback hit him hard from behind. The referee blew the whistle and pointed at the place where the direct kick would be taken from ten yards outside the right edge of the penalty box. It would be a long, difficult shot; one that would have to be bent around the defensive wall and come in at an angle that the goalie could easily cut off.

"I'll take the kick!" Frasier yelled at Pichu. "This is my shot!"

"No," Pete said, rushing in. "Cross the ball to Pichu and he'll score."

"Stay out of this, you loser," Frasier shouted at Pete, his small, angry features bunched tightly in his red face. "He took my position — now I'm taking this shot."

"If you want to win the game, cross it to Pichu," Pete said calmly. "See the light pole over there? Put the ball right on the pole and he'll score."

"No way, man," Frasier said. "This is the only chance I've gotten all season. It's mine to win."

"And yours to lose, too," Moore joined in. "You saw what he did back there, bouncing the ball off their guy. He's got a shot that's unstoppable."

"Put the ball on the pole and he'll score," Pete said. "Trust me, we can win this game."

Meanwhile, the referee paced off the 10 yards where the Westford defenders could set up their wall. The red-haired fullback was in the center of the wall, glaring at Pichu. Moore, lurking nearby, crept up behind the fullback.

"Dude, you're gonna get another spanking," Moore said.

"He tries that crap again, he'll regret it," the fullback answered, focusing his cold eyes on Pichu.

The defensive wall kept creeping forward, and the referee kept pushing them back to the ten yard limit. Meanwhile, an exuberant fan with a brightly painted face and bare chest jumped onto the field, leading the security guards on a brisk chase. They finally captured the fan and hauled him away.

The crowd turned its attention back to the direct kick, holding its collective breath, waiting for the kick and to see if USF could pull off a miracle. Then, in the silence, a single voice called out from the stands, "Ponga Boy!" Pichu looked over and saw Humberto leaning over the railing and waving to him, shouting his nickname. Another voice took up the call and yelled, "Pon-ga! Pon-ga! Pon-ga!" Other voices heard the chanting and joined in. "PON-GA! PON-GA! PON-GA!" Soon, the entire stadium was calling his name with a single voice, "PON-GA! PON-GA! PON-GA!"

Listening to the crowd, Pichu thought back to all the times the name had mocked him as an insult. Now, it was a sign of their love and respect. He turned around, looking at the crowd, waving and chanting. He let the voices and cheers wash over him and turn all the anger he had felt into forgiveness. The rain began to fall again and the lights came on and created halos in his vision when he stared up into the stands with the chanting fans. Then he realized that, at this moment, he was completely free. All he had to do was tap the energy in the air around him in the same way he had used the ocean's forces when he was a boy in Los Barriles. He became very calm and everything looked to him like it was happening in slow motion. The scene would live forever in his memory. Thinking this, and hearing the crowd, Pichu hoped his father was watching on TV and hearing the name "Ponga Boy" used as the highest form of praise. If so, Pichu felt this moment was a gift to them both, a gift to all men who worked on the sea.

Slowly, the chanting died. The referee looked around to make sure the field was clear and the defensive wall was in position. The red-haired fullback still glared at Pichu, lowering his shoulder, ready to charge. The referee held his arm up to show that everything was ready. Pichu glanced over and saw that Pete was crouching on the ground the way Humberto had done the night before, the way they had practiced so many times.

Frasier looked over at Pichu. He started to move toward the ball but suddenly stopped. Was he changing his mind? It was impossible to tell. Frasier took a step back and then started forward toward the ball again.

Across the field, Pichu began to move.

Frasier kicked the ball and lofted it toward the light pole. It seemed to hang in the air as Pichu sprang off Pete's back and, spinning like a cartwheel, turned upside down as he rose higher into the air. At the top of the arch his leg shot out and he hit the ball full force. It streaked down at a dangerous angle — and flew into the back of the net for a goal. But while Pichu was still turning in the air, completing his flip, the red-haired Westford fullback charged in and slammed into his shoulder. Pichu was knocked off balance and crashed to the field where he quickly disappeared from view, mobbed by the team celebrating the incredible winning goal.

The referee blew his whistle, signaling the end of the game. The stadium erupted in ecstatic cheering. The USF team streamed off the bench and swarmed over the pile of bodies that was already covering

Pichu. Reporters and photographers sprinted onto the field, flashes exploding, recording the jubilation. Songs and chanting broke out in the stands and whole sections of spectators linked arms and danced in celebration.

The pile of celebrating players began to sort itself out and suddenly a voice was screaming in panic.

"Get off him!" Pete was trying to clear the pile of players off Pichu. "Get off — he's hurt!"

The USF players responded to the urgency in Pete's voice and stood up, looking at Pichu's still form on the ground. He lay there unconscious, his head at an odd angle.

Quickly, the fan's celebration turned to alarm. The cheers died and the stadium became deathly quiet. Coach Jordan and two trainers hovered over Pichu. A circle of players and trainers gathered around the fallen player. Even Rev hobbled off the bench to try to help, tears streaming down his face. Several of the USF players began shoving the red-haired fullback who had committed the foul and it looked like a fight would break out. The referee hurried the fullback off the field. Still, Pichu did not move. The trainers worked on him with quick, desperate motions. A security guard ran onto the field, barking instructions into a radio. Moments later, the stadium gates opened and an ambulance sped across the field. When the crowd caught a last glimpse of Pichu, he was strapped to a stretcher, unconscious and pale, wearing a white neck brace. The paramedics carefully loaded him into the ambulance and it left through the gates. The siren wailed as it accelerated away, and the noise slowly died in the distance.

Chapter 31

When Pichu took that final spinning shot, he knew he had hit the ball perfectly. He knew the ball was in the net without even seeing it actually happen with his own eyes. He remembered turning in the air, waiting to land on his feet — when something went wrong. He crashed to the ground and saw blinding, bright stars. Everything broke apart and he seemed to rush out of himself and begin floating. He felt like he was still spinning but never landing. He was suspended in space.

Pichu's mind gave him many images to explain the floating sensation. He imagined that he was underwater, swimming in the Sea of Cortez on a warm summer day. Around him he saw all the fish of his local waters — the tuna and the dorado and even the marlin. But the dolphins stayed closest to him the whole time. One very round dolphin looked at him with an expression of recognition, as if he knew Pichu. The round dolphin seemed to dance around and around him, riding the currents. Although this dolphin smiled and looked at Pichu with kindness, Pichu felt an indescribable sense of sadness. The sadness was so powerful that there was something very beautiful about it.

The dream seemed to go on like this for days. Finally, Pichu began to wonder how he could hold his breath so long. He looked up and saw the sun through the water, shafts of light angling down around him. When Pichu turned back he saw his dolphin friend swimming off into the inky depths of the sea. Pichu let himself rise to the surface, toward the light, and he emerged back into the real world.

A bright light was shining into his eyes. The light clicked off and a doctor appeared, bending over him with, concerned.

"Pichu?" the doctor asked.

"Yes."

"Pichu, how do you feel?"

"Okay," he said. But then he tried to sit up but was stopped by the doctor.

"Whoa," the doctor said. "Take it easy. One step at a time. You've been out for almost two days. We were worried about you." The doctor scribbled intently on Pichu's chart. He moved to the door, opened it, and spoke to someone outside. Coach Jordan stepped into the room.

"Pichu," he said, looking very relieved, "you really had us worried, son. How are you?"

Pichu tried to speak but his voice was rusty and he only croaked. He tried again, "I'm good, Coach."

"Good. Good." Relief spread across Coach Jordan's face. But then Pichu saw him shoot a quick look at the doctor. The doctor's expression was unreadable.

Coach picked up a trophy on the bureau. It was a large gold statue of a soccer player with the letters "NCAA" and the date. "This is ours now. You won the game."

"Thank you," Pichu said. "But we all won the game. Pete lifted me into the air — and Frasier gave me a perfect pass. Even though he hated me he gave me the way to win the game."

Coach Jordan nodded and seemed about to speak. Instead, he set the trophy down on the side table. Finally, he pointed to Pichu's suitcase in the corner and said, "I brought you your clothes. And I also brought you these…" He held up a handful of telephone message slips and several letters. "The video clip of your goal is being replayed all over the world. You've gotten a flood of requests for interviews. And you've also had a lot of offers to play for some of the best teams in the world. They're calling you the new Pelé because of your acrobatics."

"After only one goal?"

"When you see the replay, you'll know why. It was beyond belief."

Coach Jordan sorted through the letters and pulled out three. "Looks like they want to renew your scholarship here at USF," he said, showing Pichu a letter with the university's return address on it. "Here's something from the World Cup organization. And you even got something from the University of La Paz. That's near where you're from in Baja, isn't it?"

"Yes."

"Would you like to open these now?" the coach asked.

"No thank you. I want to rest now."

"Good idea, Pichu. You rest."

Pichu leaned back on the bed as the doctor continued to examine him. He wondered if, when he closed his eyes, he could return to the dream he had been having where he could swim with the dolphins. The sensation of being back at home in the water was still with him. He didn't want to lose that beautiful feeling.

There were loud voices in the hallway and Coach Jordan looked around quickly as if he was expecting someone. He moved to the door and closed it. The voices faded away. When Coach Jordan returned to the bedside, he was wearing a different expression.

"I know this is all very sudden, but you have some very big decisions to make, my friend," he squinted, his eyes looking through Pichu.

"Decisions?"

"You need to decide which offer you will accept." He let that sink in. Then, in a different tone of voice, he added, "I was the one who spotted your talent first. So I think you can trust me to advise you. I strongly recommend that you stay here, in your country, and play for the MLS."

"In my country?"

"Well, your adopted country. I won't lie to you Pichu — the MLS is offering a package deal — I get the chance to coach if I can convince you to play. I think it's a wonderful opportunity and it's quite a bit of money. This way, we could keep working together."

Pichu closed his eyes. His head was beginning to throb. And it seemed to be getting worse.

The doctor spoke to Coach Jordan, "I think that's enough for now. He needs to rest."

"Yes," Coach Jordan said. But then he continued. "Pichu, will you accept this offer?"

"I don't know..."

"I don't mean to rush you, but when do you think you will know?"

The doctor cleared his throat. "Please... He just woke up."

"I need to go home and think about it," Pichu said.

"Good idea. Go home. And then I'll come by maybe tomorrow and we can talk some more. By the way, we're going to get you out of that dorm. I'm already working on it. And this deal I hammered out with the MLS — it includes a car for you. No more taking the bus or working in the cafeteria."

Coach Jordan picked up the trophy and paused. "Anything you want, buddy — anything at all — just let me know. Rest up now." He left, closing the door carefully after him.

The doctor turned to Pichu and said, "You were X-rayed and given a CT scan while you were still unconscious. Nothing was broken. But we have to be very careful with head injuries. Rest a little more now and then we'll see about sending you home."

"Home," Pichu said. "Yes. I'd like to go home."

"As soon as you're well, you can leave," the doctor said. "We expect that maybe tomorrow you might be ready to go home." The doctor left the room, closing the door behind him.

Pichu shut his eyes, but the dream would not return. Instead his head was spinning, and he saw stars, and waves of blood-colored liquid washing over him. He had to open his eyes to stop the horrible sensation. Finally, his vision cleared. He swung his legs out of bed and started to stand up. He had a hard time balancing. And, as he dressed, he nearly fell over several times. As he was about to leave the room, he saw the pile of phone messages on the bureau along with the three letters. He sorted through them, reading names of talk show hosts, coaches, and sports equipment companies. He stuffed them all in his pocket and left the room.

At the end of the hallway he stopped. A news crew was sitting in the lobby. Pichu reversed his direction and went out the rear exit of the hospital. It was near the emergency room and paramedics and people were rushing about and no one paid attention to him. Pichu walked around the commotion and out to the street. He stood there feeling the sunlight revive him, gaining strength as he breathed in the cool, moist air.

Walking for several blocks, he saw he was near the park where he used to play soccer on Sundays. But as he walked past the park, it was empty except for a woman in a colorful exercise suit who was jogging in circles and glancing at her watch. He kept walking, slowly, unsteadily, until he found a convenience store with a pay telephone out front. He took the calling card from his wallet and dialed, hoping there were enough minutes left for another call. His mother answered on the fourth ring.

"Hola, Mama-esta Pichu," he said.

Hearing her son's voice, Pichu's mother burst into tears and wept uncontrollably. She thanked God and Mary and Jesus many times for answering her prayers that her son would recover. And then she also thanked each of the saints she had prayed to. When she calmed down, she told Pichu how the whole village had packed into the hotel bar. They had all seen the first goal that he scored and dedicated to them. But when they saw him knocked unconscious, they fell into a state of mourning. Everyone in town seemed to be living under a dark cloud, waiting to hear if Pichu would recover.

"I want to speak to Papa," Pichu said.

"You can't," his mother told him.

"But I thought he was working the night shift," he said.

"No, Pichu, he's in his ponga again."

Pichu heard the words but was almost afraid to believe them.

"He's fishing again," his mother said. "He took his ponga out this morning for the first time. He left very early. And Pichu," she added.

"Yes, mama."

"As he got dressed, he was singing."

When she said this, Pichu could hear his father's humming song, the song without an end. He remembered the sound of his father's voice from all the years of working together in their ponga. He heard it so clearly, it was as if his father was beside him right at this moment. Now it was Pichu's turn to feel the tears burning his eyes. But they were tears of relief, tears of happiness.

"So the fish are back?" Pichu asked.

"It has improved," his mother said cautiously. "The hotel has many reservations. We are hopeful."

Pichu said goodbye, promising to call again soon. He hung up and headed for his dorm. Soon, he reached the soccer stadium and he instinctively glanced toward Humberto's little stucco bungalow. Pichu needed to thank Humberto for everything he had done. But the shades were pulled and the front door was closed. When Pichu knocked, there was no answer.

Pichu continued toward the university. As he approached his dormitory, he saw that banners were draped over the walls of the dormitory, celebrating the victory over Westford. Flowers, cards and homemade signs wishing Pichu well were arranged around the dorm entrance.

A van pulled to the curb beside him and a man jumped out. Pichu saw it was a news van and a second man was pulling out a camera and turning on a bright light. Another van pulled up and soon Pichu was surrounded by reporters and photographers. They were shouting questions, asking him why he had left the hospital, how he felt now.

"People are calling you the next Pele," a reporter said. "How does that make you feel?"

"Confused," Pichu said.

"Why?"

"I scored a goal in a college game," Pichu answered. "Pele played many years against the best defenders in the world. There is no comparison."

The reporters seem surprised by this answer.

Behind the group of reporters, Pichu saw Professor Baca appear. The professor stood watching the informal press conference.

"Take us through the final goal," a reporter said. "What was going through your head?"

"I remembered how.. I used to do a flip like that off a dock at home.

That made me happy."

The reporters don't quite know what to make of that answer.

"Happy ... until you got decked by that fullback, right?" the reporter prompted. "You going to pursue charges against him?"

"Charges...? No."

"Lots of offers in front of you," a woman said, thrusting a microphone in front of Pichu. "We've heard you'd get a million as soon as you turn pro. Do you know what you're going to do next?"

Pichu looked beyond the reporters and into the eyes of Professor Baca. He felt something odd happen deep inside him. It was as if he was seeing into his future — or what his future would be if he continued on this path: TV interviews, the attention of many fans and the money from professional soccer teams. Was this what he wanted? Pichu thought of his father at home fishing from his ponga. He thought of Angelina's beautiful face and loving voice. He thought of the hot breezes from the mountains around Los Barriles and the sun sparkling on the waves in the bay. He thought of the fishing boats leaving early in the morning and returning in the late afternoon.

"Pichu?" The reporter brought him back to the present. "Do you know what you'll do next?"

"Yes," he said, gazing at Professor Baca.

"Well? What are going to do?"

"Go home," Pichu said. "I'm going home."

He walked past the reporters toward Professor Baca. He stopped in front of him and they looked into each other's eyes.

"Why are you doing this?" the professor asked.

"I've lost my way," Pichu answered. "I don't know who I am. If I don't leave now, I may never go home again."

Professor Baca nodded. Pichu started to leave, but then he paused, smiling.

"When you visit your family in La Paz, we'll sit in the shade and drink a Coca-Cola."

Professor Baca added, "And we'll talk about why the world is the way it is."

"And how to make it a better place," Pichu finished.

"Goodbye, Pichu."

"Goodbye."

Pichu turned away. And he headed south again. He walked for a very long time. At one point he passed a trash can. He pulled out the messages he had received while in the hospital. He sorted through them slowly. Then, he threw most of them in the trash. He put one of the messages back in his pocket, with the three letters.

After several hours of walking, Pichu checked how much money he had in his wallet. He had his last week's pay from the cafeteria, only $97.34. But it was enough to buy a train ticket, with a special student pass, to San Diego. He rode the train south, sleeping most of the way. Once he arrived at the station, he went to a street corner near a home improvement center and hung out with other day laborers. He got a job building a concrete wall at a new subdivision, working beside some guys from Mexico City. Because of his injuries, he moved slowly and deliberately and his boss frequently berated him. He made friends with an old man from El Salvador who let him sleep in the bed of his pickup truck, parked beside his mobile home in a trailer park. At lunch hour at the construction site, they held a pickup soccer game. Pichu tried to play but his balance was still poor. He wavered unsteadily and fell several times. The guys from Mexico City laughed at him and teased him all afternoon, saying he had drunk too much tequila. But soon, the wall was finished and he had enough money to continue his trip south.

Pichu took a San Diego city bus to the end of the line. He was dropped off on the bridge that led to Tijuana, just outside the customs booths. He opened his wallet to count his money and spotted something. It was the telephone slip that Coach Jordan had handed him. He found a payphone and dialed the number.

"This is Professor Baca."

"Hola. Esta Pichu."

The professor was pleased to hear from him. They immediately switched to speaking in Spanish. The professor said, "Everyone wanted to know why you left and where you went."

"I told Coach I needed to go home and think things over," Pichu said.

"Yes, but he thought that meant you were going back to your dorm room."

"'Home' means one thing to me," Pichu said. "I'm going back to Los Barriles."

They talked for a few more minutes and Pichu told the professor that he had a big favor to ask. He needed a letter of recommendation to attend the university in La Paz. He decided he would continue his studies there.

"When I'm studying oceanography," Pichu said, "it makes sense to be near the waters I'm most concerned about. I'm going to devote my life to making sure my father can continue to fish. And I want to make sure I can fish, too, if I want to. And I want to see that my son also can be a fisherman, if he so chooses."

The professor was quiet and Pichu wondered if he was upset. But then he said, "I will miss you, but I respect your decision. And when I go to visit La Paz, you can me what you have learned."

Pichu realized he had one more call to make. From memory, he dialed the number of the phone in the dormitory cafeteria. In the background Pichu could hear the familiar clatter of plates and silverware and the whistling and joking of the workers. When Señor Vargas finally came on the line he was out of breath. Pichu apologized for not coming to work and not even calling to let him know what happened. Señor Vargas just laughed. "All the guys here in the kitchen saw the game. We've all been talking about your goal. No one ever saw anything like it! We will never forget it. Goodbye Pichu, and good luck."

When Pichu hung up he felt at peace. He had done everything he needed to do and he had done it properly. When he finally reached his home, he would be able to tell his father he had quit on his terms. He picked up his worn suitcase and walked across the border, back into Mexico.

Chapter 32

Pichu returned to Los Barriles on foot, walking slowly on the dirt streets carrying his suitcase. He had been dropped off on the edge of town by a work crew in a pickup truck going from La Paz to Cabo San Lucas. He eased himself down off the truck, waved goodbye and began the last leg of his journey home. Even though it was December, it was a hot day. The heat of the sun was strong on his shoulders and the sweat came freely. His feet made puffs of dust as he walked and dogs came out of the shade and sniffed his legs. They followed him for a time but then lost interest and returned to the shade, watching him until he was out of sight.

The journey south had taken several weeks. Pichu stopped to work in Tijuana and again in Ensenada, filling in as a deck hand on a fishing boat. The waters off the coast, on the Pacific side of Baja, were full of fish. The boat rode into a school of sea bass and they caught their limit within several hours. The captain felt that Pichu was good luck and urged him to stay. But Pichu took his pay and left after a week.

The farther south Pichu went, the better he felt. His sense of balance was improving but not completely restored. After sitting a long time, he had learned to stand up slowly, ready to hold onto something if he became unsteady. When he felt dizzy, it helped to look at fixed objects on the horizon. If he slept in an awkward position the pain in his neck was terrible. Often, the headaches came so strongly that he wanted to lie down and close his eyes. But when he did this, the headaches only increased. So he learned to keep moving and slowly, step by step, he felt better.

It was two o'clock in the afternoon when Pichu walked back into Los Barriles. He knew that Angelina would be getting out of school in an hour. He asked Carmen if he could leave his suitcase behind her taco stand, across from the school gates, for a few hours. She agreed, and even offered him a free #5 combination plate because she was so happy to see him. He bent over the plate of honest food and as the warm beans filled his stomach he felt his strength returning. Carmen watched him eat, smiling approvingly, her arms folded.

Pichu was standing in the shade of a manzanita tree, across the street from the school, when Angelina walked out. She paused when she saw him and their eyes met. She walked slowly toward him and he savored every step she took. He felt that it took days for her to reach him. And yet, he was happy the whole time. When she finally stood in front of him he began to speak. What he heard himself saying wasn't what he had rehearsed so carefully. It was coming from somewhere inside him he had no control over.

"I'm sorry," he told her. "I'm very sorry."

"Sorry?" she asked, confused. "What do you have to feel sorry about?"

"I'm sorry that you won't be able to say, 'My husband, the soccer superstar.'" He watched her face, waiting to see if she understood. Her expression, which had been worried, relaxed as the meaning sank in. The tension in her face began to dissolve and the sparkle returned to her beautiful, dark eyes.

"Husband?" She repeated the word to make sure she had heard him correctly.

She bent her head slightly and kissed his hand, squeezing his fingers tightly in hers. He felt something warm drop onto his fingers and saw tears falling from her eyes. She looked up at him, blinking rapidly, the tears flowing.

"If I can say, 'My husband, Pichu,' I will always be happy," she said, and hugged him.

As Angelina spoke these words, Pichu felt he had finally come home. They hugged for a very long time, standing under the manzanita tree. Carmen watched them from her taco stand and she, too, cried with joy because it was such a beautiful sight: two young people, completely in love, with their whole lives ahead of them. Then, Angelina and Pichu slowly walked down the street until the pavement became broken and dissolved into the sand of the beach. They sat on the rocks by the cove near the blowhole. Angelina rested her head on Pichu's shoulder and together they watched the spray shoot into the air. Late in the afternoon, they watched the fishing boats return. The boats came over the horizon with purpose and headed into the dock with colorful flags flapping in the wind, each flag proudly announcing how many fish they had caught.

Soon, Pichu fell back into the routine of leaving early in the morning to fish with his father. One morning, just before he left for fishing, he saw the three letters that had remained on his bedside table. They were weighted down by an unusual rock he had picked up while walking on the beach. He took the letters, folded them in half, and stuffed them into his back pocket.

In the boat, Pichu and his father, quickly caught enough fish for the day and were about to return to the dock. Pichu asked his father to wait a moment before starting the motor.

"Papa, I need your help making an important decision," Pichu said, taking the three letters out of his back pocket. He fanned them out like playing cards. "I'm not sure which direction I should go in." He held each letter out and explained the choices he was facing. "What do you think I should do?" he asked.

"The last time I had to make an important decision was this morning," his father said, a look of amusement in his eyes. "I had to decide whether to roll over and go back to sleep or go to work. I decided to go to work. I always go to work. That was my decision. These decisions are for you to make. And I know that the choice you make will the right one because you have made it."

"I don't understand."

"Delfincito..." He stopped himself and started again. "Pichu, you are a man now. You are a man when you set the course of your own life. React to the letters when you are ready. Then make a decision and live with it. I know you will be successful no matter what you do. Now, let's get to the dock before all the boats leave for the day."

Over the next few months many visitors came to see Pichu from America: coaches, sponsors and scouts. Coach Jordan tried to interest Pichu in several deals, offering him more and more extra gifts to get him to sign the contract. Pichu apologized but explained that it would be a mistake for him to accept the offers to play since he still wasn't well. His sense of balance, which had given him such an advantage on the playing field, hadn't fully returned, he said. If it did return, he might consider playing again. Until then, he would fish with his father and look into taking classes at the university in La Paz.

Things gradually returned to normal in the little town of Los Barriles. Occasionally someone would bring up the great game that Pichu had played and the amazing goal he scored. There would be a pause, and they would then turn to Pichu and ask him if he planned to play soccer again. He would shake his head and say that the injury he suffered had taken away some of his balance.

Whenever Pichu said this, Herman the German would smile and look away, as if he was trying very hard to keep a secret. This was because Herman was usually the first one on the docks in the morning. And many mornings he saw an amazing sight: Pichu dancing across the ponga boats, his feet moving impossibly fast, moving with grace and speed, all of his actions in perfect harmony with the waves below.